WHISPERS OF HER WORTH

A **HOTEL HAMILTON** NOVEL

TANYA E WILLIAMS

FIRST EDITION

Cover Design by Ana Grigoriu-Voicu

eBook ISBN 978-1-989144-39-8

Paperback ISBN 978-1-989144-41-1

Hardback ISBN 978-1-989144-40-4

Audiobook ISBN 978-1-989144-38-1

*For every woman who has whispered her worth
in the dark,*

*and for every woman still waiting to be heard in
the light.*

"Raise your words, not voice. It is rain that grows flowers, not thunder."

— RUMI

CHAPTER 1

FRIDAY, APRIL 27, 1928

lara

The lighthearted banter in the lunchroom recedes suddenly. I draw my head up to scrutinize the faces of the maids seated across from me and am trying to determine the reason for their abrupt silence when Mr. Olson, our proficient hotel manager, rushes to my side. His cheeks are flushed, and his usual prim demeanour slips further with each passing second.

"Miss Wilson, my apologies for interrupting your midday break, but we've got a situation."

My sandwich slips from my fingers onto its wax-paper wrapping. "A situation?" As the question tumbles out, my mind, always ready to leap to the worst-case scenario, narrows in on those I love most. "Louisa? Is she——"

"Your sister is perfectly well." Mr. Olson's gaze scans the gaggle of maids seated quietly around the table.

Before I can ask after my dear friend Cookie or, dare I

fret, Papa, the hotel manager gestures for me to join him. "Could you come with me, please?"

I push back my chair with my knees and stand.

An apologetic smile pulls his lips tight. "Why don't you bring your lunch? You can eat in the office."

Understanding that he won't explain the situation in the staff lunchroom, in front of the other eighth-floor maids, I gather up my lunch, stuff it into my bag, and follow Mr. Olson out the door.

As he guides us toward the back-of-house lift, his words rush out in a single breath. "Ms. Thompson has fallen ill. She is with the doctor now, but I'm afraid she is not in any shape to continue with her matron duties today."

"Oh dear." My stomach promptly twists into a knot. "Is she all right?" The lift arrives with a muted ding, and my mind dashes back to the party a few weeks ago. I noticed that night how tired the hotel matron appeared. "I've been so busy. I—I forgot to check on her."

"Did you suspect she was ill?"

The lift's snail-paced trajectory only adds to the apprehension gathering in the pit of my stomach as we descend toward the basement offices.

"No, not for certain. I only noticed she looked a touch tired at my father and Cookie's party." My chin drops to my chest as shame creeps in. William's sister is ill. Surely as his sweetheart and with him halfway across the country, the least I could have done was check in with her. "I planned to speak with her and see if there was anything I could help with, but then…" My words trail off as I consider the multitude of tasks I've taken on since the announcement of Papa's engagement to Cookie. Though the wedding to-do list is large, I am happy to tackle it to ensure their special day is exquisite. After all, Cookie has sought only the best for me and my sister since the first day we met her in the hotel's pastry kitchen. Her delight over her upcoming nuptials to my father has her beaming even more brightly than usual. My helping with the wedding plans is the least I can do for such a dear friend.

"I'm afraid there is no time for blaming yourself." Mr. Olson pulls open the lift's grate upon our arrival at the basement level. "Besides, I asked her several times myself if she was feeling unwell, and she flatly denied anything of the kind." His eyebrows lift in a telling gesture. "I don't suspect she would have been any more truthful with you than she was with me, or with herself."

We stride toward the matron's closed office door.

Mr. Olson pulls me aside before we are in earshot of Ms. Thompson's office. "Now, here's what we must do." He glances over my shoulder, ensuring the door remains closed. "You are the only one she will trust with her duties. I won't be able to convince her to do as the doctor instructs unless she knows the position of hotel matron is in capable hands. Do you understand?"

I am at once delighted and terrified. Ms. Thompson believes in me. The realization is a toe-tingling, heart-thumping, thrilling sensation. Without waiting a beat, my anxiety rears its head, determined to strike down any semblance of pride. How will I ever fill her shoes? She is a pillar of this hotel and someone I look to for guidance and counsel. Am I capable of tackling such a role, even if only for an afternoon?

"Miss Wilson." I'm pulled back to Mr. Olson's voice, stretched with worry. "I need you to be convincing in there, or all will be for naught." He gestures to the matron's office door. "She needs to see you are comfortable with taking on the role of matron." Mr. Olson stretches his palms up, pleading with me. "Please, even if it's merely a façade, I beg you to muster the appearance of confidence. She won't rest and recover without your assurances. Do you understand?"

I ignore the enormous weight of the task before me, and in a rare moment of courage, I lift my chin in defiance of my fears. "Yes, sir. I will do everything I can to ensure the matron's duties are carried out this afternoon."

"That's precisely what she needs to hear." Mr. Olson breathes a strained sigh of relief, then gestures toward Ms. Thompson's office door. "Shall we?"

The matron appears fragile, leaning back in her desk chair, with a damp cloth pressed to her forehead. Our eyes meet, and I see in her defeated expression the disappointment she feels with every fibre of her being. I've never known the woman to shy away from a challenging circumstance. A small shudder runs through me as I'm hit with the awareness that none of us are immune to hardship or illness, not even our nearly unbreakable matron.

The doctor turns toward me and Mr. Olson, clasping his black bag shut. "She needs rest, Robert." He turns his attention back to Ms. Thompson and admonishes her. "This is not negotiable. You may be a force to be reckoned with, but burning the candle at both ends is not a sustainable way of life for anyone."

Ms. Thompson's displeasure at being scolded twists her lips into a tight frown.

"I'll stop by your residence tomorrow morning to check on you, but until then"—the doctor points a bony finger at the matron—"you will go home and crawl into bed. I'm sure someone from the hotel can bring you dinner. You are not to do anything more than rest. Are we clear?"

"I understand." Ms. Thompson's voice is as small as a sullen child's, and my chest tightens in response.

"Good, I will see you in the morning." With that, the doctor leaves us to sort out the details of Ms. Thompson's care.

"Eliza, here's what's going to happen." Mr. Olson, clearly bolstered by the doctor's direct approach, takes charge of the situation. "Miss Wilson is going to take over your duties for the afternoon and tomorrow morning. I will take you home, and Cookie will bring you dinner this evening."

Ms. Thompson opens her mouth to object but is immediately silenced by Mr. Olson's raised palm. "We will figure out the rest as it comes."

She nods in agreement but asks, "What if this takes longer than an afternoon? The hotel won't run smoothly if I am chained to my bedpost."

Mr. Olson clears his throat. "You heard the doctor."

"Yes, but…" Ms. Thompson braces against the armrests as though she is planning to stand.

"No buts, Eliza, and sit back down until I'm ready to collect you. The last thing we need is you hitting your head on the way to the floor."

I smother a smile at the display of friendly affection between the two. Clearing my throat, I direct my attention toward the matron. "I'm surely a paltry substitute for your stewardship of the maids, but I promise to do everything I can to maintain the high standards you've put in place.

"Thank you, Miss Wilson. I appreciate your assistance." Ms. Thompson's gaze falls to the floor in what I assume is resignation.

Mr. Olson nods knowingly in my direction before picking up the clipboard from the matron's desk and handing it to me. "Miss Wilson, please take this and familiarize yourself with the maids' schedules. Then proceed to visit each floor, informing the staff that you will be filling in as matron for the day. Check on their progress, and make sure everything is on track."

"Yes, sir." I take the clipboard and tuck it under my arm. My stomach grumbles, the sound embarrassingly amplified in the small office.

Mr. Olson's cheeks flush. "I apologize. I forgot that I interrupted your meal. Be sure to eat your lunch before you take to the floors?"

"Yes, sir." I turn to Ms. Thompson, assuming I've been dismissed to tackle my long list of new responsibilities. "Ma'am, I hope you feel much better with some rest. Let me and Louisa know if there is anything we can do: food, company, a restful game of checkers, perhaps. Please don't hesitate to telephone if you need anything at all."

"Thank you, Miss Wilson. That is appreciated."

"I'll get to it, then." I give Mr. Olson a curt nod instead of my usual curtsy and head for the back-of-house lift.

I gobble my sandwich and apple in the stark-white staff corridor and collect my thoughts before speaking to the maids. I will let them know that Ms. Thompson is going to be fine. I'm encouraging my rehearsed monologue in an uplifting direction when it occurs to me that I've been promoted once more. My stomach flips at the thought, the same way it does when William's gaze lands on me. Who knew a dashing man and a well-earned promotion could elicit the same effect?

This is most certainly a temporary role. A day or two at best, I think to myself. But still, Ms. Thompson and Mr. Olson thought of me first. Clearly, my dedication and work ethic have not gone unnoticed. My giddiness comes to an abrupt halt when I remember it is William's sister who is unwell. There is surely no reason to celebrate when my beau's closest family member has fallen ill.

I return my lunch bag to the locker room while instilling in myself the decorum appropriate to deliver news of Ms. Thompson's health concerns. I climb the stairs to the first floor of guest suites, straightening my uniform and my spine at the top of the landing. I have a job to do.

CHAPTER 2

SATURDAY, APRIL 28, 1928

ouisa

Hovering over the newspaper spread open on the kitchen table, my nose crinkles at the faint aroma of black ink, its scent doggedly embedded despite the seven days that have passed since the edition was printed. I run a finger over the wedding announcement, my thoughts tumbling back to the crisp December morning when Cookie thoughtfully presented Papa with a box of treats for his city parks crew. She wanted to show her thanks for their work clearing the city's sidewalks of snow and ice. Who would have thought a gesture as small as holiday baking would lead to romance?

Clara pads into the kitchen, carrying her fatigue like a heavily laden grocery sack. Catching her eye, I indicate the pot of tea I brewed for her.

"You aren't going over those theatre reviews again, are you?" Clara's groggy question has no edge to it, but I sense a hint of teasing in her tone.

"No." I huff out the word and shoot my sister a pointed glare. Favourable reviews are crucial to my career. Remaining an unknown nobody isn't likely to grant me a future in Hollywood. But my habit of scrutinizing every theatre review printed doesn't help my state of mind or my acting prospects. "You don't have to remind me of the pitfalls of reading reviews." I roll my eyes with mock exasperation. "Thomas has been reminding me enough for both of you since he returned from Hollywood in February. He says hi, by the way. I met him last night to tell him about my audition for *Mr. Brown's Secretary*. We had an early dinner, since you weren't expected home at a reasonable time."

Clara delivers me an equally prickly stare as she replaces the teapot on the counter.

I ignore her look of disapproval. "If you must know, I'm rereading the engagement announcement."

Clara, cup of tea in hand, leans over my shoulder. "The wedding will be upon us in no time, and Cookie's task list is growing by the day."

I smother an exasperated sigh and sip my tea. So far, Cookie, Clara, and Papa seem more concerned with the wedding day than with our lives beyond *I do*. Each time I've tried to talk to Clara about her feelings regarding the nuptials, I've been met with a furrowed brow of confusion. With the wedding day three short weeks away, time is running out and I'm no closer to resolving my thrumming emotions. "Have you thought about how our lives will change?" I tiptoe around the topic once more, certain I am the only Wilson aware that adding a new person to our living arrangements is sure to unsettle the balance we've gained these past months.

This apartment has always been a tight fit for the three

of us, but we've managed. After months of discord, we've fallen into a rhythm that allows each of us our own space when needed. Though I would never call it a flaw, Cookie is jubilant and talkative. I fear her enthusiasm, though charming, may disrupt our family's quiet existence. Before Mama's passing, her presence in our lives was calm and steady. Never one to fuss or carry on, she led with her heart and a peaceful demeanour. Cookie, on the other hand, lives life with zealous enthusiasm. The two couldn't be more different in their approach, except for similar abilities to love deeply.

"How do you mean?" Clara hovers behind me while reading over my shoulder, confirming my suspicion that I am alone in my worries.

"Things will be different when she's living here."

I've tried to keep my fears from surfacing, but I still worry about sharing Papa's time and attention with Cookie. I admonish myself for the selfish thoughts, my bottom lip finding comfort between my teeth as I wait for Clara's response, hoping this time we can have a real conversation about the challenges that lie ahead.

"Cookie is already woven into our daily lives. I can't imagine her cheerful disposition changing anything." Clara moves behind me to read the society column. "Did you see this?" she says, and I drop the subject, accepting that we don't share this particular concern.

I angle my body to see the column and read aloud. "Miss Annabelle Evans is to marry Mr. Jacob Prescott on the twenty-sixth of May 1928." Tilting my body away from the table, I shoot Clara a questioning glance, since I am quite certain we know neither Mr. Prescott nor Miss Evans.

"Not that. Further down." Clara huffs before pointing

to the smaller font below the wedding announcement headline. "Miss Evans will be leaving her position as secretary to the honorable Judge Abernathy and is delighted to be taking on the role of wife to Mr. Prescott."

"The high-society girl is getting married and leaving her job." I return my attention to the newspaper. "No surprise there."

"Yes, but it's a good job." Clara's nose wrinkles. "Probably comes with luncheons, high tea, and a nice paycheque." She leaves the engagement announcement where it lays and settles into the chair adjacent to me. "Do you ever wonder if women actually want to leave their jobs when they marry? I mean, have you ever heard of a husband leaving his profession upon becoming betrothed?"

A laugh bursts forth obnoxiously, and my hand flies up to smother it. Clara is definitely in a mood this morning.

"You know as well as I do that such a thing would never happen," Clara says. "Though it pleases me none, I'll have you know. Polite society doesn't dictate how a man lives, but it certainly has no issue imposing rules on women. Besides, upper-crust women like Miss Evans deem marriage the ultimate goal."

Eyeing my sister with more scrutiny, I say, "Your knickers are certainly in a knot this morning." I tilt my head to one side, ensuring Clara has a full view of my raised eyebrow. "Perhaps you should try going back to bed and waking up on the right side the next time around."

Clara's cheeks turn pink. "Sorry. It made me wonder is all." Waving a hand dismissively, Clara stands and moves toward the kitchen, busying herself by slicing bread for toast.

Giving her the time she needs to sort out her early-morning grumbles, I return my attention to the newspaper, while nudging aside my worries over our future home life. Noting a similar wedding announcement, I inch forward for a closer look. Another soon-to-be bride's life will be revamped as she becomes somebody's missus. I decide to keep this awareness to myself and make a mental note to hide the society pages from Clara in the mornings. At least until she's had tea and toast.

Stepping toward the kitchen threshold, Clara offers an apology. "I suppose the day ahead has me a little befuddled. Toast?"

"Yes, please." I consider my words, not certain of how they will be received. "You know, it's okay to feel overwhelmed." I too am overwhelmed by the alterations being made to our family unit. I realize Clara and I each have a lot on our plate. "Nobody was expecting Ms. Thompson to fall ill, and with Cookie fully immersed in the role of bride-to-be, I'm sure the pressure of tackling it all is weighing on you."

"You're probably right." Clara leans against the kitchen counter, diligently standing guard over the automatic toaster until it dings. "Besides, I only have to get through this morning. Mr. Olson said Ms. Thompson will be back at the hotel by this afternoon. Surely, I can manage that."

Placing buttered toast at each of our places, Clara slides into her chair. "Do you mind if we leave a little early today? I'd like to get a better handle on the roster before facing roll call."

I smother a deflated sigh and bite into my toast, buying myself some much-needed time to shift my priorities. Putting Clara and her concerns over the day ahead of my own, I lay a hand on her forearm and press as much confidence as I am able into my sister. "Of course. Whatever will help you feel ready for the morning."

Once again, I delay broaching the subject of our changing living arrangements. Time is running out, and I worry who's going to be squeezed out of our little apartment first.

CHAPTER 3

lara

I spot Cookie bustling toward us as we turn the corner to the alley behind the hotel. In the weeks leading up to Papa's proposal, Cookie became a regular fixture in the Wilson apartment. Now, a day seldom passes without her presence in our lives. Lou and I pause, waiting for our friend to catch up.

Cookie's kind holiday gesture led to a chilly afternoon stroll through Stanley Park, which turned into a dinner out. Within a few weeks, Papa was whistling a happy tune, his good mood elevated tenfold by the time he spent in her company. Three months later, after a whirlwind romance, they were engaged. Our friend's existence in our lives is a blessing, complete with pies and sweets for our Sunday dinners. Cookie is as entwined in our lives as Louisa and I are in one another's, and unlike Lou, I can't see any drawbacks to having our dear friend become part of the family.

"How is Ms. Thompson feeling?" I ask, knowing Cookie's first priority this morning was to deliver a breakfast basket to the hotel matron.

The crisp spring air announces its presence in misty puffs as Cookie's steps quicken to match ours. I balk at Cookie's worried expression, still hopeful good news will be forthcoming.

"I'm sorry to say she doesn't look much better this morning." Cookie's weighted sigh and slow shake of her head speak of her concern.

Louisa gives Cookie's shoulder a reassuring pat. "Don't worry. Ms. Thompson is a strong woman. I'm sure she'll be up and about in no time at all."

We climb the stairs in single file, and Louisa holds open the heavy back door for Cookie and me. Inside the hotel, we are greeted by aromatic spices wafting from Chef's kitchen and by the sight of Mr. Olson. He stands before us, his face drawn and lines creasing his forehead. Panic rises in my chest, but before I can utter a word, the hotel manager waves us toward Cookie's pastry kitchen.

"What is it?" Cookie wrings her hands together nervously. "What's happened?" I lock my arm into the crook of Cookie's elbow to comfort her.

"Is it—Ms. Thompson?" Cookie asks. "Has something happened? I've only come from seeing her, less than thirty minutes ago."

A sharp whoosh of air deflates the man even further. "I wish I could say I had better news. Apparently, Eliza—I mean, Ms. Thompson." He trips over his familiarity with the matron, the situation pulling taut the usual ease with which he navigates the bounds of professionalism. "I'm afraid she will require more than a few days of rest."

"What did the doctor say?" Cookie's words wobble, an indication she's imagining the worst for her friend.

"The doctor saw her shortly after your departure. Even after another good night's sleep, Ms. Thompson remains unsteady on her feet. The doctor feels that in order for her to recover fully, she will require several weeks of rest, instead of the few days he initially expected."

"Oh my." The words are out of my mouth before I can reel them back. I was desperate to write to William last night but decided better of it, thinking the news might bring unnecessary worry. But now, with Ms. Thompson unable to return to work for weeks, I must write to him at once and assure him we will do everything we can to help his sister recover.

Before the thought has an opportunity to settle within me, Mr. Olson shifts his position, his gaze landing directly on me. "Miss Wilson, I realize this is a lot to ask, but I wonder if you will consider taking up the position of temporary matron of the hotel?"

"Me?" My arm instinctively leaves Cookie's as I contemplate Mr. Olson's request. "Are you sure?"

"I can assure you, Miss Wilson, that you are Ms. Thompson's first choice to take up her charge."

Louisa nudges me with an elbow, apparently attempting to bolster my confidence. "Well now," she says, "look at you. A proper hotel matron."

Though I'm sure she intends to be affirming, I refrain from rolling my eyes at my sister. Instead, I correct her to ensure I understand the offer being made to me. "A temporary matron." I redirect my attention toward Mr. Olson. "I'm happy to take on this morning's duties, but would it be all right if I take a little time to consider your request?"

"Of course, Miss Wilson. I hope you are aware, though, Ms. Thompson asked for you specifically. I'm not sure what we will do if you decide you're not up to the task. At any rate, please come and find me as soon as you've made your decision."

"Yes, sir. I will."

We go our separate ways. Cookie, with concern etched into her expression, heads into the pastry kitchen, and Louisa and I pick up our uniforms from the basement and then go to the locker room. Louisa knows me well enough not to press the topic, so we descend the back-of-house stairs in silence. I'm thinking of the far-reaching duties of a matron as Lou opens the locker room door to the sound of noisy maids readying themselves for the workday.

Louisa finally breaks her silence, a question burning a path straight to her lips. "Do you think you'll have to wear your maid's uniform as matron, or will we be able to go shopping?"

I do my best to dismiss her excitement at the notion of a shopping trip. "I'm not sure I'm in the mood for shopping." I tug my maid's uniform off the hanger, step a few paces away, and busy myself with getting dressed.

I feel the tug-of-war happening within my chest. On the one hand, I am delighted to have been asked to step into such a role, temporary or otherwise. But my concern over whether I'm the most suitable candidate for the position swarms around me, buzzing like a colony of bees. Adding to my uneasiness is the question of how it will appear, since it is common knowledge among hotel staff that I am in a long-distance relationship with Ms. Thompson's brother, William. The potential for perceived nepotism needles me.

Will it be assumed I am being given the position due to my relationship with the matron's brother? What if I'm not taken seriously or I can't handle the responsibilities? What if those a few years older than me are not inclined to take direction from someone younger? I do my best to nudge the pesky thoughts aside. After all, it's only a temporary position.

Still, the worries speed through my mind like a racehorse gunning for the finish line at Hastings Park. Stepping toward the small mirror affixed to the locker room wall, I study my reflection as I pull my hair into a tight bun at the nape of my neck.

Then again, what if I could try my hand at a real career? The kind that, one day, might afford me the financially stable future I am determined to secure?

After almost being evicted from our apartment at The Newbury not that long ago, I have yet to find a comfortable relationship with money. All these months later, I continue to tuck away any and all extra funds. I am steadfast in my determination to be prepared for unexpected situations, like the eviction notice we once received. A shudder runs the length of my spine, trailing my desperation to make certain I never again worry about losing the roof over my head. Maybe this is my chance to see if I am suited to a working life that would allow me to make it on my own. Louisa isn't likely to remain in Vancouver, with dreams of Hollywood dancing through her head. Besides, Ms. Thompson is sure to be back on her feet in a week or two. Just like Lou dons different characters for her theatre productions, I could use the temporary position as a dress rehearsal of sorts.

I press my lips together, considering the options. If I accept Mr. Olson's offer, I will gain a better grasp on the inner workings of a hotel matron's life. Then I will know

whether this particular career path is a suitable option
for me.

My days are already stretched thin, but I find myself
unable to let this opportunity slide through my fingers, or to
disappoint Ms. Thompson and Mr. Olson. I am certain I
can manage the wedding plans and the important job of
hotel matron if I plan my time appropriately. Yes, I almost
shout before stopping myself short and reining in my
enthusiasm. I cannot say no to this opportunity.

An image of William flits across my mind, and I am
immediately hit with a pang of guilt. "William," I whisper,
his name barely audible among the incessant chattering in
the locker room. I hadn't considered his thoughts on all of
this. Should he be a factor in my decision? Our relationship
is a mere four months old. Surely I don't require his
opinion. My thoughts reel back to the newly engaged Miss
Evans and Mr. Prescott from the newspaper, and I wonder
if I would also be expected to give up a well-paying job for
marriage.

Before diving down that particular rabbit hole, I give
my head a firm shake and remind myself that accepting the
temporary matron position is an act of generosity. I will be
helping out William's sister, for heaven's sake. Mr. Olson did
say that Ms. Thompson asked for me specifically. I pat the
bun at the back of my neck, guiding the rogue strands into
place. I've already made up my mind, and I know it cannot
be changed. The prick of an unfamiliar sensation
resembling rebellion insists this decision is mine alone.

I take one final glance in the mirror, pivot, and move
toward the locker room door. It's ridiculous to think
William will be anything but pleased by my choosing to
assist the hotel and his sister. William is a forward-thinking
man. He is surely comfortable with women working for a

living, since his sister chose a life with a career. Or did she? My steps falter as the thought occurs to me. "I don't actually know how Ms. Thompson came to be a hotel matron." The words slip quietly from my lips as Louisa bumps into me from behind.

"Clara, what are you doing? You can't stop in the middle of the exit. You're blocking the path to the door." Lou's voice is laced with annoyance for less than a second before it transforms into a teasing tone. "I don't know if you've heard, but we've got a new matron today, and none of us wish to be late for roll call."

A chorus of laughter erupts behind me, ensuring my cheeks are flaming red as I step to the side and allow the maids to file past.

Once the locker room is empty, I silently count to thirty, determined to steady my nerves. I take a deep breath, tug open the locker room door, and head straight to the basement.

Mr. Olson's office door is open, but I knock anyway. His head snaps up. "Yes, Miss Wilson. What can I do for you?"

"You asked me to let you know when I'd come to a decision, sir." I take a tentative step into the room.

He puts his pen down and interlaces his fingers on top of the desk, all of his attention on me.

"I would be honoured to accept the position of matron, temporarily, sir. That is, well…" I feel a rush of heat dash toward my cheeks as I fumble over my words. "What I mean to say is that I will remain in the role until you no longer require my assistance."

Mr. Olson's smile conveys not only gratitude but also relief. "I am very pleased to hear it, Miss Wilson. I will admit I was a tad worried you might decline. I am confident the standards our guests have come to expect will not be impacted with your guiding hand at the helm."

"Thank you, sir." I resist the urge to curtsy, unsure of how to address the man now that our positions have put us in working proximity of one another.

"You should know the position comes with a wage increase, given it may entail longer workdays and more complex situations than you are currently accustomed to."

"Thank you, sir." A thrill of excitement courses through me, and all I can think is how a bigger paycheque will ease my budget-conscious mind. A bigger nest egg means more financial stability for me and my family.

Mr. Olson gestures to the chair across from his desk. "Please have a seat. We can go over the details quickly before you report for roll call."

For the next fifteen minutes, Mr. Olson explains everything I need to know to fill Ms. Thompson's shoes while she is away. Though many of the details will be acquired through the doing, the linear task list does wonders for my anxious mind.

I am comforted to learn that Mr. Hamilton has insisted on continuing to pay Ms. Thompson while she recovers, with the caveat that I can seek her counsel if ever the need should arise. With the most important duties gone over, Mr. Olson hands me the clipboard I worked from yesterday and explains the day's priorities.

"You'll attend roll call for each floor, from the bottom to the top. The maids are accustomed to expecting you at the times listed on each floor's roster. I've penciled in your arrival time to each floor in the top right-hand corner." He points to the clipboard in my hand, and I flip the pages to gain a grasp on how much time I am allotted per floor.

"Thank you, sir. That is helpful."

"During roll call, you will provide direction on general tasks, tend to any specific guest needs or requests, and inform the maids of who is on rotation for hallway duties and such."

"I understand." I nod my head with confidence. My experience as a maid offers far more insight than I might have considered. I am keenly aware of what is expected of us in each guest room, in the hall, and even while maintaining the lift's polishing regimen.

Mr. Olson clears his throat. "I have no doubt you are qualified in directing the maids in their duties, but if you find yourself in an unfamiliar situation, I invite you to seek my counsel." His head moves back and forth, as if he'd rather not speak of such things. "There are times, Miss Wilson, when situations of a more personal nature affect those employed at the hotel. I wish I could be more specific and offer you advice, but honestly, I seldom foresee trouble until it's upon us. All I can say is, you'll know it if you see it."

"Yes, sir. Thank you." His warning leaves me a touch unsettled, but given my state of already being behind schedule, I decide now is not the time to ask more questions.

Mr. Olson removes his pocket watch from his vest. "You'd best be off, then. First, check in with Mr. Reynolds at the registration desk for any changes to the guest list. The first-floor maids will be filing into line." He examines the watch in his hand. "You'll want to be on the first floor in fifteen minutes."

Without waiting another minute, I stand, gripping Ms. Thompson's clipboard, and head for the hotel lobby, my eagerness battling with hesitation as I wonder what today will bring.

CHAPTER 4

SATURDAY, APRIL 28, 1928

*L*ouisa

"Have you heard how Ms. Thompson is doing?" Jane Morgan, the upper-class debutante whom I once incorrectly assumed would make neither a good friend nor a good Hotel Hamilton maid, has proved me wrong. Now thick as thieves, we work side by side most days, confiding in one another with honesty and affection.

As I pivot to face her, my head shakes slowly to convey the seriousness of my response. "I'm afraid she's not well. It could be weeks before she returns. Clara is hotel matron again today and has been offered the temporary position until Ms. Thompson has recovered."

Jane steps around her cleaning cart, placing a comforting hand on my shoulder. "We're all worried for her, Lou. Perhaps we could organize a get-well basket to cheer her while she is away."

"That's a good idea. I'm sure she'd appreciate knowing

we are thinking of her." I tap a finger to my bottom lip. "I'll check in with Cookie. She may know if there are any items the matron favours."

Jane adds a stack of towels to her cart and checks her wristwatch. "If the matron were here, she'd be telling us to get a move on. Roll call in thirty minutes."

We push our carts to their designated stations, tucked out of sight yet easily accessible upon the completion of roll call, and head for the back-of-house stairs to retrieve more supplies from the basement.

We are a few feet from the stairwell when Mrs. Kent, a guest from room 538, rushes toward us, a determined expression lining her features.

"Mrs. Kent, can I be of assistance?" The woman has been kind and accommodating over the past few days, even playing music on her and her husband's portable radio while I clean their room. The addition of music to an otherwise dreary day as a maid has been a much-appreciated distraction.

"Oh, Miss Wilson. I am so glad I found you. Come quickly. They are about to announce the verdict."

Mrs. Kent grabs my hand and tugs me down the fifth-floor hallway. Glancing back over my shoulder, I see a group of maids following close on my heels. They need little convincing, since Mrs. Kent's arrival at The Hamilton included several trunks and a determined message. In the few days since she and her husband checked in to the hotel, Mrs. Kent has made it a point to inform every fifth-floor maid of the importance of the legal action taking place in Ottawa. Mrs. Kent's words trickled through the hotel corridors, giving us a clear understanding of what we, as women, have to gain. From the guest floors to the locker room, every maid employed by the hotel is now aware of the crucial nature of such a verdict.

"Women in Canada have been waiting on this verdict for years," Mrs. Kent said the first day we met. Though I hate to admit it, until the newspaper began reporting on the case in March, I didn't realize a concern existed. British Columbian women petitioned for and won the right to vote in 1917. Though the law is far from inclusive, I somehow managed to convince myself we were on the right track. Despite the topic of whether women will be deemed eligible to be appointed to the Senate only beginning to fill newspapers for the past month, according to Mrs. Kent, petitions and women's group platforms having been advocating for change for far longer than I realized. As women seek equality, independence, and a voice within federal decision-making, Canadian women have apparently been holding their breath for the result of this legal petition, referred to as the Persons Case in the media.

Behind me, the other maids pile into Mrs. Kent's room. I stand beside her as she clutches my hand from her seated position on the bed I've yet to tend to.

Mrs. Kent's eyes bore into mine. "This is it, Miss Wilson. This may be the very thing that changes the course of history. Women will be able to advocate for women, children, the elderly, and the poor once we are appointed to the Senate. In Canada, Parliament cannot pass a single law without the Senate's approval. This is how we will make our country better. Women's voices shall finally be heard."

CHAPTER 5

SATURDAY, APRIL 28, 1928

lara

As I climb the stairs toward the back-of-house corridor, the giddiness inside me swells with each step. This is an excellent opportunity for me. It occurs to me that this might be precisely how Louisa feels when she takes on a new role in the theatre. I've never had the opportunity to pretend to be anything besides boring, *do the right thing* Clara.

"This is an adventure," I say boldly to myself as I move through the corridor, toward the hotel lobby, intent to check in with Mr. Reynolds, the front desk manager, before starting roll call on the first floor.

I give myself a pep talk as I move swiftly down the hall. William will appreciate how I'm helping out at his sister's request. He will be proud of me for having the courage to embrace this opportunity. The thought of marriage surely isn't on his mind at this juncture in our relationship. With most of our communication taking place through letters, we are getting to know one another at a slow and steady pace, which is exactly what I prefer. Even if a future together is on William's mind, his being all the way across the country means I can put it out of mine for the time being. I wave off all concern regarding William, assuring myself this is the right decision for both of us.

I slip through the swinging door with a spring in my step and stride with confidence to the front lobby desk. Mr. Reynolds is nowhere to be found. Mr. Sampson, Mr. Reynolds' subordinate and a curmudgeon if ever there was one, is occupied with a guest. The exhausted-looking young woman has in tow two children, a mountain of luggage, and a plainly dressed woman I presume to be a nanny.

"I understand, Mrs. Tyler." Mr. Sampson's haughty response is tightly reined in but barely veiled. "As I mentioned, your husband telephoned to say he would be arriving late this evening instead of yesterday afternoon, given the train's unfortunate delay, and he gave no indication that you were arriving ahead of him. Your suite was given to another guest after your husband informed us of the change in your plans. The suite your husband reserved is simply not available at this time."

I clamp my lips closed and bow my head to keep from drawing attention as I overhear their exchange.

"What do you suppose I do, then? My husband is occupied in meetings all day. I have Mr. Tyler's children, his luggage, and an appointment of my own in less than an hour." The woman's frustration oozes from every pore, and it occurs to me that even life as a high-society wife isn't necessarily easy or simple to navigate, especially without the aid of one's husband.

On the other hand, I know all too well how the high expectations of those who can afford the Hamilton suites are not always reasonable. The day has barely gotten on, and this woman is attempting to check in to a suite that has likely not yet been vacated by last night's guests.

"We'd be happy to store Mr. Tyler's luggage." Mr. Sampson tries again, though his smile is forced rather than genuine.

"Do you propose to store Mr. Tyler's children too?" The woman's eyes narrow as the sarcasm she's spewing lands on the registration desk in front of Mr. Sampson's folded hands.

"No, ma'am. We are unable to store *your* children." His flat reply with an emphasis on "your children" leaves me feeling slapped by the insinuation that the woman's children are entirely her own responsibility and not her husband's. Regardless of this woman's growing annoyance or her unusual request, the slight in Mr. Sampson's words lifts the hairs on the back of my neck.

A quick scan of the children tells me all I need to know. They're wearing rumpled clothing and drawn faces, and the littlest one has a thumb stuck firmly in her mouth. This family is travel weary and barely able to stand, much less negotiate early access to their suite.

I slide the clipboard from beneath my arm and quietly flip the pages to the roster of eighth-floor suites. Searching for the last name Tyler, I find the suite in question and confirm it is very much occupied. Wishing to get on with my own day and cognizant of the first-floor maids awaiting my arrival, I move a finger down the list until I locate a vacant suite.

"Mr. Sampson, if I may." I take a small step forward, aware my current status as hotel matron is not reflected in my eighth-floor maid's uniform. "I imagine Mrs. Tyler and the children are quite worn out from their lengthy travels. I wonder if Mrs. Tyler would find suite 815 suitable for her stay? The suite is currently available and ready for guests." I press a demure smile into place and steal a glance in the woman's direction before facing Mr. Sampson straight on. "I am quite sure Mr. Reynolds will be willing to accommodate an early check-in, given the situation." My eyes shift to the children, small and looking to be on the verge of collapse. I incline my head in their direction, hoping the man will take the cue and realize his lack of a solution will result in having two cranky, overtired children lying about the hotel lobby until four o'clock.

Mrs. Tyler opens her mouth to respond but is cut off.

The man's superiority knows no bounds. "Miss Wilson, I have this in hand." The smirk lining his lips only makes my point for me. The man appears to believe he is above the concerns facing women, guests of the hotel or otherwise.

Ignoring his rudeness, I turn and introduce myself to the woman. "Pleased to make your acquaintance, Mrs. Tyler. I am Miss Wilson, the hotel's matron." I state my temporary title clearly while positioning my clipboard, clasped tightly in my hands, in front of my apron.

"Ah." Mr. Sampson stutters slightly. "Yes, Miss Wilson. Perhaps you are right." He turns his attention to Mrs. Tyler, whose gaze is sliding back and forth between Mr. Sampson and me as she tries to understand what has transpired between us.

Mr. Sampson clears his throat and addresses the woman. "It appears we have suite 815 available for immediate check-in, if that will be suitable for you, ma'am."

Mrs. Tyler's posture visibly relaxes, and for a moment I

worry she might collapse right in front of me. "Yes, that will be quite fine." Turning to face me, she adds, "Thank you."

I say nothing more and simply offer a polite nod as a realization floods my being. I am aware, for the first time, of the authority a position such as matron of the hotel offers, even for a simple maid like me.

Within minutes, the children, nanny, luggage, and Mrs. Tyler are being loaded onto the lift for their journey to the eighth floor.

I return my attention to Mr. Sampson, choosing to ignore the previous encounter, and inquire if any new guests or requests need to be added to my roster. Then I head to the first floor of guest rooms.

Angling my chin to maintain a presence of confidence, I tug on the door and step onto the plush blue carpet of the first floor. The maids are lined up and ready for roll call.

Everything goes smoothly on floors one through four. I am getting the hang of this, I think to myself as I climb the next set of stairs to the fifth floor, where Louisa is working. She will be proud of me for standing up to Mr. Sampson. My black oxfords sink into the thick carpet, and I allow a small smile to emerge when I think of the story I will share with my sister on our walk home this evening.

The emptiness of the hall stops me short. Unlike floors one through four, this hall has not a maid in sight. Panic shoots through me like a lightning bolt. Are they playing tricks on me? I check my watch and then the fifth-floor roster. I'm right on time. Not even a minute late.

I move quickly through the hall, determined to locate the fifth-floor maids. I'm on edge as I turn each corner, in the event they are planning to jump out at me as a prank on my first official day.

A kerfuffle of some variety is taking place at the end of

the hall. As I draw near, I realize the sound is coming from inside guest room 538. A few maids are huddled close and spilling out into the hall. Upon seeing me, their chins drop to their chests, and they part like the Red Sea.

I am about to open my mouth to offer a reprimand for their unbecoming behaviour when I spot a guest, seated at the end of an unmade bed, her eyes glued to a box radio on top of a short table.

"You are listening to CKWX. The news is official out of Ottawa this morning. The Supreme Court of Canada has issued a ruling with regards to the Persons Case. They have ruled that women are not—I repeat, are not— qualified persons."

ouisa

I can hardly believe my ears. Crackling across the airwaves, the radio broadcaster explains how the Persons Case came to be.

"The Valiant Five is led by Alberta's first female Magistrate, Emily Murphy, and includes Henrietta Muir Edwards, Nellie McClung, Louise McKinney, and Irene Parlby.

"Also known as the Alberta Five, the group began their crusade because, despite women being allowed to run in federal elections since 1921, they have not been permitted to partake in the Senate. The Senate has resisted the pressure to appoint women into its folds stating that the British North America Act does not recognize women as 'qualified persons.'

"Mrs. Murphy herself has battled sexism since 1916, when a lawyer in her own courtroom first challenged one of her rulings. The lawyer argued that because a woman was not a person in the eyes of the law, Mrs. Murphy should not be taken seriously as a judge.

"It is widely known that Mrs. Murphy was outraged by these comments. However, they continue to plague her legal career. After years of having her authority challenged, in 1927, Mrs. Murphy and the four other women decided to put an end to what they deemed a senseless interpretation of the British North American Act and asked the Supreme Court of Canada to determine if women could be appointed to the Senate.

"It has been confirmed with today's ruling, likely much to the dismay of women across the country, the prevailing attitude of both the Senate and the Supreme Court of Canada is that men are the only 'qualified persons' in our country and therefore the only ones able to be appointed to the Senate.

"In a nutshell, the Supreme Court of Canada's unanimous verdict says women are not 'persons' under Canadian law."

A collective gasp sucks the air from the room.

Mrs. Kent, who is the wife of an Alberta businessman, squeezes my hand in hers. When she called me into her room only moments before the broadcast began, she indicated that she and her husband have been following the story closely. They brought their thirty-pound portable radio while visiting Vancouver in case the verdict was decided while they were here.

I imagine my blood is boiling. Mrs. Kent's hand, locked in mine, is cold as ice in contrast to my hot and pulsating skin. "This isn't the end," she tells me above the dissent darting around the room.

Knowing little of how court proceedings such as these

are conducted, I have nothing to offer in reply. My expression, though, must read as skeptical.

Mrs. Kent stands and meets me eye to eye. "A woman's worth shall never be determined by a group of privileged and closed-minded men, Miss Wilson. Even if all we hear is the faintest whisper of it from our own lips, our worth is not theirs to take. Cling to that truth. It is how we will remain strong during the storm."

The volume of disquiet rises another octave in the room, and from the corner of my eye, I note Clara's agitation lifting with it.

"You are right, Mrs. Kent." I take her hands in both of mine, an unlikely gesture between maid and guest, but the news here today has bonded us in more ways than I would have ever imagined. I feel as though a steel rod is replacing the distasteful news bristling beneath my skin. "This is only the beginning."

"Ladies. Ladies, please." Clara's voice wavers from a few steps inside the guest room. "I believe we've taken up enough of"—she flips a page on her clipboard and scans what I presume is the names of fifth-floor guests—"Mrs. Kent's time. If you'll all return to your stations, we will begin roll call in two minutes."

Several of the maids filter past Clara, thanking Mrs. Kent for her kindness as they go.

My sister looks like a tadpole swimming upstream, and I wonder how she is taking this news. By the concerned look on her face, I'd hazard a guess that she is less worried about her current state as a person and more troubled by how to get the maids back on track this morning.

Clara's perplexed expression informs me it is not certain she will join this fight. I recoil at the thought, as I feel the beginnings of a bumpy road ahead for us. Without my sister's steady presence at my side, I worry I may not be strong enough to stand against those who assume incorrectly that women are inferior. Whether she knows it or not, Clara's practical nature and thoughtful approach to life instill in me a belief that I can face challenges head on. She is the quiet thread of encouragement, even when she doesn't understand my view of the city and its goings on. I've never known her to abandon me entirely. I'm not sure I am capable of fighting this particular battle without her support.

I shake the woeful musings from my mind with the sharp whip of my head. If I begin defeated, there is no possibility of succeeding. Stiffening my spine, I decide I must remain resolute with or without Clara's support. I will stand up for women and our right to be considered persons in this country. We stand no chance at being deemed equal without representation in the Senate. I have no grasp on how to accomplish such an endeavour. All I'm sure of is that I can't sit idly by while women are made to be voiceless in their own lives.

I'm the last to leave Mrs. Kent's room, and as I cross the threshold, I hear Clara apologizing for any inconvenience.

True to form, Mrs. Kent informs her that she invited the maids in to hear the verdict. "This case will impact those maids too. They have every right to know what they're up against."

I pause, out of sight but close enough to eavesdrop on Clara's response.

"Yes, I'm sure you're right. If you'll excuse me, ma'am, there are many guest rooms that need our attention."

"Of course." Mrs. Kent offers her understanding response before asking one more thing of my sister. "Don't be hard on them though. It really was my idea for the maids to join me to hear the verdict."

"I have no intention of being hard on anyone, ma'am."

I slink away from room 538, in a hurry as Clara moves toward the threshold. Though Clara seemed to agree to not reprimanding us, I'm uncertain I'll have her on my side of this situation. I feel my resolve wobble at the thought of losing Clara's support. With Papa's time and attention wrapped up in Cookie and wedding plans, I've already felt the sting of being pushed aside in my own home. I think back to last week's dinner. Cookie and Clara worked side by side in our little kitchen. Though dinners are far tastier with Cookie's involvement, my exclusion from such activities pains me more than I've admitted.

I settle into the roll-call line with the others, disappointment and agitation cloaking my every move.

"Do you think our right to vote will be revoked too?" I hear Rosemary fret three spaces down from me. "I'll only be of age by the next election. I was looking forward to casting my ballot."

"What about our jobs?" Gwen Russell chimes in. She's only recently returned to her position after a New Year's Eve scandal almost cost her everything.

"I can't imagine men wanting to become maids anytime soon," Roselyn, a maid from the opposite end of the line replies. "I haven't seen any evidence of an inclination to clean up after themselves in my house. With four brothers, I can tell you it isn't in their nature."

This gets a laugh from the rest of the group, but it's cut short as Clara appears from around the corner.

To her credit, she doesn't mention the gathering in the guest room. Though she doesn't mention the verdict either.

Instead, she focuses her attention on the tasks for the day before sending us on our way to tackle them.

I see her check her wristwatch as she rushes from the fifth floor. I suspect our interruption of the day's duties has put her behind schedule, and for that, I am sorry.

Letting the others go ahead of me, I take my time gathering my cleaning cart before venturing toward my assigned guest rooms on the opposite end of the fifth floor. As I meander down the hall, my mind whirs. The chatter coming from behind partially closed guest room doors is punctuated by the occasional thud of furniture being positioned with more force than necessary. The maids' clear view of their importance within the country they call home has been turned on its head.

I feel the tension grow like a heat wave as it spreads through the gaps in the doors and into the hallway. Even if the awareness comes with a hefty dose of unease, it assures me I am not alone in my disapproval of today's verdict. I am not alone at all.

Two hours later, I manoeuvre my cart back toward the storage cupboard, ready to rest my feet and eat my lunch. The angst over today's news hangs in the air. Maids, having clearly forgotten where they are, speak with raised and somewhat angry voices as they travel in clusters of three and four about the fifth-floor hall.

A flung-open guest room door draws my attention. The maid inside steps into view as she pummels a pillow before tossing it carelessly toward the bed. I cringe at the thought of Clara bearing witness to any of this unruly behaviour. There must be a better way. Even I'm aware that this behaviour will only cause more harm than good.

I am comforted by the awareness that these women, these maids I spend countless hours working alongside, are not the wallflowers I presumed them to be. Not when it comes to something as important as our freedoms.

A flash of a bellboy's uniform whips my head around. He is running down the hall. Quick on his heels are two fourth-floor maids with broomsticks and feather dusters in hand. The maids are new to The Hamilton, and since they work one floor below mine, I haven't made time to properly introduce myself. Perhaps that was fortuitous, given their current behaviour. I have barely made sense of the scene when Clara steps into the hall from the back-of-house stairwell.

She takes one look at my startled expression and follows my gaze to the end of the hall.

"It's not up to me," George's usually timid voice cries out as he turns the corner, barrelling straight toward us. "Louisa, please help me." George's pleading spurs me into action. Once he is safely behind me, I angle my cart to block the path to him.

The maids come to an abrupt stop, their faces flushed and their weapons raised.

"What exactly is going on here?" Clara's voice commands their attention and mine. I have never heard my sister embody such strength.

Realizing the matron of the hotel is before them, the maids drop their arms to their sides.

Clara turns her attention to George, who is cowering slightly behind me. "George, please explain yourself."

"It wasn't me, Miss Wilson. Honest, it wasn't." George gestures to the fourth-floor maids. "I was delivering a newspaper to a room on the fourth floor when these two came chasing after me. Said something about it being unfair that I'm paid a higher wage than they are. I've no idea what they're going on about, but I don't set the wages. I simply do as I'm told."

One of the maids with an attitude unbecoming her job description can't seem to help herself. "It's not fair. We do all the hard work, and you sit around on your duff all day."

"That'll be enough out of you, Miss Monroe." Clara points in the direction of the stairwell. "Off you go, both of you. I will see you in Ms. Thompson's office in five minutes."

A guest room door opens, and a man steps out. "Is everything all right? I heard shouting."

Clara's face transforms instantly, and she greets the hotel guest with a sincere smile. "My apologies, sir. There is no trouble at all. Can I offer you a complimentary tea service for the interruption?"

The guest hesitates, considering the offer.

"I have it on good authority that our pastry chef has recently pulled a fresh batch of scones from the oven. We'd be happy to deliver the service to your room." Clara inclines her head in a knowing angle. "I've not met a person yet who can resist these particular scones."

"Well, all right. That does sound quite enjoyable." The guest nods his thanks and ducks back into his room.

"George, Miss Wilson." Clara takes charge, directing us away from the guest's room and toward the storage cupboard.

"What a day." I lift a single eyebrow, eliciting a true smile from my sister's lips.

"I am sorry for the trouble, Clara." George, familiar with hotel etiquette but also with us, offers an apology as a friend.

"I realize it wasn't you who caused the commotion.

Next time, though, try to run toward the basement instead of a guest floor, would you?"

"I'm hoping there won't be a next time, if I'm being honest." George's cheeks flush. "I always knew there was a reason to steer clear of the maids. I won't let my guard down again."

Clara and I exchange a look. "This isn't your doing. The maids are riled today because of the Supreme Court ruling."

George looks between Clara and me with a blank expression.

"This morning the Supreme Court ruled that women are not considered persons when it comes to gaining a seat in the Senate." Clara provides the context for the upheaval.

"Well," George says with a shake of his head, "sounds to me like the Supreme Court hasn't met the likes of our maids."

"You may very well be right about that." Clara smiles while giving his forearm a reassuring squeeze. "Don't you worry about those maids. I'll be sure to keep them busy for the rest of the day. But please ensure a tea service with warm scones is delivered to our guest."

"I'll get right on it. Thank you, Miss Wilson." George ducks his chin and heads for the back-of-house stairwell.

"You okay?" I ask as I push my cart into the cupboard and lock its wheels in place. "That was quite the display."

Clara's shoulders slump in defeat. "I'm not oblivious. The ruling isn't fair, Lou, but—"

"Hey," I place both hands on Clara's shoulders, steadying her in the only way I know how. "The ruling isn't fair. There is no 'but,' Clara."

Clara washes her hands over her face. "I never expected to do battle with the maids. I never expected to find myself dealing with a warranted outrage while positioned on the opposite side." Her eye roll speaks volumes about the conundrum she's found herself facing. "Now I'm in charge, and I don't see how I can ignore these sorts of transgressions when we've got a job to do. Honestly, that's about all I can focus on right now."

"I understand." My head quirks to the side, drawing her eyes up to meet mine. "It's good to know we agree on the unfairness of it all. That helps. Maybe we can keep work separate and discuss what we think and feel about the ruling at home, like sisters."

"I'd like that." Clara's eyes pool with moisture. "Now, I've got to figure out what to say to those unruly maids."

"Don't let them off the hook for their behaviour." I tug at the hem of Clara's apron, straightening it into place. "But do so with compassion. A little compassion goes a long way."

We say our goodbyes as I head for the locker room to retrieve my lunch, while Clara descends the employee lift to the basement to deal with the wayward maids. I cannot condone the behaviour I've witnessed since the verdict was announced, and yet I know that our stance against the verdict must be made clear. Tapping a finger to my lips, I feel the corners of my mouth lift as an idea begins to take shape.

CHAPTER 7

SATURDAY, APRIL 28, 1928

lara

The subdued clanging of the descending lift is good company for my ruminating mind. Less than halfway into my first official day as hotel matron, I've already gotten a taste of Mr. Olson's warning about managing the maids. An exasperated sigh sails past my lips as I realize how blissfully ignorant I was of the conflicts that can arise within these walls. I certainly didn't expect to encounter two maids chasing poor George around the fifth floor. I might even consider the shenanigans amusing if I weren't responsible for wrangling them in. No wonder Ms. Thompson worked herself into a state of exhaustion.

The Supreme Court decision touches every single woman among us. The concern is real and, I admit, warranted. I'm certain today's outburst won't be the last of the backlash. I'd be naïve to think otherwise. But my job is to ensure the maids remain on task, regardless of what is happening in the news. I can hardly puzzle out the circumstance before me. I never would have imagined I'd be dealing with the ramifications of a Supreme Court verdict in my role as hotel matron. Uncertainty hums through me as the lift bumps and rattles toward the basement. I could certainly use a bit of guiding insight now.

Over the past few months, William's letters have provided unwavering support and wisdom. Posted across the country to me are encouraging words and probing questions that make me consider my perspective in a new light. An image of William flits through my mind, and I wonder what he, as a lawyer, is making of today's verdict. I long to hear his voice and his words of encouragement on the matter.

I think back to his recent letter and feel my cheeks flush with colour.

Dearest Clara,

Although winter has yet to thaw from the city, I find myself warmed by continual thoughts of you. Just yesterday, in the middle of a deposition, I found myself daydreaming of our New Year's Eve dance. The poor court reporter had to clear her throat several times to draw my attention back to the matter at hand.

Since dancing with you that evening, I have been buoyed by your presence in my life, even if *that presence takes the form of a beautifully penned letter. To answer your question, yes, I was teasing when I asked how all four Wilsons are going to fit in your apartment once Cookie moves in. Though there is an underlying truth. Even in happy times, challenges often arise. Being aware of potential conflict is the surest way to maintain a level head. I hope you are able to avoid feelings being hurt as you settle in as a new family of four.*

I am aware of the conflict awaiting me in the shape of two misbehaving maids. As William said, if I remain aware, my level head will prevail. Tucking William's calm, matter-of-fact wisdom into my being, along with Louisa's reminder to be compassionate, I infuse my body with a confidence I don't yet own and stride down the hall, doing my best to mimic Ms. Thompson's commanding presence. The dank smell that permeates the basement floor fills my nose as I anticipate the difficult conversation before me. This may not be an easy road, but it's the one I am determined to explore. I turn the corner and spot the two maids, waiting in front of the closed office door, heads hung in shame.

This is up to me and only me. I am certain, given my newness to the position, Mr. Olson would be kind enough to step in and take care of this unruly behaviour, but if I'm going to succeed—I mean, really succeed—at being matron of The Hamilton, then I must do as I promised. It is my obligation to serve Ms. Thompson and the hotel well.

Today, that means facing this conflict head on.

"Ladies." The maids shuffle to one side of the office door, allowing me entrance to the shoebox-sized office. "Please take a seat."

My eyes dart around the room. I haven't even stepped foot in Ms. Thomson's office in my capacity as matron, and I feel like a fish out of water. "You can pull up an extra chair from the hall." My voice wavers far less than I expect as the three of us settle into hard-backed chairs.

"I don't believe I need to point out the undisciplined nature of your conduct. Running amok anywhere in the hotel is not permitted, but doing so on a guest floor is an indiscretion worthy of immediate dismissal."

One of the maids, Marjorie, snaps her head up. "I can't lose this job, Miss Wilson." Tears spring to the girl's eyes, and for the first time, I wonder how often Ms. Thompson has to put aside her sympathies to do her job.

Biting down on the inside corner of my cheek in an effort to remain stoic, I say nothing and instead let the girl fill in the blanks.

"My mother used to take in laundry, you know, as a way of helping my family pay our way." The girl swipes a frenzied hand at the tears trailing furiously down her cheeks.

"And now? Does she no longer take in laundry?" The question is out of my mouth before I realize my mistake. I want nothing more than to pull it back in, but heaven help me, I already know what is coming next.

"No, miss. My mother passed two months ago. My pa is working double shifts in an effort to pay off the burial."

"I am sorry for your loss, Marjorie." My voice cracks, reminding me of a time when I too couldn't mention the loss of my mother without shedding tears. I remind myself that showing emotion is not a weakness. I can only be myself in this position. I can take cues from Ms. Thompson's example, but if there is anything I've learned at The Hamilton, it's that being true to myself is the first step in doing the best job I am capable of.

"If you need this job so badly, then why would you behave in such an unbecoming fashion?"

The girl's shoulders shrug in response.

"Miss Wilson." The other maid speaks up.

I believe her name is Marie, and I make a mental note to check the fourth-floor roster once this meeting is finished.

"Yes."

"We are sorry for causing such a disturbance. We realize our actions could very well have serious consequences, but you see, miss, the fear—it took on a life of its own. When we heard our lives meant little to the country we call home, I don't know. We apologize, miss. The fear of not knowing what will happen to us took over. We never meant to cause any harm."

"Your actions are not acceptable, but I do understand your reaction to today's news." I turn my head in Marjorie's direction. "You will apologize to Mr. Baker at once. He is not to blame for this dreadful ruling, and you'd be best served with him as an ally instead of a combatant. Am I clear?"

"Yes, miss," the maids answer in unison.

"I fear we have troubled roads ahead, ladies. The Hotel Hamilton has always had the best interests of its staff in mind. That goes for the women and the men. We don't know what is to come next, as far as rulings and laws, but I promise you we will weather whatever comes our way together."

"Yes, miss."

Still feeling the need to assert myself as hotel matron, I lift my voice to what I hope is a commanding octave. "If I see either one of you put a toe out of line, our next conversation won't be as cordial. Do you understand?"

"Yes, miss."

"You may go. But first, you will quietly find Mr. Baker and offer your sincere apologies. Then you will return to the fourth floor, where you will clean the remainder of the guest rooms on your roster before offering to take up the hall duties, including the polishing of the lift." In this moment, I wish I had mastered Lou's single eyebrow lift. The sight of it would be sure to let these maids know I mean business.

I flip the pages on my clipboard. "You can let Miss Parey know that you will be doing her and your co-workers a favour by taking care of those extra duties this afternoon."

I sense from them a desire to argue. I tilt my chin a fraction, indicating my reprimand is not to be questioned.

"Yes, miss."

Both maids stand and move toward the open door.

"By the end of day, ladies. Even if that means you work a tad later than usual. If you need to telephone home to inform a family member you'll be tardy, you can use the phone in Mr. Olson's office."

"Thank you, miss." The maids file out, solemn and properly reprimanded.

The moment they are out of sight, my chin drops to my chest as the exasperation of the past thirty minutes releases in a hiss of air.

"Well now. You surprise me, Miss Wilson." Mr. Olson is leaning against the door frame with a cheshire grin lifting his cheeks.

A laugh that I wasn't anticipating erupts from my throat. "To be honest, I think I surprised myself, Mr. Olson."

"You did well." He steps into the office and slides into one of the chairs. "The verdict though…" Mr. Olson shakes his head. "This will not make your position any easier. The women are sure to be outraged. I can't blame them. The ruling is downright absurd. No, I can't blame them. Not one bit."

"Do you think it might help if you or Mr. Hamilton were to address the staff? Let them know their positions are secure within the hotel. Maybe even go as far as telling them you, too, do not agree with the Supreme Court ruling."

"That can be arranged. I'll have to speak with Mr. Hamilton first, and of course, if there are ramifications further down the line, we will have to take each one in stride." Mr. Olson looks to the ceiling, deep in thought. "I never thought it would come to this. How do five small-minded judges stuck in the 1800s roll back decades of progress?"

"I wish I knew. My primary concern right now is how we will manage the issues within the hotel should things escalate."

Mr. Olson stands, stuffing his hands into his pants pockets. "We will proceed one day at a time, Miss Wilson." He taps a finger to the side of his nose. "In the same manner women have done since the beginning of time. If I've learned anything from working with a female-led roster, it's that one should be cautioned not to underestimate the resilience of women. I'd go as far as to say that when women band together for a mutual purpose, you'd best stay out of their way entirely or risk being run over."

"A wise notion, indeed, sir."

"I'll let you get on with the rest of your day, Miss Wilson."

I check my watch and decide a few minutes of organizing myself is in order before I venture back above stairs to check on the progress being made on each guest floor. Hopefully, the maids will resist demonstrating their defiance with regard to the Persons Case verdict, at least for the remainder of the day.

CHAPTER 8

ouisa

I woke this morning with a plan, and it's a doozy. I had intended to share my idea with Clara first, but by the time I slipped my feet out from under the covers, she was already gone. Over the past two days, I've thought about little other than the verdict that came as a slap in the face to Canadian women. More than aware I cannot stand idly by, I've been racking my brain for a course of action. In the wee hours of another sleepless night, my idea for resistance rang through loud and clear.

Padding into the kitchen, I am surprised to see Cookie and Papa whispering across the table from one another as Papa digs into his hearty breakfast.

Cookie's presence in our kitchen before the workday has begun sends a ripple of panic through my chest. "What time is it? Did I oversleep?"

Papa lifts his head with a delighted expression, which I

admit has been present more often since Cookie's arrival in my father's life. "Good morning, Lou. Care for some breakfast?"

Swivelling to face me, Cookie beams. "No need to fret. You aren't the least bit late. I'm early is all. Clara mentioned she was planning to head to work at an ungodly hour." The disapproval in her voice is accompanied by a slight roll of her eyes. I smother a smile, knowing her mild reprimand comes from a place of concern. "I thought the least I could do is make sure the two of you got a fine start to the day." She gestures to the teapot she's pouring from. "Tea?"

"Yes, please." I accept the cup of steaming brew, inhale its earthy aroma, and take the sole remaining chair at the kitchen table. My sleep-weary mind does the math. "You realize we're going to need another kitchen chair before the wedding. We can't keep pulling up Papa's armchair each time we all share a meal."

Cookie stands and begins puttering about the small galley-shaped kitchen, her cheery disposition firmly in place. "We were just discussing that very thing." Filling a plate with sliced ham, warmed-up roast potatoes, and scrambled eggs, she pulls cutlery from the drawer before setting it all before me.

"Thank you." A nervous chuckle is waiting impatiently at the base of my lungs. "We are used to tea and toast. Keep this up and we are going to need a bigger apartment to fit our expanding girths."

Papa and Cookie exchange a look that perplexes me, halting my fork before it reaches my mouth. With a surge of trepidation, clammy perspiration emerges on my palms. I feel the exclusion from their private conversation and wonder how stable the ground beneath me actually is.

I am about to inquire further when Papa laughs good-naturedly. "We are going to start bringing some of Ruby's things over, a little at a time. With the wedding a few weeks away, we thought it best to get a jump on it."

I chew and nod, still wrapping my head around Papa's use of Cookie's Christian name. I do my best to assuage my ruminating mind with the assurance of their ever-present concern and love for Clara and me. Waving off my unfounded disquiet, I locate an appropriate response. "Should we make some room first, or do you have another plan in mind?"

My reply, apparently not sounding as untroubled as I hoped, spurs Cookie into action. Reaching across the table, she covers my hand with hers. "Not to worry, it'll only be a few boxes at first. I'm sure we can tuck them to one side for the time being."

Reminding myself that Cookie has only ever had my and Clara's best interests at heart, I deliver a stage-worthy smile. "Clara and I can make room in our closet, if you need."

Papa pushes his chair back and stands. "Awfully thoughtful of you, Lou." His warm, calloused hand rests on my shoulder for the briefest of moments. Too brief, if I'm being honest. "Well, I'd best be going. May is the prettiest month to be immersed in the gardens."

My laugh comes naturally. "You say that about every month."

Papa winks in my direction, and I feel the depth of his love for me in that one small gesture.

Cookie walks him to the door, giving him a well-stocked lunch sack and a kiss on the cheek before bidding him farewell for the day.

Papa is one of the good ones, I tell myself as I scoop the

last of my potatoes onto my fork. We are all lucky to have him in our lives. As Cookie's potatoes melt in my mouth, I nudge aside any concern and concede that we're lucky to have her too.

Turning my attention back to the day ahead, I mull over the plan that, even in the bright of a fresh day, seems perfectly appropriate for the current times. My mind reels back to the Persons Case verdict. Despite not having the chance to speak with Papa about my plan this morning, I am buoyed by the memory of his ardent response to the verdict. *Foolhardy* and *shortsighted* he had called the Supreme Court judges.

I turn over the words printed in yesterday's newspaper. Delivered in dramatic and compelling fashion by Mary Ellen Smith, a member of the British Columbian legislature, the sentiment leaves me feeling both empowered and distraught.

The iron dropped into the souls of women in Canada when we heard that it took a man to decree that his mother was not a person.

"Well, he's off." Cookie swallows her last bit of tea and begins cleaning up in the kitchen. "I'd better get a move on. Clara is putting me to shame, heading into work even earlier than me."

"Typical Clara," I say. "She'll do that until she's got a handle on things." I lift my plate from the table and move toward the kitchen, determined to help with the dishes, considering Cookie is still technically a guest. "Thank you for breakfast. And don't worry about Clara. This is how she works through challenges. First, she tries to control everything in sight. Then she tries to anticipate all the possibilities, which of course, she can't. If things get to be too much for her, I'll know."

"You're a good sister, Lou. I've packed you a lunch and

made an extra one for Clara in case she forgot amidst her early escape. I'll wash up here. If you can be ready in ten minutes, we can walk together."

"Are you sure?" Guilt creeps in. I know Clara would insist on doing the dishes herself.

"My hands aren't so fragile that another load of dishes will cause them any harm," Cookie teases and shoos me off with a tea towel clutched in her hands.

The telephone rings, and I rush to answer it, eager for news about my recent auditions. I've been on several since *All Soul's Eve* wrapped up at the beginning of April. "Wilson residence."

I listen silently, with Cookie watching me the whole time.

"Yes, this is Louisa Wilson."

Bubbles of excitement stir within me.

"Of course. Thank you. I will see you then. Goodbye."

I hang up the telephone and pivot to meet Cookie's expectant gaze.

"Well, out with it, then." Cookie beams, clearly guessing the news is favourable.

"I've been called back for a second audition for *Mr. Brown's Secretary*. The director wants me to read for the role of the secretary."

Cookie returns to the kitchen, and I hear dishes plunk into the soapy water as she sets to scrubbing them. "Look at you. Another leading role, is it?"

My head bobs vigorously as excitement runs through me. "I'd better get going or we'll both be late."

I call out to Cookie as I move toward the bedroom. "I have to make a quick stop along the way. If you have time for that, I'll be ready to join you."

In the locker room, I gather as many of the hotel's maids as I can and tell them my plan. I wait impatiently as they exchange questioning looks and murmurs I am unable to decipher. The beating of my heart thrums in my ears as the seconds tick by. With the room crowded and buzzing with conversation, their deliberation feels hours long and I begin to question my resolve. Perhaps I should have run the plan by my sister before announcing it to all of The Hamilton's maids.

Hushed whispers echo through the locker room. "What does she want us to do?" "Can we be dismissed for such a display of disobedience?" "A lower wage than the bellboys is better than no wage at all." The maids' worries bounce off the hard surfaces like an out-of-control ping-pong ball. I cringe at the truth of my decision to not tell Clara. When she wasn't at home this morning, I managed to convince myself that she wouldn't want to be included in any show of resistance. Temporary or not, she is currently a hotel manager. Besides, we agreed to keep our conversations about women's rights between us as sisters and out of our place of work. Of course, that was before I decided to bring the issue into the hotel this morning, front and center.

In this moment, with uncertainty staring me in the face, I long for the support of my sister. My bottom lip slips between clenched teeth as I attempt to calculate my misstep. With Clara's steadying support, I can do anything. Without it, I fear my stark, knee-jerk boldness is sure to waver.

Straightening my posture along with my resolve, I hold my desire for resistance strong within me, trying to ignore the worry that I may be the sole maid in this hotel with a fire in my belly big enough to risk admonishment from the hotel managers. Will these ladies join me? Can we be a force of resistance to demonstrate that women will not be ignored? None of us have the skills or knowledge to take on the Persons Case verdict in a legal manner, but we can show our displeasure. At the very least, we can come together to remind ourselves of our common belief that a woman's voice in the Senate is the next logical step in ensuring all women's right to equality.

Jane is the first to respond, her head bobbing as she steps forward. "A show of resistance?" Her eyebrows quirk up momentarily before dipping as her expression morphs into a determined smirk.

All it takes is Jane's endorsement. Everyone quickly jumps on board with my idea. After a few giddy moments and a litany of excited whoops, the girls move into position. One after another, a crooked line emerges in front of the small, oval mirror hanging on the wall.

"What are we calling this?" Jane, who is unsurprisingly first to be situated in front of the mirror, swivels her head toward me. The deep red hue of the lipstick pokes out from its gold tube.

I tap a finger to my still-bare lips as a bubble of exhilaration rises within me. "How about the Resistance Red Brigade?"

Jane's red-stained lips smile back at me. "I like it." Smacking her lips together, she steps away from the mirror and passes the lipstick to the next maid in line.

I am thrilled with the maids' enthusiasm. Fifteen minutes later, we parade out of the locker room, dressed in our maid's uniforms, with our lips painted deep red, and with our spirits lifted in unity. The desire to chant something empowering brews within me, but fitting words do not appear.

We take to the back-of-house stairs as a group and bid our first-floor counterparts a successful day as they file from the stairwell onto the first floor of guest rooms. A surge of excitement courses through me as our group bids the second-floor maids a good day.

By the time we've reached the fifth floor, I can barely contain my enthusiasm. I try my utmost to focus on the task of restocking my cleaning cart, but everywhere my gaze lands, all I see are the bright faces of strong women determined to make a statement. My cheeks ache from my wide smile. In this moment, I couldn't be prouder.

Hazel, one of the quieter maids among us, draws our attention. "It's time," she says, looking up from her wristwatch.

"Roll call, ladies." I march from the supply cupboard to our designated location in the hall and wait for the hotel matron to arrive.

Right on time, the door leading to the back-of-house stairwell squeals open and Clara steps onto the plush, blue-grey carpet of the fifth floor, her regular eighth-floor uniform swapped for the most demure dress from her closet. Her gaze sweeps the line of maids until she catches me in her sights. Though her unease is likely invisible to everyone else, I note the slight squint of her eyes and drawn nature of her downturned mouth.

All I can think is that she knows, and for the first time since the maids agreed to join me, I consider the wrath of my sister's disappointment. I conveniently set aside any concern over Clara and her new role as matron before leaping in and committing to the plan. There will be a price for my decision.

That I am certain of. My only hope now is that my rash actions today won't cost me the favour of my sister. I may be strong, but in reality, though I hate to admit it, I need my family's backing to help prop me up, especially when I am venturing beyond what is deemed acceptable for a young woman in Vancouver.

After delivering our day's roster and last-minute instructions, Clara dismisses us—but not before holding me in place with a steady stare.

"Miss Wilson, please see me in my office in thirty minutes."

She doesn't even wait for a reply, and before my red-stained lips part to speak, Clara has vacated the fifth floor, presumably on to her next task of the morning.

My trip to Ms. Thompson's basement office feels more like a slink than a stroll. I feel my shame battle my desire to come out swinging and prove my point. I knock lightly on the open door.

"Come in." Clara's voice is clear but difficult to read. Inside, her head is bent over a stack of papers in front of her. "Close the door, please, and take a seat."

I swallow a lump in my throat and wonder for the first time if my sister will fire me over my attempt at resistance.

Normally I wouldn't hesitate. I'd race ahead, eager to get my side of the story out, but something in my sister's demeanour holds me back from saying anything at all.

Clara straightens the papers and places them to the side of the desk before meeting my gaze. Her lips twist in what I assume is contemplation. When she folds her hands together on top of the desk, I realize fully that I'm in for it.

"How could you, Lou?" Her pretense of calm vanishes. "You know how important this position is to me. I'm already fighting an uphill battle, with the maids unsettled and Ms. Thompson unwell."

My bottom lip makes its way between clenched teeth. "I'm sorry, Clara. I didn't think—"

I'm not given the chance to finish my sentence, as my sister is clearly ready to quarrel. "No, you didn't. Is this purely another case of what Louisa wants coming before everything else? 'Cause if it is, I'm not interested."

"How could you say that?" I stand, pushing the chair back with a squeal. "Do you think I want to be demoted simply because I am a woman? Do you think it's okay for our legal system, the one that is supposed to protect all Canadians, to strip us of our rights, our voice, our humanity? I thought you understood the unfairness of this ruling."

Clara stands to meet me eye to eye. "I do understand the unfairness. But what do you possibly think you and a handful of maids can accomplish? We have no power, Lou. We never have."

"How can you say that? We won the right to vote. Women infiltrated the workforce in a big way during the war. We are on our way to greater equality. Well, we were until the verdict."

Clara's expression reads as defeated, but I am struggling to understand why. "Really?" She pushes, her voice rising an octave. "From where I stand, a woman has two options in life. Marry or remain a spinster and work."

Clara's hand flies to cover her mouth, a sure sign she's said too much.

"What are you talking about?" As the question hangs between us, I glimpse what is brewing beneath the surface. This argument has little to do with the verdict or the lipstick. Clara's worry is about her view of the life before her. My sister is scared of her own future. Her own choices. My heart squeezes in my chest at the realization, and I wonder if she is even aware of the worry she's holding tight.

"We may not have the authority we are looking for right now. But Clara, we certainly won't ever have it unless we stand up, together. That's the point of the Resistance Red Brigade."

Her lips quirk into a hint of a smile at the mention of the organized front's name, and I push forward, determined to make my sister understand. "Have you even considered what this means for our future? If we let these lawmakers write us out of our own lives, we will pay dearly for decades to come."

"I'm aware of how bad this is." Clara slumps into her chair, forcing its swivel into motion. "I'm certainly not blind to the ramifications of the verdict, Lou. I also know we would be nowhere if it weren't for Ms. Thompson, Mr. Olson, and The Hotel Hamilton. We owe it to them and to Mr. Hamilton for giving us a chance when few might have. The last thing I want to see is a feud between maids and bellboys over the inequity of pay, no matter how warranted the discussion is."

I open my mouth to protest, but Clara's raised hand forces me to reconsider.

"A riot isn't going to benefit the maids. It certainly isn't going to change the beliefs of society at large, and if you ask me, there is a difference between standing up for oneself with boldness and an all-out war against the very people who support our efforts on a daily basis."

"You're right. The thing is, I can't sit idly by and let those who believe a woman should have no voice think it's okay." I return to my chair and prop my elbows on Clara's desk. "I'm aware you have a job to do, and I'm not trying to undermine you. I promise you I'm not."

"But…?"

"But I think if you let the maids have this win, with the lipstick brigade, you'll improve morale while also bolstering their belief that they can stand up for their rights in a respectful manner. You might be surprised. An empowered woman is a force to be reckoned with, don't you think?"

Clara leans back in her chair, and I'm certain I can hear the wheels turning in my sister's head. I allow her time to consider a path forward. I bite the inside of my cheek to prevent myself from saying another word and taste a hint of blood.

With an abrupt movement, Clara places both her hands flat on top of the desk and stands. "Fine. You can wear your lipstick in protest. Just don't get it on the pillowcases."

I jump to my feet and reach for her hands. "You won't regret this. I promise you won't."

She holds her tongue on the topic of regret, choosing a neutral question instead. "Where'd you come up with the name? The Resistance Red Brigade, was it?"

I give her hands a squeeze of gratitude before pivoting toward the door. "The suffragettes wore red lipstick to demonstrate their resistance to the exclusion of women from voting. I figured if it worked for them, it might work for us too."

"Well, I'll give you this much, when greeted by an entire floor of maids, it certainly makes a bold statement."

I smile, pleased with her comment. Wearing Clara's approval like a feather in my cap, I turn toward the door and make a mental note to press my sister further about the options a woman has available to her in life.

CHAPTER 9

lara

Earlier this morning, Louisa returned to the fifth floor with a skip in her step. I'm grateful to have made amends with my sister while also maintaining my decorum as hotel matron. I spend the first part of the day poring over the schedule for the upcoming week, which takes more hours than I anticipated. By late afternoon, a worry has settled in beside me, keeping me company as I tally up each maid's workdays while ensuring their days off rotate fairly. With a hotel filled with maids, the task is daunting at best and mind-numbingly frustrating at worst.

Though I have yet to make time to speak with Mr. Olson about the events of this morning, I am quite sure he has seen the maids' staged resistance. How could he not have? Today, every single maid is smiling with dark red lips. I have to admit the protest looks remarkably good on them. If I weren't currently filling in for Ms. Thompson, I might have considered painting my own lips to brighten the day with quiet resistance.

I close the scheduling book and heave myself to standing. The long day is adding weight to the already heavy week ahead. Walking the short distance down the hall to the manager's office, I steady myself with a slow exhale before knocking on his door.

"Come in." His baritone voice echoes beyond the closed door, and I gently push it open.

"Mr. Olson, I was wondering if you can spare a minute of your time."

"Of course, Miss Wilson. My door is always open for you." He leans back in his chair, pencil twirling between his fingers. "I don't suppose this has anything to do with our entire roster of maids wearing shockingly bright red lipstick, does it?"

"Well, yes." I feel the heat of a blush and admonish my emotions for being so transparent.

He gestures to a chair across from his desk. "I assumed I would be privy to the full story at some point today." His good humour seems intact, which bodes well for me.

"My apologies for the delay. I've had my nose in the schedule." I take the offered seat and cross my ankles.

Waving off my concern, he leans forward, amusement written across his face. "Is it true they are demonstrating a united force against the Supreme Court decision?"

"I'm afraid so."

"Marvellous. We have the right sort of women lining our halls, Miss Wilson. Industrious yet respectful."

"I am relieved to hear you think so, sir, since I've given them permission to protest with their chosen shade of red lipstick, provided they are careful not to stain the linens." I feel my posture relax and allow my back to rest against the hard chair.

Mr. Olson positions his elbows on top of the desk. "I really shouldn't be surprised, given your level-headedness to this point, but I have to say that your allowance of this lipstick thing does intrigue me. I would have expected you to put a stop to any show of force, especially one so vivid."

I let out an embarrassed laugh. "If you must know, it was my bull-headed sister who convinced me. Her heart is in the right place, and she managed to empower the maids without causing tension among the rest of the staff." I stifle another laugh. "And I didn't have to save poor George from an attack of brooms and dusters."

"I'd call it a successful day, then." Mr. Olson chuckles as he pulls his pocket watch from his vest pocket. "What time did you arrive this morning?"

I feel my cheeks warm again. "I'm still trying to gain my footing."

"What time?" Though I'm certain he means business, I sense a teasing tone in his question.

"I arrived at half past five."

"Well then, it's time for you to pack up your things and head home for the day. I can guarantee the work will still be here in the morning."

"Yes, sir." I thank him and stand, glancing at my wristwatch. If I hurry, I can walk home with Louisa and Cookie.

Movement at Mr. Olson's door draws my attention. "Papa? What are you doing here?" Without waiting for a reply, I step forward, a flurry of awful scenarios flooding my mind.

"Can't a father come see his daughter doing important work?" His teasing tone erases my distress like magic.

Tilting my head to one side, I let him know I'm still waiting for an answer.

"I've come to see Mr. Olson." Papa looks past me, smiling and nodding at the hotel manager.

"Oh, is it about the wedding?" I look between the two men, knowing Cookie has asked Mr. Olson to do the honour of walking her down the aisle. Her family, still living in Ireland, won't be able to attend the ceremony.

Papa's smile never leaves his lips. "No, darlin'. I've come about Ruby's wages."

I feel my eyebrows converge in question, not understanding.

"Since we'll be married soon, I've got to sign the paperwork transferring her salary to my name." He says it so matter-of-factly that I feel my body sway, pushed back by the boldness of the admission.

"Your name?" Though I know this is likely not the time or place for such a discussion, I find myself unable to edge out the accusing tone from my voice.

"Clara, are you all right?" Papa takes hold of my arm to steady me. "This is how things are done. Ruby has made it clear she prefers to continue as head pastry chef at the hotel. I assumed you knew."

I force a tight smile. "Yes, I did know she was staying on. Only—" I stop myself from saying more. My gaze drops briefly to the floor as I try to regain my composure. "I shouldn't keep you." I step around my father, letting his hand fall away from my arm.

At the threshold, I glance over my shoulder. "I'll just tidy my things, then perhaps we can all walk home together." I do my best to add a semblance of levity to my delivery. "It will be a treat to enjoy an evening stroll, all of us." I press another smile into place. "I'll meet you by the pastry kitchen?"

Papa nods, though I can tell by his downturned expression and the concern in his eyes that he is aware of my unease.

My head is swimming as I return to Ms. Thompson's office, determined to tidy up before my departure. The news of Cookie handing over her hard-earned salary to Papa forces me into the chair with a thump. I'm aware Cookie's decision to remain employed as a married woman is unusual, but she assured me when the topic first arose that she had no designs to bear children at her age. Nor did she imagine herself sitting about the apartment waiting for the rest of the family to return from their workdays, not when she could be useful at the hotel.

I had admired her gumption and assumed her training and talent as a pastry chef afforded her a certain amount of acceptance among the working class. Besides, it isn't as if Papa runs in high society, where conventions must be followed at the risk of one's business ventures. I hadn't understood that forsaking her wages was an expected part of the arrangement. I have no idea if there is another way or if Cookie even wishes for a different outcome. All I know is that I would never do such a thing. If I were maintaining employment to ensure my individual financial security, I wouldn't be interested in handing my salary over to a husband, no matter how eager I was to be married.

A knock at the office door catches my attention. "Hazel, what brings you down here? I'd have thought you'd be eager to get home. Don't you have tomorrow off?"

Sliding the oversized scheduling book into the drawer, I reach for my spring jacket and search my friend's face. She hesitates, still waiting quietly outside the open door.

"I do." She hesitates and then adds, "Miss."

I wave off her deference while tugging my mind away from my spiralling thoughts to give her my full attention. "I think when there are no other maids around, you can still call me Clara. I promise I'm no different than I was on Saturday." My friend visibly relaxes as I coax her into opening up. "What did you want to talk to me about?"

"You look as though you are heading home for the day. I didn't mean to intrude."

"Hazel, please sit down. Clearly something is troubling you."

I relinquish my hold on my jacket and take a seat opposite her. The hard-backed chair groans as I swivel to meet her straight on and note the worry lining her features.

"Well, it's… Something dreadful has come to my attention." Hazel is typically quiet, but I've always felt she is more likely to be herself with me. She twists her fingers together. "Do you remember Miss Perkins? Well, her name is Mrs. Whitmore now. The maid who left the hotel's employ to marry her sweetheart."

"Yes, of course I do. Her vacating the position on the eighth floor is the reason I was able to move up." My mouth floods with the taste of metal as foreboding fills the small office. I resist the urge to shrug it off, not wishing to unnerve Hazel further. "What's happened?"

"Her husband was killed in a work accident last month. I got word this afternoon when I popped out at the midday break."

"Oh my heavens." My fingertips lift to cover my mouth, which is falling inelegantly open with the news. "How is she?"

"To be honest, she doesn't look well at all. Her husband

is—I mean was—the full extent of her relations. Well, him and the baby she is carrying."

My heart plummets toward my stomach. "Oh my goodness. I am so sorry to hear this. Is there anything we can do?"

"That's why I came to see you. With no income and no family support, I fear her future is grim. When her child is born, they will surely have an uphill road. I hoped you might have an idea of how best to assist them."

My head shakes, stuttering in its trajectory as my voice trembles. "I don't. Not at the moment." As soon as the words leave my lips, I realize my mistake.

Hazel's eyes fill with tears. "I haven't got much to offer them, but I simply can't leave them to fall into poverty."

Hazel's mention of poverty stops me cold. "Of course you can't. We won't. Leave this with me. I will think on it some more. Once the shock of the news has subsided, I'm sure we'll be able to find a way to help them."

My friend stands, though I fear it's on shaky legs. "Thank you, Clara. I made plans to meet Mrs. Whitmore for tea next week." Hazel's shrug is filled with defeat. "I thought the least I could do was treat her to a simple meal."

"You are a kind friend, Hazel. Don't you worry. Together, we will think of something." I stand and step around the desk to embrace my friend in a supportive hug, doing everything I can to infuse her being with hope.

Climbing the stairs to the corridor that leads to the back door takes every ounce of energy I have left. With a heavy heart and mind, I fear a restful sleep will not be mine tonight.

Mrs. Whitmore is in a dreadful situation. How did something so joyous turn into a disaster with a lifetime of difficulty ahead? The poor woman chose marriage, thinking it would see her through happily for the remainder of her life. Now, she has no job, no income, and no husband.

This day feels as if it will never end. Between Lou's lipstick brigade, Cookie's wages being diverted to Papa, and Mrs. Whitmore's dire situation, I am beyond exhausted. Adding to the upheaval is my admission to Louisa. I hadn't meant to speak the words out loud. If I'm being honest, I'm not sure I even realized how I was feeling until the words flew from my lips.

I always imagined I would do as Mama did. I would marry for love, raise a family, and create a home. I never considered that I might desire anything other than marriage. Now, though, with a prominent position within the hotel, temporary though it may be, I find myself unable to ignore how valued, respected, and worthy I feel as The Hotel Hamilton's matron.

Would I choose marriage to William over a career? Or would I live without his companionship but with financial stability and a career that provides me with a sense of value? Given the news of Mrs. Whitmore's situation, if I had to choose right now—though it breaks my heart to think it—I'd pick financial stability over anything. That's the thing about having previously teetered on the edge of financial ruin. The dread of it never seems to let you be.

My anguished sob stops me halfway down the corridor. I cannot invite the fears of poverty back into my life. I've worked too hard to grow beyond them, and yet, a single mention of another woman in need draws me back to square one. Even with the promise of love, marriage, and financial security with a husband who is a good earner, a woman can still land in a heap of despair, with a broken heart and an empty cupboard.

I shake myself free of my angst, determined to do

better for both Mrs. Whitmore and myself. I will do whatever it takes to ensure she is taken care of. I'll leave no stone unturned. I have no idea how I will manage such a task. All I'm sure of is that I must.

Straightening my posture, I tuck my anguish out of sight and proceed down the corridor with my head held high. I am the matron of this hotel, temporary or not. I cannot let anyone see me as weak. If I am going to fall apart, I'll do so in the seclusion of my own bedroom.

Laughter filters into the corridor as I make my way toward the back entrance. A smile comes easily as I spot Masao laughing with Papa, Louisa, and Cookie.

"What's all this about?" I tug on the arm of his jacket teasingly. "You look like you're having far too much fun, young man."

"Miss Clara!" Masao exclaims while gesturing toward Louisa. "Why is Miss Louisa dressed up like a geisha?"

"A geisha. My word." A bubble of laughter spills forth. "Ah, I see what you are saying. Her ivory skin and bright red lipstick."

Louisa rolls her eyes.

"But she's missing the beautiful, sleek black hair and the kimono," I say.

Masao erupts with giggles, spurring each one of us into a fit of laughter.

As our chortles subside, Cookie retreats to the pastry kitchen to fetch a sweet treat for the boy and Louisa grabs her opportunity with both hands.

"Actually, I am wearing this geisha lipstick, as you call it, in protest for women's rights."

"Huh?" Masao's dark eyebrows crowd together on his forehead.

"Some men in Ottawa decided that women were no

longer considered people. This lipstick"—Louisa taps her bottom lip—"is a quiet resistance to let them know that women are indeed people."

"Oh." Masao's face scrunches up in a question. "Why do you do that? My mother and grandmother say it's better to stay quiet and go unnoticed. That way nobody will make a fuss."

I feel the ground shift beneath my feet. Louisa and I exchange a look, our eyes as wide as our open mouths. Of course, Masao's mother and grandmother are all too familiar with prejudice, being not only women but Japanese women. Right when you think you're making progress toward a solution, somebody reshuffles the deck.

Cookie bustles toward us, a sweet-scented cinnamon bun in hand. The mood quickly changes as Masao takes a large bite, smearing glazed icing from cheek to cheek.

Cookie's gaze narrows on me. "Clara, you look as though you've had a day. Why don't you all head on home. I'll walk Masao home and stop by Ms. Thompson's on the way."

"Are you sure?" I begin to protest but have little energy to insist further.

"I left a casserole for you three in the refrigerator this morning. Cooked it last night at home. All it needs is a warm up." Cookie guides Masao toward the door. "I know how full your week is, Clara. I only want to help."

"Thank you." Louisa and I say at the same time.

"Ruby, you've outdone yourself with kindness again. Won't you join us for dinner? We'd be happy to wait, or we could join you in dropping this young man at home." Papa's coaxing gives Cookie reason to pause, a delighted smile lighting up her features.

"You three go ahead. I'll have a proper visit with Eliza

and an early evening for myself." She places a hand on Papa's sleeve. "Besides, sometimes a father needs time alone with his daughters."

Papa is about to protest, but Cookie waves him off. "I'll come by bright and early in the morning and see you before you head off for the day."

With the final word issued by Cookie, we say our farewells and breathe in the fresh scent of a May evening in Vancouver. As we stroll toward home, I hide the unease I've gathered throughout the day beneath a forced smile, not ready to share the burden with Papa, or even Lou. The news of Mrs. Whitmore's situation has unsettled me more than I care to admit, and with it comes uncertainty over my own future.

CHAPTER 10

MONDAY, MAY 7, 1928

ouisa

My Resistance Red Brigade is going strong. Stepping into the locker room first thing Monday morning, I am delighted to see our plan of action has yet to lose steam. I worried that commitment to the cause would lessen after some of the maids took days off from the hotel. But here they are, a committed group of women, all sporting red lips as they ready themselves for the workday.

Though the shade varies among the lot of us, I am bolstered by the success of our joining together to show the country that women won't stand for the ruling, even if only within the walls of The Hotel Hamilton. Quiet resistance is the key. We will not accept the Supreme Court's decision, but neither will we wallow, fret, or cause a scene.

Between last Saturday's audition, which I'm sure will grant me the lead role, and the maids' continued dedication to the lipstick brigade, I'm almost giddy as the fifth-floor maids line up for roll call. From my vantage point at the end of the row, I look down a straight line of crisp white aprons over blue uniforms. Pleasant but determined-looking faces fuelled by a shot of gumption and a dab of red wait patiently for today's instructions.

Thirty minutes into the day, I am called to room 503, where a distraught Gwen is furiously scrubbing a corner of bed linen over the bathroom sink. As I step into the tight space, I see that Gwen's tears are running as fast as her hands are scouring.

"Gwen." I place a calming hand on her shoulder. "What's happened?"

The maid who fetched me quietly disappears to give us privacy.

"I don't know how it happened." Gwen sniffles between words, but her head remains bent toward the bedsheet between her hands. "One minute I was making the bed. The next, a streak of red was staring back at me."

I tilt my head to get a look at the girl's face. Placing my hands over top of her frantically moving ones, I compel her to stop. "Let's put this down for a minute and take care of you first."

I remove the soiled linen, dropping it to the floor behind me. Placing a gentle hand beneath Gwen's chin, I nudge her face up. With the lipstick's impressive staying power, I recognize time is of the essence.

"Gwen, hand me that clean cloth."

The girl glances behind her to retrieve the washcloth, and as she turns back toward me, she glimpses herself in the mirror.

Her anguished wail catches me off guard. Her cry is

warranted. A streak of red has bled from Gwen's lip and down her chin, leaving a trail resembling that of a knife cutting through a slice of meat.

"Hush now. You don't want everyone to come running, do you?" I take the cloth from her hands and run warm water over it. "Now hold still while I fix this."

I dab gently at first, with no success. When I scrub harder, Gwen grimaces but doesn't protest. The stubborn line of lipstick chooses to smear instead of lift. I position one hand on Gwen's chin in an effort to keep her from checking our progress in the mirror.

"This won't do," I mutter to myself and instantly regret it, as Gwen's eyes grow wide with terror.

"What a mess I've created. I'll be sacked for sure."

"Nobody's getting sacked." I run the cloth under warm water and try again. "I don't suppose you have any cold cream in the locker room?"

Gwen's head shakes slowly back and forth.

"Actually, I have an idea." I step back, examining our lack of progress. "Have the guests for this room checked out already, or are they coming back later in the day?"

"They've checked out. Why?" Her chin, rubbed red, wobbles slightly with her words.

I place the washcloth on the sink's corner and step past the discarded sheet. "Stay here. I'm going to close the door, and I'll be back in a jiffy."

"Where are you going?"

"If you want me to help, you're going to have to trust me, Gwen." Considering our shared history, which resulted in a scandal with a despicable guest and Gwen's leave from the hotel for several months, I am certain she will acquiesce.

"I'll wait here, but Louisa, please hurry."

I waste little time consoling her and instead dash down the back-of-house stairs, thankful for my theatre experience once again. I know exactly how to remove the lipstick from Gwen's chin. Makeup is a constant presence in any production. Both the men and the women apply it for shading and more. Getting it off at the end of the night, though, can be a lengthy endeavour. Anyone who's spent hours smudging and smearing with little result knows to reach for cold cream or glycerin if they want any hope of getting home before dawn.

Flying through the corridor, I come to an abrupt stop at the threshold of a short hallway. This is the junction between the kitchen, the hotel lobby employee access point, the back-of-house corridor, and the pastry kitchen.

I inhale a steadying breath, straighten my apron, and walk calmly toward Cookie's pastry kitchen. Popping my head inside, the aroma of sweet treats makes my mouth water.

"Are you looking for me?" Cookie startles me from behind.

I clutch a hand to my chest. "You scared me."

"Well, that's a sure indication you're up to no good." Her words may be serious, but the mischievous smile tugging her mouth upward tells me she's my ally.

"There's been an incident with—" My lips twist as I consider the mess I am likely responsible for creating with my Resistance Red Brigade. I lean toward her and lower my voice. "With the lipstick. I was hoping you had some glycerin we could use for the cleanup."

"Ah, I see. I suppose you'd like your sister to remain unaware of this incident?"

My head bobs up and down ardently in agreement with Cookie's assessment.

"I'll give you the glycerin on one condition." Cookie moves past me toward her supply cupboard.

"What's the condition?" I follow close behind her.

"I told your father I'd be over to help with dinner, since Clara and I are working through the final plans for the wedding. On our way, I'd like to stop by Spencer's. Do you think you can help me choose a shade of red that is suitable for my ruddy complexion?"

Cookie hands me the jar of glycerin with a cheeky smile.

"Of course I can, but your complexion isn't ruddy. It's glistening with bride-to-be enthusiasm."

"Oh, is that what it is?" Sounding far less than convinced, she turns her attention to the glycerin. "Don't scrub too hard or you'll end up with a red spot either way."

"Thank you. I will bring the bottle back as soon as we're done with it."

Bottle in hand, I dash back up the stairs to room 503.

Ten minutes later, Gwen is lipstick free, relieved, and putting the final touches on the bed in the guest room as I turn my attention to the soiled sheet. I let the glycerin trickle over the stain before placing the corner over the edge of the bathtub, hoping time will do most of the work.

I chuckle to myself, knowing a few months ago I would have run straight to Clara for help. I've come a long way as a maid, and since my sister is currently in charge, the more I can accomplish on my own, the better.

I pick up the feather duster, catching Gwen's eye as I do. "I have to wait for the glycerin to work. Might as well make myself useful."

"I won't forget this, Louisa. Thank you."

A few minutes later, I return to the room I was cleaning before being called to help Gwen. The first round of glycerin faded the red streak in the sheet, but it didn't remove it entirely. Unprepared to admit defeat and risk the Resistance Red Brigade's success, I brought the sheet with me for a second round of glycerin treatment.

With the sheet soaking in a hearty dose of glycerin in the bathroom sink, I turn my attention to the room at hand. Being extra careful of my own painted lips, I strip and remake the bed, plumping the pillows against the headboard. I am hoisting the vacuum from the back of my cart when someone I never thought I'd see above stairs steps into the room, her mood foreboding her presence.

Jing may be slight and short of stature, but as the hotel's head laundress stands inside the guest room, she appears rather imposing indeed.

I bolt upright, taking the vacuum's handle with me. "Jing, what brings you to the fifth floor?"

"Miss Louisa." Jing crosses both arms over her chest. "I have a—how do you say?—bone to pick at you."

Knowing English is not her first language, I waver on whether she wants me to correct her phrasing. "Do you mean you have a bone to pick with me?"

Jing grunts in acknowledgement.

Stepping around the vacuum, which takes up a fair share of the space within the small guest room, I move toward Jing. "Have I upset you? I'm not sure how. It's been weeks since we've seen one another."

"You tell all the maids to wear bright red lips. That is the problem."

"Yes, that was me." Pride over our quiet resistance straightens my posture. "We are demonstrating our independence against—" I am not afforded the opportunity to finish my explanation.

"Red lips make Jing's work very difficult."

My head tilts sideways in question. "How so?"

"Too many stains."

Understanding dawns on me, dismantling my pride one vertebra at a time. "You're telling me the maids have been getting lipstick on the sheets?"

"On the sheets, the towels, the pillowcases. It's everywhere. I even have chair cushions that are marked red." Jing points an accusing finger at the wingback chair and its accompanying cushion.

"Oh my goodness. I am truly sorry. I had no idea." My mind reaches back to the sheet soaking in the bathroom. How naïve of me to think I had avoided a catastrophe. Gwen's sheet is clearly not the first casualty of my well-meaning brigade.

"You fix, Miss Louisa." Jing's plea strikes straight to my heart.

"Yes, I will fix it." My hands wring together as the battle between taking a stand against the verdict and making life harder for another woman rages inside me.

Jing's head bobs once in understanding before she turns on her heel to leave.

"Wait, Jing." I take a few quick steps toward her. "I'm truly sorry for the inconvenience. I did not intend to make your work more difficult. What can I do to help? Should I gather a few maids and help you in the laundry with the stains? I am sure—"

"No more red lips."

"No more red lips. Got it," I repeat with a defeated nod of my head.

Jing leaves the fifth floor as quickly and as silently as she arrived, but her departure does little for my disappointment or my remorse. I wanted to make a difference for women's rights, but all I ended up doing was creating extra work and strife for other women. That was not my intention at all. Once again humbled by the enormity of the task of standing up for all women, I immediately feel small, all over again. The familiar saying about a path and good intentions flits across my mind, souring my mood, and I question whether I can truly make a difference.

CHAPTER 11

MONDAY, MAY 7, 1928

lara

With less than two weeks to go, the countdown to Papa and Cookie's wedding has consumed every spare ounce of my time and energy. Between the hotel, Hazel's pressing desire to give Mrs. Whitmore promising news this week, and my continual ruminations, I haven't had the chance to speak with Louisa. I've been burning the candle at both ends for more than a week. A weary sigh slips from my lips, and my heart aches for my sister's camaraderie and insight. Despite sharing a bedroom, we've been ships passing in the night. Louisa, eager to secure her next leading role, has filled her schedule with auditions, and I've filled mine with more tasks than I'd like.

Cookie and Lou left the hotel an hour before me, saying something about stopping for a splash of colour. Though I had little time to inquire as to what they were giggling about, I am pleased that my sister has finally dropped her wariness over Cookie joining the Wilson clan. I've downplayed her comments for weeks, hoping Lou would embrace the coming changes. After all, they're beyond our control. I am doing as William suggested and being aware of potential conflicts while maintaining an open heart.

I walk home alone, relishing the quiet reprieve one can only find once the stores are shuttered. Solitude in a bustling city is a rare occurrence, so tonight I intend to enjoy every moment of it as I stroll toward home.

The door to our third-floor apartment is shut tight, but it can't mute the flurry of heated words coming from within. I retract my hand from the doorknob and take a step back, contemplating my options. The thought of retracing my steps away from The Newbury and finding a quiet café to wait out the disagreement unfolding inside feels like a cool breeze on a sweltering day. With my eyes and mind focused on the closed door, I don't hear him come up behind me.

"Clara?" Papa's voice is gentle, yet I can pick out the concern wrapped around his words. "What are you doing out here?"

"Papa." I whirl to face him. "I—"

There's no need for me to finish. Louisa's voice, loud and clear, bursts through the solid wooden door as if it were merely a curtain. "I can't believe you dragged me into Spencer's for some resistance red when all along you were cozying up to the other side."

Papa's eyebrows lift high into his forehead. "I don't suppose we can ignore whatever it is that's got your sister worked up." His shaking head tells me he too would rather hightail it out of here and head for calmer waters. "Sounds like it's going to be a long night."

His sad smile is my only comfort as he reaches past me and opens the apartment door.

I sneak in behind Papa, hiding in his shadow as we make our way into the apartment. As we move down the hall to hang our spring jackets, he glances into the kitchen with a weighted sigh.

"Joseph?" Cookie's voice cracks with emotion as she calls out in what I interpret as a plea for help.

Papa wraps an arm around my shoulders, and together we head into the eye of the storm.

"Evening, Ruby." Papa, reading the room, moves to Lou first and places his other arm around her shoulders. "What are my girls up to tonight? We could hear you clear across town."

The statement, though directed at Louisa, is delivered with a chortle intended to smooth the friction in the room.

Louisa ignores the comment, pivots, and directs her wrath squarely on me. "Did you know?"

I glance up at Papa, but even he can't shelter me from my sister's accusatory tone.

"Did I know what?" My gaze travels between Cookie and Lou.

The huff comes with enough force to take a sailboat clear out of the harbour. "Did you know Cookie is handing over her salary to Papa when they wed?"

Dread plummets from my chest to my shoes. I swallow hard as I kick myself for not having made time to discuss the matter with Lou. She is sure to think I've been keeping it from her, when in truth, I've been trying to come to terms with the knowledge myself. It was a punch to the gut when I learned it's common practice for a woman's paycheque to be given to her husband for him to manage. The troubling notion has had my stomach tied up in knots, making me wonder what I would be willing to give up should I decide to marry in the future.

Louisa shakes off Papa's arm, crossing her arms and tapping her toe. She's onto me. "I see. So you did know."

It's a statement, not a question.

"I've been so busy, and we haven't had time to talk, and…" My excuses do me little good.

"I'm alone in this, then, am I?" Louisa juts her chin up a notch, her eyes flashing between Cookie, Papa, and me, a sure indication she's more hurt than angry.

I despise the idea of hurting Cookie, or Papa for that matter, but if I'm to be honest, I've got to say so now. "You aren't alone. I understand why you're upset, and I agree with you. But we can only decide what is best for ourselves. This"—I gesture between Papa and Cookie—"is between them. Not us."

Lou's lips purse into a pout, unwilling to concede the point. "But she wanted to show her support of the resistance. Dragged me to the shops and spent oodles of time picking the perfect shade of red."

"Two things can be true at the same time, Lou." I offer a small smile in Cookie's direction. "A woman can desire rights and recognition for women while being content to have a loving, mutually respectful relationship with her husband. I can't say I'm sure it's how I want things to be in my life, but I also know you and I have been pooling our wages with Papa's since the moment we started working at The Hamilton. And Papa has discussed every purchase and debt with us since that day. He hasn't spent our earnings as if they were his alone. We've done it together, as a family."

Louisa's mouth twists as she contemplates my logic. "Yes, but—"

This time I don't let her have the upper hand. "No buts,

Lou. Think about the discussion we had regarding the telephone. The three of us went round and round over whether to spend the money or not. Do you remember how we solved it?" I don't wait for her reply. "Papa worked overtime hours for a full month to afford the installation on his own, and do you know why?"

Louisa's shoulders slump forward, a sure sign she knows she's lost this battle. I press forward, my tone taking on a soothing note. "Because he wanted us to be able to telephone him if we were going to be late. He didn't want us worrying over his worry. He did it for us, and even still, we all had to agree before he would spend the money on the telephone."

Stepping forward, Papa wraps Louisa in a hug. "I should have thought to discuss the matter with you, given how we've relied on one another since moving to The Newbury." He looks over his shoulder at me. "With both of you. I'm sorry I didn't consider your feelings when it comes to how our family finances are changing."

Cookie's voice is as quiet as I've ever heard it. "I didn't realize it would upset you so, Lou." Her hands twist within one another. "I never meant to disappoint you. Like Clara said, I do wish for women's rights to be strengthened, but I also wish to be a part of this family. You all mean the world to me, and since you've been contributing financially, I only wanted to do the same."

Louisa acquiesces with an apology of her own, humbled by the awareness of her regular contributions to the family pot. Despite her appearance of understanding, I am more than aware the conversation between my sister and me is far from over. One day, after the high emotions that come with organizing a wedding have faded, I am quite certain we will revisit the topic. Until then, I will do everything I can to ensure our home is a happy one as our little family of three becomes four.

I exchange glances with Cookie and spot the moisture gathering in her eyes. She loves us with everything she's got. When things start to get crowded in our little apartment, all I have to do is remember that.

CHAPTER 12

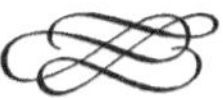

SATURDAY, MAY 12, 1928

*L*ouisa

This morning's telephone call is a welcome bit of
distraction. Since Jing's appearance on the fifth floor several
days ago and the heated discussion about Cookie's wages,
I've found myself brooding over how to positively impact
the fight for all women's rights. All women, including Jing.
Worried my thoughts are beginning to resemble Clara's
typical pattern of overthinking, I've pushed myself to focus
on other topics. Sadly, this has been less successful than I
would have liked, and I fear my crankiness is at an all-time
high.

Today, though, I've turned a new leaf. I stare at my
complexion in the bathroom mirror before reaching for my
red lipstick. Instead of plumping pillows and making beds, I
am heading to the director's office to pick up the script for
Mr. Brown's Secretary and begin the first day of rehearsals.
The telephone call offering me the role of the secretary

couldn't have come at a better time. I'm ready to dive in and sink my time and attention into something I can control.

Thomas was the first person I told. A brief telephone call with the man who is eager to see me succeed set the tone for a jubilant morning. After a quick bite of toast and a half cup of tea gulped while standing over the kitchen sink, I grab my bag and head into the warm spring morning, with Thomas's encouraging words tucked in my heart.

Thankful for a day off from the hotel, I take in the blue sky above. Not a cloud in sight, I think as I make my way toward a small park nestled in between two office buildings.

Having grabbed the script from the director's office, I lay my spring jacket on the bench and sit with my face angled toward the sun. A few warming minutes later, I pluck the script from my bag and begin reading. Eager to be immersed in the story, I set my enthusiasm on high and wait for the play to wash over me.

Forty-five minutes later, the hard bench forces me to shift positions. I glance up from the pages and feel my brows knit together. It isn't only the bench that is rubbing me the wrong way. The character of Mr. Brown's secretary is flat. She has skills but is so stoically demure she doesn't take any credit for her role in Mr. Brown's success.

"Nothing more than a cardboard cut-out." I say to myself, tossing the script onto the bench beside me.

I stand to stretch and pace back and forth in front of the bench. Running a hand through my waves, I try to examine the character from a different perspective—one that will bring life and meaning to her. Given the play's title, I assumed Mr. Brown's secretary would be a pivotal element to the story, but sadly, this woman is simply a prop for good ol' Mr. Brown. The play is intended to be humorous, but from what I've read so far, the only one getting the laughs is Mr. Brown himself. That won't do. That won't do at all. Women, especially now, need to be seen as versatile, intelligent, witty, and capable of doing the job at hand.

Deciding a change of scenery might provide the inspiration I require to fully embrace the secretary's role, I head for the café across the street and a much-needed cup of coffee.

Settled at a table in the far corner of the diner, with a steaming mug of dark brew, I open the script to the opening scene.

The New York city offices of Mr. Brown. Mr. Brown's secretary, Agatha Taylor, is seated at her desk when Mr. Brown blusters into the office, late as usual. She stands to greet him.

Agatha Taylor: Good morning, sir. Your coffee and your paper.

Agatha hands coffee and paper to Mr. Brown.

Mr. Brown: Good morning, Miss Taylor. Take this down, will you?

Agatha is seated at her desk (typewriter) with fingers poised.

Mr. Brown: Ahem.

Dear Mr. Samson, I am pleased as punch to accept your invitation to...whatever that dinner thing is.

(Sound of monotone typing.)

Agatha: The annual Business Review gala, sir.

Mr. Brown: Yes, yes, that. Tell him I'll be there with bells on.

Agatha: *(Typing)* I look forward to an evening within your dignified company.

Mr. Brown: Yes, that! That's what I meant. You really do know how to make me sound like an Oxford man.

Agatha: I wouldn't dare, sir.

"You may be flat on paper, Agatha Taylor, but I will make you shine." I dig a pencil from my bag and begin writing notes in the margin, adding a raised eyebrow here and an eye roll there. I practice the words out loud a few times, working on the timing and deadpan delivery. This is how I'll do it, I decide. My contribution to the play will be putting my own stamp on this character. The audience will adore Miss Taylor once I'm through with her.

I relish the buzz of anticipation as I step into the rehearsal hall. A makeshift set is positioned atop a basic wooden platform, but I can make out the bones of an office setting. Striding to the front of the hall, I say hello to the others and play my usual first-rehearsal game of guessing who is portraying which role.

The director, Max Barker, joins us and makes introductions. I'd heard of Mr. Barker's theatre accolades, but I'd never met him until the first audition. I recognize a couple of names from other productions, and when a young woman arrives a few minutes later, I do a double take before recognizing her. Ana left the audition for *All Souls Eve*, with her friends in tow, after Eve Dumont decided the role would be hers. I give Ana a brief but friendly wave, pleased that our paths have crossed again.

After a head count to ensure all are present, the director asks us to turn to the first scene in the script. A man named

Archie, who is a few years older than me, is playing Mr. Brown. We climb the two steps onto the stage before he shakes my hand in introduction. I see in an instant why Archie is the perfect actor for Mr. Brown. His vivid and plentiful facial expressions are sure to get laughs from the audience at every turn.

I am bolstered by this insight. With a talented actor beside me and a director credited with a long list of commendations, this production will be a lot of fun. The director moves a few pieces of office furniture before offering me the seat behind the desk.

"Let's read through the first scene and see what we're working with." He removes himself from the stage, standing in the corner in a contemplative pose, his chin resting in one hand. "Let's begin."

Archie comically struts into the pretend office, and I smother a smile.

I read my line and stand to hand him an imaginary coffee and paper.

When my next line comes, I add my signature eyebrow lift, which elicits an appreciative smile from Archie. I turn toward the make-believe audience and roll out a deadpan glance, along with a significant pause to add weight to my dialogue.

We are sailing through the first scene, the harmony between my and Archie's characters clicking into place, when the director interrupts with a loud "Wait, wait, wait."

Both of our heads swivel to take in his direction.

"Miss Wilson, can you stick to the script, please? We've got a lot to get through this afternoon."

"I'm sorry, did I misread something?" I am flipping pages, searching for my misstep.

"No, Miss Wilson. You didn't misread anything. There's no need for theatrics is all."

I almost laugh out loud but catch myself when the director's serious expression remains intact. No need for theatrics. Isn't that the whole point of a play?

"Okay, again," the director hollers from the edge of the stage.

"But, sir. My apologies for interrupting. I'm not sure what you are referring to. I'm merely testing out options for my character's personality."

An impatient whoosh of air leaves the director's lips. "Miss Wilson, your character doesn't need a personality."

My chin drops, leaving my mouth agape. It's the murmurs from the rest of the cast that assure me I'm not wrong in my reaction to this comment. Smothering my desire to unleash a witty retort, I remind myself of the man's extensive theatre experience.

Understanding dawns on Mr. Barker, and he jumps to correct himself. "What I mean to say is that today is simply about reading through the script together. There is no need to read too much into your character at this time." He grins in my direction, but instead of eliciting understanding, his smile makes me feel uneasy. "Your character doesn't need a personality today, Miss Wilson."

"Yes, sir." I stuff my opinion out of sight, not wishing to appear disrespectful, but my elation over this new role is deflating like a popped balloon. Summoning my desire to remain professional, I remind myself, this is an opportunity to learn from this man.

"From the beginning," the director calls out before stepping back to the sidelines.

I do as I'm instructed and simply read my lines. No embellishments. No eye rolls. Not even the slightest lift of my voice. By the time five thirty arrives, I am bored beyond measure.

"That's a wrap," the director announces as he closes his script and walks toward the hall's entrance.

Archie catches my arm lightly as I step from the stage. "If it makes a difference, I preferred the first take."

I feel my cheeks flush and offer him a quiet thank you before heading for the door.

As I near the door, I give the director a polite nod. As soon as I've passed him, his voice booms out again. "Archie, join me in my office, will you?"

"Figures," I mutter while pushing open the rehearsal hall door with more force than necessary. I feel the director's eyes on my back as I rush from the building.

The walk to The Newbury feels all uphill, despite the sidewalk having no incline at all. My mind whirs with emotion-tinged questions—questions I wouldn't even ask myself under normal circumstances, since taking my eyes off my goal of becoming a Hollywood actress simply isn't an option.

Tonight, though, after a disappointing rehearsal, I let the irrational thoughts ping-pong through my mind. How is it that Archie was not only permitted but expected to showcase his talents for Mr. Brown, when poor Miss Taylor was shoved into a box? And why was Archie invited back to speak with the director and I wasn't? I see where I stand in this production, and I don't like it one bit.

CHAPTER 13

SATURDAY, MAY 19, 1928

lara

The early-morning telephone call pulls me from a restless
sleep.

"Wilson residence." My attempt to edge my sleepy state
from the greeting is unsuccessful.

"I woke you." William's voice is lined with concern.
"Shall I call back in an hour?"

I laugh as my heart swoops with delight. "Don't be silly.
I'm awake now."

"I'm sorry. I didn't want to miss you, and I wasn't sure
what time you'd be leaving for the church."

"You've nothing to apologize for. I should already be
up." I lean a shoulder against the wall, relishing its
invigorating coolness. "Cookie kept us up going over the
plans for the day."

His soft chuckle sends a delicious shiver over my skin.

"In other words, she was too excited to sleep and you were her company?"

"Yes, that's an accurate assessment of the events." I try but can't smother the smile in my voice.

"I spoke with Eliza last evening. She said she will be at the ceremony but not likely to make the reception. The doctor advised her against attending at all, but she told him plainly that she was going to the wedding."

I stifle a laugh, imagining the matron telling the doctor what for. "That's kind of her. How is she feeling?"

"Getting better every day." I can picture him shaking his head with a knowing smile. "So much better, in fact, she had the energy to berate me about not yet securing a train ticket to Vancouver. I suspect she was hoping I'd arrive in time for the wedding."

I snap to attention. "Oh, I didn't realize you were planning a trip." The idea of seeing William exhilarates and terrifies me. "I thought you weren't able to leave Toronto due to the court case you're working on."

"Yes, this one has been delayed several times over, and since I'm uncertain of when things will resume, I've been reluctant to leave town. Eliza assured me when she fell ill that I didn't need to make the trip to check on her. Perhaps boredom has overcome her now and she's desperate for some fresh company."

A light sigh of relief slips past my lips, and I admonish myself for being relieved by the lack of an imminent visit from William. "I'm sure it isn't easy being housebound. I'll stop over for a visit soon. After today's celebration, I'm certain I'll have a touch more time on my hands. Perhaps that will help."

"Would you? Clara, thank you. I know she would enjoy

a visit with you." William pauses before lowering his voice and adding, "Come to think of it, so would I."

The sultry nature of his words brings a flush of warmth to my cheeks. My heart leaps ahead of my mind. "Me too." The confirmation is out before I can think better of it.

"I'm pleased to hear it." The low rumble of his acknowledgement sends my stomach flipping. "I hate to let you go, but I'm sure you have a thousand things to do. I only wanted to wish you and your family luck and happiness today."

My smile grows wide at his thoughtfulness—or is it his heart? "Thank you. I will be sure to pass on your well wishes to Cookie."

"Enjoy the day, Clara. I am truly happy for all of you."

"Thank you." Just when I thought it wasn't possible, my heart swoons a little more for William Thompson. "Goodbye."

After months of planning, I can hardly believe the day is finally upon us. I stand behind the oversized wooden doors of the sanctuary, where the organ plays quietly, and I imagine guests settling into the moulded-wood church pews. I release a slow breath, trying to settle my nerves as I tick off the list that's been embedded in my mind since the date was set. The centre aisle leading to the altar is lined with spring flowers tied with broad white ribbons. I positioned them in place earlier this morning, the blooms mixing delightfully with the faint scent of candle wax and the church transforming before my eyes.

With Cookie's unending list of tasks, I've been so busy I haven't had time to feel nervous. That is, until this moment.

The organist pauses before serenading the wedding guests with one of my mother's favourite hymns. This is my cue. The song that never fails to move me floats in the air, and I feel butterflies take flight within my rib cage. The tall, ornately carved, wooden doors are pulled open with a well-timed whoosh. All heads pivot in my direction.

Pasting on a smile, I take a tentative step forward while trying to time my movements to the music. My gaze lands on Papa, and I feel adoration emanating from him. His love for Mama transcends time, distance, and even death. This song is his gift of thanks to her for teaching him not only how to love but how to recognize it from another. If someone had asked me a year ago, I would have said my father would never remarry. Once ignited, though, it didn't take long for the spark between Cookie and Papa to develop into something more.

I take careful, slow steps toward the altar, feeling Louisa's presence a few paces behind me. The bouquet in my hands shakes slightly, despite my best efforts to still the emotions running through me. As I near my father, I resist the urge to wrap him in an embrace, choosing instead to take my designated place across from him as Cookie's bridesmaid.

Louisa takes a final step and falls into line beside me. She gracefully turns toward the guests and the doors at the threshold of the narthex, once again closed. The vibration of the bridal chorus thrums through my body as everyone in attendance stands to face the back of the church in anticipation of the blushing bride.

The doors are pulled open by two men in matching dark suits, who stand as though steel rods run the length of their spines. A beaming Cookie dressed in a bias-cut, tea-length satin gown appears in the doorway, a large bouquet of flowers draped across her arm and Mr. Olson at her side. The flowing embroidered veil flatters her every curve, making her a vision in white. I hear Papa's sharp inhale, and I glance in the nick of time to watch him place an emotional hand over his heart.

Cookie's gaze remains locked on Papa's as Mr. Olson guides her down the aisle, her hand in the crook of his steadying arm. Papa, I notice, cannot hide his delight, and his smile grows wider with each step she takes. I feel the prick of moisture at the corners of my eyes and press my lips together, futilely attempting to stay my happy tears.

A warm welcome from the minister is followed by a short prayer before the guests reclaim their seats. The ceremony begins with the reading of 1 Corinthians 13. The minister's booming voice recites the familiar passage.

"Love is patient" echoes around the nave as my gaze scans the rows of guests, all present to show their love and support for my father and Cookie. I note Ms. Thompson's presence, making eye contact with the matron while delivering an appreciative smile.

My thoughts shift to William and his telephone call this morning. His thoughtfulness knows no bounds, and even though it unnerves me at times, I know I am fortunate to have his light shone upon me. Despite my unease over the choices that lie ahead, our weekly letters and monthly phone calls have prompted imaginings of a future together. In moments when I'm missing him dreadfully or during a particularly tiring day at the hotel, I let my thoughts wander and my heart warm to the idea of being a lawyer's wife in a quiet Toronto suburb. When my defences are down, the notion of such a life feels less claustrophobic than it does when I'm thriving and independent. Such imaginings are perhaps made easier by the safe distance between Vancouver and Toronto.

Cookie turns to me, handing me her bouquet, which I juggle with my own smaller one. I look on, a genuine smile upon my face as my father recites his vows.

"I, Joseph, take thee, Ruby, to be my wedded wife, to have and to hold from this day forward, for better, for worse, for richer, for poorer, in sickness and in health, to love and to cherish, till death us do part, according to God's holy law. In the presence of God, I make this vow."

I swipe a tear from my cheek as Cookie repeats after the minister.

"I, Ruby, take thee, Joseph, to be my wedded husband, to have and to hold from this day forward, for better, for worse, for richer, for poorer, in sickness and in health, to love, to cherish, to obey, till death us do part, according to God's holy law. In the presence of God, I make this vow."

The word "obey" catches me by surprise. I resist the urge to shake my head with disbelief, not wanting to disrupt the ceremony or the pile of curls Louisa so carefully heaped into place this morning with an excessive number of bobby pins. Surely the wording was a mistake. Papa's vows mentioned nothing of the sort, and yet Cookie—dear, sweet Cookie who has already signed over her salary to my father —has just agreed to obey him for as long as she lives.

I snatch a look in Louisa's direction but find my sister smiling as she watches the happy couple exchange rings. Surely, she must be acting. My sister, outraged by the state of women's rights, must be aware something is amiss. Is this what marriage truly means for women? All my worries over my future rise to the surface, bringing a fiery flush to my cheeks.

Louisa nudges me from behind, whispering, "Are you okay?"

I remind myself of where I am and of my role here today as Cookie turns toward me to accept her flowers back into her arms. Her wide smile begs me to respond in kind. I've no desire to ruin her special moment, so I nudge the unease from my mind while coercing my expression into one of complete joy.

A few minutes later, with vows exchanged and gold rings placed on one another's fingers, the official union is complete. The entire ceremony took less than an hour. On cue with the quiet organ music, I thrust my concerns over the wedding ceremony to the back of my mind and focus on the next tasks in my charge. I obediently adjust Cookie's veil and wish her well for her first steps down the aisle as Mrs. Wilson.

The minister introduces Joseph and Ruby Wilson to the congregation in a hearty announcement. The guests stand as the bride and groom make their way down the aisle at a slow pace but with delightful joy.

Louisa and I fall in behind them and are escorted outside by Papa's groomsmen. My arm is linked with Mr. Murray's, and Louisa accompanies one of Papa's friends from the city parks crew. As the sun shines high in the early-spring sky, my head spins with the list of duties I am responsible for at the upcoming reception. Until the job was bestowed upon me, I had little knowledge of the looming task list necessary to ensure a wedding reception is enjoyed by all.

Mr. Hamilton, at the request of Mr. Olson, generously offered a small banquet room at the hotel for the wedding reception. Cookie, using the hotel's pastry kitchen and ingredients she purchased herself, has worked into the last several nights to prepare treats and an elaborate wedding cake that is sure to have all the guests talking.

Cookie, thankfully experienced with hosting large events, has been giving me impromptu lessons so I can take charge as she enjoys the day. We've spent oodles of time together going over every detail to ensure the day's success. I am both honoured and overwhelmed by the responsibility. Despite the unease roiling within me, my only desire is to make Cookie proud today.

Though invited to both the ceremony and the reception, Chef insisted on staying in the kitchen, offering his gift, with Mr. Hamilton's permission, of a sit-down luncheon for today's festivities. Eager to arrive at the hotel before the bride and groom, I excuse myself from the crowd the moment Papa and Cookie are swept into the back of Mr. Olson's automobile. Louisa joins them for the journey, sliding into the front seat for the short drive to the photography studio.

Thankful that a few highly capable eighth-floor maids are already adding the finishing touches to the banquet room, I catch the first streetcar and release an emotional sigh, telling myself I can do this. All will be well. Once their wedding has been thoroughly celebrated, I can take the time to consider my next steps.

Arriving at the hotel, I use the main lobby entrance, hoping to reach the banquet room as quickly as possible. The doorman opens the door with the flourish of a slight bow and says, "It's an exciting day here, Miss Wilson. An exciting day, indeed." I do my best to summon a brilliant smile and hurry past in a flurry of spring air and chiffon ruffles.

I wave a quick hello to Mr. Reynolds, the registration desk manager, whom I once assumed to be a perpetual stick in the mud, as I set my sights on George. The affable bellboy sees me coming and rushes to open the swinging door that leads to the back-of-house corridor.

"Hello, George." I step from the hotel lobby into the bright white hallway.

With a flush of colour on his cheeks, George steps into the hallway behind me. "Mr. Olson told me to let you know that I am to be at your disposal. There's nothing we wouldn't do for our Cookie."

"Thank you, George." I give his arm a quick squeeze of appreciation and step toward the corridor. I refrain from dashing down the hall at a full gallop and instead force my legs to maintain a brisk but ladylike pace until I am out of sight.

As I climb the stairs to the second level, the joyful sound of my friends' happy work seeps into the hallway like an ocean's tide coming to shore. After the double doors are swung open, it takes only a moment for Rebecca to spot me at the threshold. Rushing forward, white linens in hand, Rebecca embraces me in a fierce hug.

"Oh, Clara. Everything is absolutely perfect. Ms. Thompson called earlier in the week and insisted we put out the best of the best. The boys have been polishing the silver since last Tuesday. It's so shiny we could use it as a looking glass."

Eyeing the transformed banquet room, I feel fresh emotion rise within me. "I don't know how to thank you. I'm certain I wouldn't have been able to handle this myself."

"Don't be silly. We're thrilled to be a part of Cookie's big day." Rebecca presses my hands into hers. "Now, come see the centrepiece. I want to make sure everything is precisely as you imagined."

I'm thankful for the busy distraction. An hour speeds by as we put the finishing touches in place. Bellboys and maids work together, filling water jugs, setting tables, lighting candles, and dimming the lights to a soft glow. The crystal chandelier tugs my gaze upward as the lights dim and the well-positioned candles flicker and dance around the room.

Across from the banquet room, the lift dings. Mr. Tuppary, the lift operator, steps out and announces as quietly as I've ever heard the man speak, "They're here."

A flurry of activity follows as ten or so Hotel Hamilton employees cram into the lift's cage and descend to the lobby level. Several others dash down the hall to the back-of-house stairs. I am left wondering what to make of the commotion when Rebecca takes my hand and guides me to the balcony railing overlooking the high-ceilinged lobby below.

I peer over the rail, taking in the gleaming wooden beams that, without fail, cause my breath to hitch each time I admire them. I drop my gaze to the hotel lobby. A wave of gratitude brings another round of fresh tears. Among the polished tiles, marble registration desk, and dark wood tables adorned with fresh flowers are two straight rows of hotel employees. The lines run from the red-carpeted steps, beyond the gold-trimmed glass doors, and all the way to the lift, which is open and waiting for the newlyweds. The Hotel Hamilton staff have come out, one and all, dressed in their best to welcome Papa and Cookie to their wedding reception.

Rebecca gives my hand a reassuring squeeze as I covertly wipe a tear from my cheek. "Just think, Clara, you'll be next. I can hardly wait for the day I witness you become Mrs. William Thompson." My friend, clearly filled with wedding exuberance, gushes. "You as a high-society wife. No more making beds or scrubbing bathtubs for you." Rebecca lets out a shrill giggle. "I imagine you'll have your own maids to tend your beautiful two-story house with a wraparound porch. Oh, and a nanny too. You know, for the little ones that are sure to come along."

Rebecca's words are enough to knock me over, but when she inadvertently bumps into me without pausing for breath, I find myself grappling with the rail to steady myself. "I do hope you'll remember those who knew you before you stepped into the life of the elite." Rebecca's laughter cascades from her lips like a crystal chandelier plunging from the ceiling, tinkling on its descent until it shatters against a polished marble floor.

A shiver so deep it feels yanked from the depths of my soul forces chill bumps to prickle my skin. My turn next. I shudder at the thought. I've no want of a large house that requires a single maid, much less more than one. I certainly never dreamed of having my children raised by anyone but me. It's true William's career places his income, and thus his privilege, heads above my own. Until this moment, I haven't considered the true impact of our societal gap.

Though I'm certain she means no harm, surely Rebecca knows me well enough to realize that I don't seek the embellishments of the upper crust. Besides, I love my job at The Hamilton. I am proud of myself for achieving the role of eighth-floor maid and even prouder of my time as hotel matron. In my temporary position, I have guided maids with a gentle hand and an encouraging word. Every day presents me with the satisfaction of a job done well, even if it's accompanied by an aching back and sore feet.

I shake my head as Rebecca turns her attention back to the hubbub in the lobby. I have little time to scrutinize the fear that her proclamation has driven into the centre of my being. A loud cheer arises from the lobby, drowning out everything, including my wayward thoughts.

Hoots and hollers of "congratulations" and "look at the happy couple" infiltrate the two floors of the hotel's front entrance. Rebecca calls down from the balcony, cheering and waving with those below. I coerce a delighted expression and fix it in place, determined to put aside for now the choice between William and a career, knowing it may very well be the most difficult decision I'll ever have to make.

CHAPTER 14

SATURDAY, MAY 19, 1928

*L*ouisa

I wiggle my fingers in a wave toward Thomas. Despite him being back in Vancouver and my life for the past three months, I've yet to tire of seeing his handsome face. He's arrived at the hotel ahead of the bridal party and is patiently waiting with a few other guests for the reception to begin. His tall frame leans comfortably against the hotel's brick façade as I slowly make my way into the hotel with the bridal party, sans Clara.

Papa and Cookie are stopped a few paces into the building by a warm welcome from the hotel staff. As soon as I am able, I skirt the long line of well-wishers and head straight for the second floor, where Clara watches the scene below. My heels sink into the plush blue carpet as I rush forward.

"Thank heavens you're here." I embrace my sister in a hug fit for a lengthy time apart, rather than the short ninety minutes since I saw her last. "I had no idea a few photographs could be so vexing. I was ready to pull my hair out when the photographer demanded yet another pose, which is sure to be identical to the first twelve."

"Speaking of hair." Clara motions to my soft curls, haphazardly dancing about my face. "You look lovely as always, but Cookie did request our hair be styled up today. Why don't you head to the washroom and freshen up? I'm quite certain the happy couple will be several more minutes. We still have time to get the receiving line in place before the guests arrive."

My hand goes to my waves, tucking a strand behind my ear. "The wind kicked up a bit as we were leaving the photography studio, and I was focused on getting Cookie back into the car without mussing her hair. Lord knows how long it took to get that veil to stay put in the first place."

"You've got time." Clara gives my arm a squeeze. "Meet us in the banquet room when you're ready." Her words are pleasant and delivered with a smile, so I'm not sure why I feel a ripple of unease running through my sister.

When I return from fixing my hair, Hazel, the most timid maid The Hamilton employs, ushers me into the receiving line. With Clara to my right and Paul, the groomsman I've been paired with for today's events, to my left, I am anchored in place, as I prefer to be. I catch a glimpse of Thomas as he ducks out of the line of guests waiting to greet their hosts, choosing instead to stand in my line of sight and watch the goings on. I feel a blush warm my cheeks as his intense gaze lands on me.

"Is that your beau?" Paul asks, his chin jutting in Thomas' direction.

"Yes, that's Thomas Cromwell."

"I remember your father mentioning he was an aspiring director. I hope his time in California was a success."

I take in Paul's kind expression. It's no wonder he's Papa's closest friend from the city parks crew. "It was. He was invited to spend time on the set of a motion picture. Came back with a fire in his belly." I laugh at the memory of Thomas talking non-stop for hours his first day back in Vancouver, as excited as a small child who had been to the circus for the first time.

"And you? Your father said you were a hit in *All Soul's Eve*." Our conversation pauses as a couple I've never met offers their congratulations before moving on to Clara and Mr. Murray.

"That is kind of him to say, but then again, he is my father." A knowing smile stretches my lips. "We wrapped up the play about a month and a half ago, so now it's on to the next role."

"No rest for the weary?" Paul teases before shaking hands with his and Papa's boss and introducing me. "This is Joseph's eldest daughter, Louisa."

"Ah, the actress. Bound for Hollywood, I hear." The portly man exudes enthusiasm, and I can see why my father speaks highly of him.

"That's the plan." I offer a polite curtsy. "I have a few more credits to gather, but eventually…" My words trail off as more guests enter, increasing the noise in the room.

Papa's boss tucks his chin and whispers closer to my ear. "Stay the course, Miss Wilson. You never know which decision will be the one that sends you soaring." He issues an encouraging wink before stepping in Clara's direction.

"Thank you, sir." My words are quiet, given the trouble I'm currently facing with the director of *Mr. Brown's*

Secretary. I'm ready to soar, I think. If only that blasted director would let me do my job.

My mood is elevated again when Masao appears before me. "Well, my friend," I say to the boy who stole my heart the very first day I made his acquaintance. "I am very pleased to see you here today."

"Miss Louisa, I have never been in this part of the hotel. It is very nice." The boy's eyes are as big as saucers when he spots the wedding cake waiting safely on a table in the corner of the room.

I say hello to Masao's parents, greeting them with a traditional Japanese bow. "Thank you for coming. Cookie and Papa will be so pleased to see you here."

"We cannot stay long. We do not wish to intrude," Masao's father informs me stoically.

"You are invited and welcomed guests. You are our friends. Besides"—I wink at Masao—"you won't want to miss Cookie's cake."

Masao's expression pleads with his father as his small body twists in anticipation.

Masao's father relents. "If you insist, we can stay a short while." He is a proud man but also one who knows all too well how the world works. Vancouver may be a progressive city in many ways, but for a man of Asian descent, the anti-Asian riots of 1907 don't seem that long ago.

I glance up and spot Thomas beaming at me. We've spent several days a week together since his return from Hollywood. With my work schedule at the hotel, our theatrical endeavours, and the wedding planning, some days we've only had time for a quick coffee at the local diner or an afternoon stroll through one of the city's parks. I don't expect the busyness of our schedules to change in the near future, given my new role in *Mr. Brown's Secretary,* but I've felt closer to Thomas these past few months. It seems true that absence makes the heart grow fonder, and I can't imagine not having him in my life.

A few hours later, the luncheon is complete. As hotel staff bustle from table to table, clearing plates and refilling water glasses, Chef pokes his head into the reception. Papa stands and publicly thanks him for the fine meal. Chef's cheeks flush with colour at the hearty applause from the guests.

For the first time, I see the tender side of a man who, from all appearances, rules his kitchen with an iron fist. His French accent adds depth to his toast of happiness and long lives for Papa and Cookie. Chef vacates the banquet room with speed, a proud man with his emotions getting the better of him. As he leaves, I catch a glimpse of him wiping rogue tears from his cheeks. Our eyes meet, and his shy smile is quickly covered by a single finger pressed to his lips.

"Our secret," I mouth and incline my head in gratitude.

Papa and Cookie stand and move toward the three-tiered cake resting on the small, square table.

Thomas leans in. "Cookie really outdid herself with that cake."

"Almost too pretty to eat." I say, nudging his arm with my elbow.

" 'Almost' is the key word there, Lou. I don't know a person living who could resist one of Cookie's treats." Thomas licks his lips in anticipation, and I stifle a laugh.

Without needing direction, the guests stand and form a line for a piece of cake. Thomas and I step back, allowing the others to go ahead of us.

My gaze scans the beautifully decorated room, the guests eager for cake, and the wide smiles of the bride and groom. I am happy for them. Truly, I am.

I turn my attention toward Thomas but spot over his shoulder one of Papa's coworkers sneaking a sip from a flask. The hairs on the back of my neck stand on end, but I give him the benefit of the doubt. Clearly this man is unaware of Papa's demons.

When Thomas' eyes find where mine are fixated, his head jerks back in reflex. "That isn't right." His murmured words assure me my initial reaction is not out of line.

"What should we do?" I whisper behind his ear.

A heavy sigh is his only response. Without waiting a beat, Thomas strides over to the man.

I follow him, staying close enough to overhear the conversation.

"Sir, I am not sure you are aware, but this is a family celebration. As you can see, there are women and a few children present. There is no alcohol permitted at the reception. I kindly ask that you put it away or vacate the premises."

I feel my resolve strengthen, relieved to have Thomas, with his assured manner, by my side. But then a whiff of alcohol reaches my nose, and I recoil.

The man shrugs off the options with a joke. "I promise I won't offer Joe any, if it makes you feel better."

I stomp the three paces to the man, outrage fuelling my movements. "Sir, I insist you dump the contents of your flask or vacate the reception."

The man sways on his feet, clearly inebriated despite it being early afternoon. "Aren't you the actress? I thought you were off to Hollywood. What's keeping you here?"

I feel the prickle of irritation running the length of my spine. "I do intend to go to Hollywood, but it takes time and work and…" I let my words falter as I try to ascertain why in the world I feel compelled to explain myself to this man.

"I'd've thought you'd be eager to leave, now that old Joe's time and attention will be elsewhere." He inclines his head toward Papa and Cookie, their heads bowed together as they transfer a piece of cake onto a guest's plate.

"If you're referring to my father, his name is Joseph. I am quite sure he has earned that courtesy, sir."

The man doesn't seem to register my words. His leering gaze is locked on Cookie. "A daughter can't compete with a warm body between the sheets."

My mouth falls open, but before I can respond, the man continues his diatribe. "Even if she is on the plump side."

I pay little heed to the volume of my voice. "I'll have you know that Cookie is fully welcome in our home and our hearts. She is a good woman, and she loves all of us. How dare you dirty a beautiful union with your unseemly remarks."

Before I can continue, Thomas grabs the man by the bicep and drags him toward the exit. "I think you'd better take your party somewhere else."

Before Thomas can close the double doors, the man utters one more sneering comment. "Be ready to fly, girlie. You're about to be pushed from the nest."

Thomas returns to my side, wrapping a protective arm around my shoulders. I am shaking like a leaf in an autumn rainstorm.

I look up to see my father watching me, a perplexed expression moving across his features. He's about to set down the knife he's been using to cut the cake, and I instantly understand I must steady myself or risk ruining the happiest day he's had in years.

I shake my head, letting my father know everything is

fine and then lean into Thomas' embrace. "Thank you," I whisper into his shoulder.

"I am sorry you had to witness such distasteful behaviour."

"I'm fine." I pull away, aware my proximity to Thomas isn't likely to put my father at ease.

Forcing a smile, I gesture toward the dwindling cake line. "We'd better get in line or we'll miss out entirely."

Though I'd like to believe the inebriated man was entirely misguided, his words ring a touch too close to home. I've put off my worry over how Cookie moving in will change our lives. And I've felt a stab of guilt each time a hint of concern over the matter has the audacity to flit across my mind.

I love Cookie. We all do. She is a dear friend, and she makes our father happy. But what if Papa doesn't have time for me anymore? What will happen to our late-into-the-evening discussions about life and current events within the city? Will he still want to hear about my day or only about Cookie's? I'm afraid we are destined to lose the close relationship that has blossomed between us over the past year. And I don't know whether I will have the strength to chase my biggest dreams if Papa isn't there to cheer me on. What if that man was right? What if inviting Cookie into our lives and our home means there won't be room for me?

I can be strong. I try to convince myself that everything will work out just fine. Haven't I proved my resilience several times over? I push aside my self-centred thoughts and remind myself that this change in our lives is a happy one.

Thomas dips his chin and lowers his voice. "Are you okay? You look as if the weight of the world snuck in and landed on your shoulders. Don't give him any mind, Lou.

He was drunk and rude and not worth a moment of your consideration."

My smile comes easily, though not genuinely at first. "You are right." I take another step closer to the cake table. When I steal a sideways glance at Thomas, I catch him watching me. He's still concerned. Though he's made me exceptionally happy these past months, I may have underestimated Thomas' true impact in my life. Maybe I've been thinking about this all wrong. Perhaps as I grow older and our lives change, Papa's involvement in my life is supposed to take a step back, with Thomas filling in the gap. What if it's Thomas who will cheer me on with unbridled adoration? My smile widens as I sneak another look his way. I could get used to that, I think. Even if things change with Papa, I'll have Thomas, and surely I can count on him.

CHAPTER 15

TUESDAY, MAY 22, 1928

lara

I drag my overthinking mind with me this morning. I had grabbed an apple and one of Cookie's biscuits before heading to work early, determined to tackle the stack of papers covering the desk in Ms. Thompson's office before roll call. Walking the sleepy streets, I relish the cool morning air while marvelling at the uncommon quiet of a city on the verge of a new day.

Mrs. Whitmore's devastating predicament has pressed on my mind with increasing force since Saturday afternoon, when we waved farewell to Papa and Cookie from the train station platform. Though their honeymoon was brief, they arrived home last night atwitter with news and stories to share. The Agassiz, the Canadian Pacific Railway train with a regular route between Vancouver and the village of Agassiz, was apparently the highlight of their time away— save for the two days and nights they spent soaking in hot springs and enjoying the natural and architectural beauty of the recently rebuilt Harrison Hot Springs Hotel.

I arrive at The Hamilton's back door in time to spot the first glimpse of the sun peeking above the horizon. I feel my faint smile over Cookie's delight fall from my lips as I tug open the heavy door. The past few nights, my dreams—or rather, my nightmares—have been filled with the dreary future that lies ahead for Mrs. Whitmore and her unborn child. Having been unable to locate a solution before Hazel's arranged tea time with the former hotel maid, I'm determined to set something in motion this week.

Yesterday, I brought my concern to Mr. Olson, after exhausting the government assistance offerings. Even the newly funded Old Age Pension program, for those over the age of seventy, rarely provides the assistance promised. Most are either blatantly turned away or humiliated by a strict and intrusive application process until they abandon the request. A shiver runs through me at the thought of being unable to support myself once my working years are through.

Churches and community organizations seem to hold the most promise of help, but they are stretched thin as they continue to support widows with young families from the Great War. Although Hazel can offer only a cup of tea and a listening ear, she has arranged another meeting with the distraught young widow this week. This time, I plan to send her with news of how we at The Hamilton might help.

As Mr. Olson and I chatted, I gained yet another level of respect for him and his inclination to do right by others. We talked through the possibility of employment, but in her condition, a job as a maid is unsuitable physically. It could very well cause a scene if a guest were to witness a pregnant woman cleaning their room. Despite Mrs. Whitmore's accomplished skill set, being reinstated as a maid is not the solution.

We decided on a temporary approach while committing to revisiting the options once Mrs. Whitmore's child is born. The plan is to appeal to the kindness of the hotel staff. We are prepared to collect donations of all kinds. From baby clothes to furniture to the all-important dollar, every little bit will certainly make a difference for Mrs. Whitmore's future.

I check my wristwatch and find the hour has flown by. The bellboys and porters for the day shift are sure to be gathering in the lobby to await instructions from Mr. Reynolds, who is an unrelenting stickler for hotel propriety. Though I used to consider the man a fuddy-duddy, as hotel matron I have seen his desire to keep the boys under his charge in line.

If I were a maid, I wouldn't even consider approaching the man as he hands out orders for the day. With my temporary role as matron to bolster me, I settle my hesitations with a slow exhale and climb the stairs to make my request.

George's friendly face greets me, reminding me to relax. I am here for Mrs. Whitmore, after all. I force my knees to steady as I wait for Mr. Reynolds to spot me.

"Ah, Miss Wilson. Can we be of assistance?" Mr. Reynolds addresses me with a cordial expression.

"Good morning, Mr. Reynolds. If I may, I would like to take a moment to make a request."

"Certainly, Miss Wilson." Mr. Reynolds makes a show of stepping aside while gesturing for me to proceed.

I decided during my ascent to the lobby to invoke the good name of the hotel manager to give my plea added weight. "It has come to Mr. Olson's and my attention that a former eighth-floor maid has fallen on hard times." I meet the gaze of each bellboy, porter, and doorman in turn, hoping my imploring eyes will help loosen their pocketbooks. "You may remember her as Miss Perkins." A few heads bob up and down. "She left the hotel's employ to marry, but sadly her husband lost his life in a work-related accident."

Mr. Reynolds' audible gasp trips me up for a split second, since I am quite certain he never knew the maid.

I clasp my hands in front of me and lower my gaze. "Miss Perkins, who is now Mrs. Whitmore, is in a dire situation. I'm sure you can imagine the grief and financial pressures she is facing, but in addition to this heartbreaking news, Mrs. Whitmore is expecting her and her deceased husband's first child."

Mr. Reynolds, quite unlike himself, steps forward. "You are seeking donations, Miss Wilson?"

I am startled by the man's astute response. "Yes, we are hoping if everyone pitches in, together we can help lighten the financial burden for Mrs. Whitmore."

"Say no more. You'll have our full cooperation." Mr. Reynolds turns his attention to the line of impeccably dressed men. "You heard Miss Wilson. If you cannot donate financially, I'd like you to consider raiding your cupboards and appealing to your mothers and wives, since their generosity is certain to outshine ours. When one of our own is in need, it is our duty to pull together in any way we can."

I thank them all for their time, and Mr. Reynolds dismisses them to their work.

"Miss Wilson." Mr. Reynolds stops me at the door that leads to the back-of-house corridor. "Thank you for bringing this to our attention. I suspect most women might be inclined to limit the request to the ears of other women, so your candour is appreciated. You see, Miss Wilson, my brothers and I were raised by my mother alone. She found herself in a similar predicament to Mrs. Whitmore's, and it was the generosity of others and her sheer determination to raise us right that kept food on our table and a roof over our heads."

I place a hand on Mr. Reynolds' forearm. "Thank you for sharing your experience with me. I am grateful for your support, as I'm certain Mrs. Whitmore will be."

"I'll be happy to donate financially, but I wonder if I might accompany you when you deliver the donations? I realize I don't know Mrs. Whitmore personally, but I feel as if my experience might shed light on a rather bleak situation."

"I am sure that can be arranged. I will let you know the details as soon we have confirmation."

"Thank you, Miss Wilson."

I return to the basement to gather my clipboard, lost in the knowledge that even when life feels dark and heavy, a glimmer of hope can shine through from the most unexpected direction.

I decide to inquire with the kitchen, laundry, and maintenance staff before assigning the first-floor maids their day's duties. My spirits are lifted again and again as each hotel employee embraces the idea of helping Mrs. Whitmore. My faith in humanity is steadily climbing out of the dungeon, where it's been since the blow of the Supreme Court verdict.

Pushing the distasteful thoughts of the ruling aside, I focus on the good all around me as I make my way to the first floor. I expect to be greeted with a row of freshly painted red lips, but instead bare faces stare back at me this morning. I noticed the dwindling number of lipstick-clad maids but assumed their decision to go without the bold shade was personal. Now, though, with not a single maid smiling demurely in resistance red, I wonder if there is more to the story. I resist the urge to inquire further and instead turn my attention to the task at hand, repeating my request of assistance for Mrs. Whitmore.

Like those I've asked before them, the first-floor maids show concern for our former eighth-floor maid and promise to give thought to how they might best help in her time of need. Though I'm certain they require no reminder, I am compelled to share my thoughts, especially in lieu of the missing Resistance Red Brigade.

"Not all decisions are determined at a Supreme Court level. Some are made with our individual hearts. Each time we choose to step up and offer assistance to another, we grow stronger together. We can change the world, ladies, and it starts with us helping out when one of us struggles. Lifting one woman up lifts us all up."

With the first floor complete, I climb the stairs, feeling uplifted by the progress I'm making. I am eager to relay the news to Hazel and help ease her worries.

With Mrs. Whitmore consuming my thoughts for days, I have conveniently set aside my other concerns. But with a solution in the works, I can no longer avoid the question that is desperate to taunt me.

I surely wouldn't be where I am today if it hadn't been for Mrs. Whitmore stepping down. Her leaving the hotel's employ created a vacancy for an eighth-floor maid. My position as an eighth-floor maid helped me gain the skills Ms. Thompson saw as necessary for a temporary matron. So why, I wonder, do I feel as skittish as a cat dangling over a bathtub?

The foreboding is like a wall of cement in front of me. Regardless of whether I choose marriage or a career, my entire future seems uncertain. Mrs. Whitmore's experience is sadly not unique. Though William's work is aristocratic in nature, if I choose marriage over a working life, there are no guarantees. If he were to perish, I can't say my life would be any less shaky than Mrs. Whitmore's currently is.

The light thumping of my footfalls slows as I near the second-floor landing. Then again, if I choose a career, who will come to my aid should I fall ill? Without a husband or children, whom could I count on for support?

I try with all my might to shake off the ridiculous spiralling thoughts. I have Louisa, Papa, and even Cookie. Surely, I will never be left alone.

I tug on the second-floor hall door and consider how Ms. Thompson might view this line of thinking. She did choose a career. At least I think it was her choice. I wonder if she regrets her decision, given her current predicament. I shake the troublesome worries from my head as I stride toward the straight line of maids.

I force a confident smile, and my step hitches at the awareness. Does Ms. Thompson hide her worries behind a confident smile too?

I busy myself with pretending to examine the roster before addressing the gathered maids. I won't let this line of thinking derail the remainder of my day. Instead, I make a decision to visit Ms. Thompson after work, just as I promised William I would.

Women must support women, I remind myself. With William on the other side of the country, the least I can do is check in and make sure his sister is doing well. Regardless of the choice Ms. Thompson made, I will ensure she knows someone close by is looking out for her. I make a mental note to obtain Ms. Thompson's home address from Cookie before heading there this afternoon.

"I hope I'm not overstepping," I whisper to myself while standing on Ms. Thompson's front stoop. Tucking the bag under one arm—Cookie insisted I bring chicken soup and fresh-baked buns—I lift the door knocker and rap it twice against the wood. Since I telephoned ahead, Ms. Thompson is expecting me.

I hear movement beyond the closed door as I crane my neck, taking in the quaint English-style garden. The lavender by the front gate is small this early in the season, but its fragrant bushes remind me of Mama and her love of gardening. I note the round wrought-iron table and matching chairs, imagining myself seated there with a cup of tea in the early-morning sun. The house is charming and more affluent than I might have imagined, given Ms. Thompson's status as an unmarried woman.

The sturdy wood door opens with a yawn, and Ms. Thompson, hair cascading around her shawl-covered shoulders, greets me with a warm smile. "Aren't you a sight for sore eyes." She steps aside, gesturing me inside. "Please come in."

"I hope I'm not intruding." I take a step inside and am surprised to find the small entryway to be cozy and inviting. I scold myself for having thought Ms. Thompson would wish to reside in a home that is anything but inviting. Then again, I've only known her in the hotel, and I must have incorrectly assumed the dark, damp basement office suited her well enough.

"Please, I'm bored out of my mind most days." The

matron points at the bag tucked under my arm. "Plus, I believe that delicious aroma is Cookie's famous chicken soup."

"She insisted," I say as I hand her the bag, "and she baked a fresh batch of buns to go with it."

"My mouth is watering at the thought of it." Ms. Thompson turns to the left, where the entryway opens up to a tidy living room. "I'll put this in the kitchen. Please make yourself comfortable."

"You have a lovely home." The room is weighted by a fair-sized hearth and a solid-looking sofa positioned with a view out the front window. I notice a few feminine touches around the room but not as many as I might have expected for a woman who lives on her own. There exists a subtle sense of order among the furnishings and decorative touches. Then again, I remind myself, Ms. Thompson is sure to run a tight ship at home, just as she does at the hotel.

Ms. Thompson returns with a tray laden with a teapot, cups, and accompaniments. "Thank you. It's far from grandiose, but this little bungalow is quite suitable. The yard is small, but the minimal maintenance the property requires is a blessing."

I take the offered cup of tea. "How are you feeling?"

A forced smile diminishes her true frustration at the prescribed rest. "I will admit I am much happier being busy. Alas, I pushed past what even I thought was reasonable. This is my penance. At any rate, this is where I'll be until the doctor sees fit to say otherwise."

"Well, you should know you are very much missed at the hotel. Everyone looks forward to your return, once you are recovered."

"Mr. Olson tells me you are getting on quite well,

despite the challenges." Ms. Thompson's raised eyebrows leave no question that she is aware of recent events in The Hamilton. She and Mr. Olson must talk regularly about the goings on at the hotel.

"Thank you, ma'am. I'm pleased to hear I am offering capable assistance." I sip my sweetened tea, suddenly feeling awkward with our casual conversation and no hint of an impending task on my end.

Ms. Thompson narrows her gaze on me. "Clara—may I call you Clara, since we are away from the hotel?"

"Yes, of course, ma'am."

"Eliza is fine." She waves a hand in the air, clearing the room of pomp and circumstance. "Tell me, what brings you to my little corner of the city?" Her questioning expression is lined with a smile. "I appreciate the visit and dinner, but I suspect you are here for something else."

"I never could fool you, ma—" I stop myself short, swallow hard, and finish. "I mean, Eliza."

"Out with it, then." She is teasing now, and I find myself warming to my mentor and her familial resemblance to William.

"You heard about Mrs. Whitmore?"

"The poor dear. Yes, Mr. Olson filled me in. I've been collecting a few things here and there with her in mind. I've even started on a baby blanket, though my knitting skills are a tad rusty." She gestures to the knitting basket tucked at the foot of her chair.

"Yes, it's a dreadful situation." I clear my throat as I stall for time. "The thing is, it got me thinking about the choices we must make as women. Mrs. Whitmore chose marriage, whereas you chose work."

"Well." Ms. Thompson draws out the word before leaning back in her chair.

"I realize it's none of my business. I—I don't have anyone else to ask is all."

"You are wondering why I chose to work at the hotel?" Her head dips in question before she adds, "Is that all there is to your question?"

I sense the matron has narrowed in on what I hoped to disguise.

"I'm concerned because Mrs. Whitmore married for love and now is in a terrible situation. Then I thought of how you might not have someone to help you in your difficult time right now, since you chose a life of work." The sigh leaves my lips in a rush of frustration. "You became aware of my family's financial situation when you hired me. You know that my father put us in a precarious position and we came close to losing the roof over our heads." I suck in a sharp breath to steady my emotions. "I suppose I'm wary of the prospect of not being able to support myself. I've been disappointed by someone I loved before." I sneak a glance at her from beneath my lowered eyelashes. "I don't suspect I'm willing to let that happen again, and I wondered if you could shed light on how a woman is expected to make the right choice to ensure her future well-being."

"Ahh, I see. Your concern has more to do with ensuring a safe and happy future than anything else?" Ms. Thompson takes a thoughtful sip from her teacup.

"I never thought about it that way."

"I'm sorry to say, Clara, I don't have a crystal ball to offer you. Everyone's future is uncertain, my own included. We must simply make decisions based on the information we have before us."

We sit silently, sipping our tea for a few minutes as I consider her words.

Placing my empty teacup on the squat table, I bolster my courage to ask a question that risks sounding impertinent. "How did you know you were making the right choice?"

"I didn't." Her laugh emerges, abrupt and controlled. My choice was…" She trails off, considering her words. "Unconventional. But it was mine to make."

The Persons Case verdict pokes at me mockingly, and I smother the scoff that rises like a knee jerk to a doctor's mallet. "Seems like that may be changing for women now."

"You're referring to the Supreme Court decision?"

I bob my head in reply.

"The news out of Ottawa is disturbing, but I wouldn't be so sure of the outcome just yet. Those women fighting the good fight are strong and tenacious. They won't leave it be. I am certain of it."

"I hope you are right." I glance at my wristwatch, noting the hour. "I should go. I don't want to intrude on your dinner hour. Thank you for seeing me." I stand and move toward the front door.

"It was lovely to see you, Clara, though I suspect I wasn't as much help as you hoped. Perhaps it's time for you to look outside of the usual options. Society doesn't change its opinion on what is right or wrong all by itself. People make changes, which are eventually accepted by society. If you want a different choice than the ones you see before you, keep digging until you find an option that suits you."

"Thank you, ma'am—Eliza." I step over the threshold and onto the cobblestones lining the path to the front gate. "We look forward to having you back at the hotel."

Less reassured than I hoped to be, I wave goodbye and head for home, thankful that a good meal and a quiet apartment await me there.

CHAPTER 16

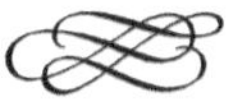

TUESDAY, MAY 22, 1928

ouisa

My back is pressed flat against the wall as another one of Cookie's treasured pieces of furniture is squeezed past me into the apartment. Doing my best to keep the door ajar, I hold my breath and my tongue, willing myself to not be the fuse that sparks a heated discussion over the state of our apartment this evening.

Cookie follows the dresser on its path to Papa's bedroom. "Let's set it under the window and see how it fits." Her excitement is evident, though not at all contagious.

With the dresser clear of the door, I release my grip. The door swings toward closing until it's met with a muffled complaint.

I yank the door back open and Clara steps through, rubbing her shoulder with one hand while the other clutches a brown paper bag of groceries.

"I'm sorry. I didn't see you standing there."

She shoots me a weary look but refrains from saying more on the matter. "What's all this?" Clara stands on tiptoe, her chin lifted in the direction of Papa and his friend Paul's retreating frames.

"Moving day." My reply is flat.

"Oh, I—I thought everything was already here." Clara's nose crinkles in question as she lowers her voice. "How much more is there?"

A shrug is all I can offer before Cookie reappears from the bedroom, a wide smile leading the way.

"Hello, Clara. Well, it's a little tight, but there's room enough to open the drawers, so we can be thankful for that."

Papa and Paul appear in the hall, perspiration dampening their foreheads.

"Hey, darlin'." Papa wipes his face with a palm and steps forward to take the grocery bag from my arms.

Cookie, not winded in the slightest, rouses the troops with her announcement. "Only one more piece of furniture to go, and then I'll set to making dinner." Turning to Paul she adds, "You'll stay for dinner, won't you?"

"That's very kind of you, Ruby, but I expect Marjorie is waiting on me at home. Besides, I'm not sure there is room for an extra guest tonight." His tone is teasing but honest to a fault.

Cookie takes the bag of groceries from Papa and begins unloading the items onto the only free square of counter space in the kitchen. "Another time, then."

Clara and I observe the goings on like we're watching a photoplay, transfixed and a little alarmed at the small amount of space available in the kitchen. Cookie, it seems, has spread every kitchen item she's ever owned across the tight space of our galley kitchen and dinner table.

My sister and I exchange a look, and then Clara steps forward. "Can I give you a hand with that?"

"Oh no, I've got it all under control." Cookie's smile is genuine, making my heart squeeze at the train wreck I sense coming our way. "Besides, I want to put things where they make the most sense to me, since I'll be doing the cooking."

Though she doesn't utter a word, I feel my sister deflate. In this apartment, it's been Clara who's shopped for groceries, planned our meals, and cooked for us. She's the one who's baked bread, biscuits, and scones. She's the one who scrimped and saved until we were on our feet again. This is Clara's kitchen. At least, it was. I want to reach out and wrap my arms around my sister, but I know doing so will only result in a distraught Clara and a bewildered Cookie.

Braver than I expect her to be, Clara presses forward as Papa and Paul head out to retrieve Cookie's final piece of furniture. "I thought we might share the load of cooking, since we're both working and living here. You, of course, are welcome to take over the baking, since you're a master at it."

Clara's words and the olive branch she's offered do little to open the conversation.

With a wave of her hand, Cookie dismisses everything Clara's said. "You'll have your own house to run one day too. This is the least I can do to contribute."

The apartment goes silent, save for the sound of Cookie puttering about the kitchen Clara apparently has no further domain over.

I reach for her hand and tug my sister close, whispering

in her ear as I guide her into the living room. "She's trying to lighten the burden for you. I know it doesn't feel like that right now, but you've said yourself that Cookie loves us. She's only trying to do right by us."

Clara searches my eyes, but a single nod is her only response.

A few minutes later, the apartment door opens again as Paul and Papa enter, grunting with the weight and awkwardness of some large item in the narrow hall.

"Where do you want it?" Papa asks over his shoulder as Cookie emerges from the kitchen, a towel draped over her shoulder and a delighted expression lighting up her face.

Without hesitation, Cookie points to the spot in the living room where Mama's trunk sits.

I smother a gasp and squeeze Clara's hand in mine.

Papa mumbles for Paul to set the chair down where they stand before turning to meet our stricken faces. He opens his mouth to speak, but Cookie beats him to it.

"This was the only piece of furniture I brought with me when I came over from Ireland." Cookie moves to stand beside us. "Was my mother's, it was. Oh how I worried over it during the passage." Cookie's elbow nudges Clara's arm, causing her to bump into me. "With the high seas and salty air, I thought the rocker stored deep below decks might be a goner before I made it all the way to Canada." Her enthusiasm turns sentimental. "I sat in that chair every night for months with an ache so deep in my heart from missing Ireland and my family. Now that I have all of you, it feels perfect to welcome my mam's rocker into our home." Cookie swipes at a tear rolling down her cheek.

Glancing at Clara, I see tears streaming down her face, and I know in this moment, my sister is having to say goodbye to our own mother all over again.

Cookie looks from Papa to us, confusion blooming in the creases of her forehead.

Clara clears her throat and shakes her head. Not looking at Papa or me, her gaze remains fixed on Mama's trunk, but her words are intended for Cookie. "It's a lovely rocking chair. What a nice addition it will make."

CHAPTER 17

lara

I have not yet gotten my bearings. I've been overwhelmed
by the fanfare of the wedding and now the stress of
attempting to fit Cookie into our lives and our small
apartment. We've been packing and unpacking boxes for
the past few weeks. With all of her possessions crowding
ours, I find myself scurrying to pack and store too many
pieces of our lives.

Last night, the remainder of Cookie's things arrived at
The Newbury, and suddenly our haven after busy days
became too small. The last straw, which sent Louisa and me
to our shared bedroom to grieve, was the arrival of
Cookie's favourite rocking chair. There was no need to have
a lengthy discussion about it. Cookie's chair is important to
her, and it's going to stay. I don't begrudge my friend her
memories and mementos of her past; I simply hadn't

realized her joining our lives would mean the eviction of Mama's trunk and all her memories. Off they went to the dank bowels of The Newbury basement.

My feet are sore and my neck aches. I'd like to blame the pain on the frenzy of moving or my long hours at the hotel, but I fear it's from walking on eggshells in our new living arrangement. I have no desire to hurt Cookie's feelings, so I reach for every bit of my courage and strength to ease the growing tension.

I've become accustomed to smiling first and speaking second, thankful The Hotel Hamilton has been great training for such niceties. Yesterday, after a particularly difficult evening, I decided to reclaim a bit of time for myself. This morning, I am taking the long way round on my walk to the hotel. Moments alone to consider and reflect have been in short supply since Papa and Cookie first announced their engagement.

I let gravity carry me down the hill toward the water's edge, the salty air whipping my hair about my face more forcefully as I near the ocean. Begging off Cookie's offer to walk together this morning took both gumption and a good excuse. Knowing that her usual arrival at the hotel is a full hour earlier than my own, I crammed a butter biscuit into my mouth and chased it with a hot cup of tea to get an even earlier start.

I was already dressed in my spring coat, with my hand upon the apartment's doorknob, when Cookie emerged from my father's bedroom. The expression that lit her features, confusion lined with a hint of sorrow, should have initiated a complete about-face from me. Instead, I pushed out an excuse in a rush, telling her I woke with a strong desire to visit the ocean's edge.

Nudging aside my guilt over Cookie's potentially hurt feelings, I inhale the misty ocean air, determined to consider what is truly troubling me. I've had little time to reflect on my knee-jerk reaction to Rebecca's comment at the wedding reception, about me being married soon. Between Rebecca's assured statement and Cookie's statement—made last night while reorganizing what used to be my kitchen—I've felt pushed onto a track I didn't realize I'd agreed to.

Cookie's words lift in my memory with the ocean breeze, taunting me. *You'll have your own house to run one day too.* Though I'm certain she meant well by shooing me out of the kitchen, saving me from the extra work at the end of a long day, her comment stung. Tears pricked my eyes as I bit my tongue, desperately holding back the reminder that before she moved in, I did have a house of my own to run.

A slow sigh slips past my lips. Cookie isn't to blame, she's simply trying to embrace our new living situation, unaware of where the emotional landmines might be hidden. If I had any sense, I realize far too late, I would've sat down at the kitchen table with my friend and talked through my worries. I step over a water-tossed log and onto the sandy beach. I might have even told her of my concerns about marriage in general. Perhaps she would have had some advice to give, especially since she has made the bold decision to marry while remaining head pastry chef. Though the fact that she is handing over her wages to Papa pleases me none—and concerns me plenty when I consider the implication for my own situation—her decision to work and marry is evidence that our social expectations aren't the norm in all parts of the world. In rural Ireland, Cookie told me, it's common practice for all members of the family to work and contribute how they can.

I adore William, that much is true. He makes me laugh. He makes me happy. With his ever-present optimism, he sees the good in me and in others, despite his career as a Toronto lawyer bringing him into daily contact with humans amidst stressful situations. But marriage isn't something I expected to consider so soon, especially with the immense pride I've found in the role of hotel matron.

Perhaps I had convinced myself that, with him living on the other side of the country, our relationship would bloom more slowly than couples who enjoy closer geographical proximity. I figured I had time to dream and plan without committing to something as permanent as marriage, at least not right away. I'll admit I can be slow to come to terms with change, both the good and the challenging, but the pressure of others' expectations for my life is more than I can handle. I'm aware the usual trajectory of courtship leads to marriage. I suppose I desire more time to relish dreaming about a future with William. Perhaps then I'd be more inclined to give up what is sure to be deemed my selfish pursuit of a working life filled with purpose and value.

While most girls are hanging their hats on a marriage proposal that will take them out of service, I find myself fretting over the thought of not having The Hamilton to go to every day. My head shakes of its own volition, pointing out the absurdity of my thoughts. Of course I want to marry William. It's true. I feel it with my whole heart. However, I am unable to concede the point, since I also desire a life and career of my own. I've experienced the pure bliss of successful work and others believing in my abilities. How can I be expected to give that up for marriage?

I rest against a log, damp from the ocean air, to remove

my socks and shoes. The desire to sink my feet into the sand overcomes me. Taking a step forward, the cool sand grounds me, even as its ever-shifting granules unsettle my equilibrium. I laugh at myself and the comical epiphany. The sand and William's presence in my life are remarkably similar: steadying yet disconcerting.

My mind drifts back to William's telephone call last Sunday while my gaze fixes on a gull sailing higher with the breeze. As always, I was delighted to hear his voice. His laugh, whether boisterous or deep-throated, never fails to bring a smile to my lips. I admire his forthright nature. His assuredness is comforting, while his occasional boyish shyness melts my heart every time it shows itself.

Show itself it did during our conversation about the wedding. I filled him in on the events, skipping my concern over the word "obey" during the ceremony. I anticipated the change in him a split second before he spoke. "Clara, I have something important I'd like to speak with you about." William's words filter through my memory. I'm not sure if I replied or simply waited for him to continue. "But I don't wish to do so over the phone."

By then, with Rebecca's words reverberating through my mind, fear was thrumming through me, fuelling my dismissive response. "Well then, it seems like you'll have to wait until I see you again in person."

I forced a teasing laugh in an attempt to lighten the mood, and being good-natured, William replied with his own laughter. "Yes, I suppose I will."

We hung up shortly after, and I've been kicking myself ever since, hoping I didn't put him off completely with my abruptness. I've contemplated writing him a letter, but the words have yet to come. Calling this situation awkward is an understatement, if my instincts are correct and William wishes to have the one conversation I'm not yet prepared to have.

Is it possible to love someone without being fenced in by the expectations that come with their social status? William's life includes obligations that without question overwhelm me. I didn't set out to snag myself an aristocratic gentleman and a life of luncheons and society galas. I prefer to spend my time quietly in the background, filling my days with work at the hotel. William, I admit, does not carry the self-importance I've witnessed in so many men of influence. He is humble, kind, and genuine. I stare out at the horizon, with a telling sigh. I could go round and round with arguments for and against my options, but in my heart, I know what I truly desire. I'm just not sure I'm brave enough to insist on having it all. What I want is to remain working at The Hamilton and to marry William Thompson.

I am keen to keep my independence and my earned wages, and to eventually gain a permanent position as hotel matron. Marriage to William may mean giving it all up. I shake my head, refusing to let either one of my dreams flounder.

"There must be a way for me to do both." I say the words out loud, determined to find the solution. Even Ms. Thompson told me to keep searching until I find an option that works for me. So search I must.

Frustrated by the circular nature of my ruminating thoughts, I take several steps forward and sink my bare feet into the frigid water of the Pacific Ocean. The shock of the cold does exactly what I need it to do. Everything except the numbing sensation disappears from my awareness.

Tortured thoughts, gone. Worry over our new living arrangements, vanished. My heart, swelling with love for William, remains strong, but the angst that accompanies the feeling fades into the background like a curtain closing on one of Louisa's plays. I close my eyes and let the tide's rhythm pull me from reality, one biting wave at a time.

CHAPTER 18

WEDNESDAY, MAY 23, 1928

ouisa

"The man was downright rude." In room 513, the first
bathtub of the day is benefitting from my pent-up
frustration over the drunken man at the wedding reception.
The angrier I grow, the more frantic my scouring becomes.

"Have you heard how Ms. Thompson is doing?" Jane
asks, not taking her eyes off the sink she's polishing. "Clara
said yesterday she's still recovering. Poor thing."

I barely register Jane's question, my mind moving on its
one-way track. "I mean, seriously. Who would say such a
thing? Pushed from the nest. I never. Like he has any insight
into our family's situation at all."

"Louisa." Jane's exasperated tone pulls me from my
incessant ramblings. "You've been ruminating on this for
days. Don't you think it's time to move on?"

I feel my brow furrow as I glance over my shoulder at

Jane. Clearly, she doesn't understand, I think before returning my attention to the tub.

"Of course you could always work on your own roster for a spell." Jane's warning is lighthearted enough, but I suspect it's lined with truth. "If you continue on about the rudeness of a complete stranger at an otherwise delightful celebration, I will leave you be for the rest of the day."

"Fine. I apologize. You're right. It's just that, well, things at home aren't simple either, and it's making me feel unsettled is all."

Jane moves and wipes down the large oval mirror above the sink, carefully resting one hand on the sink's edge for balance as she spritzes the mirror with a cleaning solution. "You didn't expect everything to fall into place so easily, did you? You're starting anew. I'd think you would be more inclined to embrace the excitement of a new season of life."

I crinkle my nose at the sharp scent of vinegar. "I know it has only been a few days, but the apartment is a tad small." I cringe at the admission, knowing Jane lives in a regal mansion with an expansive view of the ocean. I conceal my embarrassment and lean into the humour of the situation. "I think we'd have been pressed for space if a mouse had moved in."

Jane laughs in response. "There you go. You have to accept these changes are going to take time. It'll all work out in the end. You'll see."

"When did you become so wise?" I stand from my kneeling position and toss the rag onto the cleaning cart, a stone's throw beyond the washroom door.

"Blame it on all the time I've spent in your company," Jane teases as she follows me out of the washroom.

I reach for the feather duster and give my friend a

sincere smile. "Papa is smitten with her. It's sweet, really. I am happy for them—truly I am—but I can't help but wonder how long Clara and I will be permitted to tag along on their coattails."

"I don't think your father or Cookie consider having you and Clara in their life to be a burden. Honestly, Louisa, I'm not sure what you're worried about. Cookie is part of your family now. I'd welcome her with open arms if she came to live with me, even if only for the scrumptious treats alone."

With a light sigh, I turn my attention toward dusting the desk in the far corner of the room. "You may have forgotten, but your house is far more spacious than most. If the shuffling of furniture, dishes, and Mama's possessions are any indication, I have a feeling we'll be pushed out of the apartment in no time. Maybe not directly by Papa or Cookie, but surely by the sheer volume of belongings crowding us out." I force a lighthearted laugh, aware it falls flat when Jane's eyebrows lift toward her hairline. "I know. I'm probably overreacting. Either way, I'll remain where I am until I'm no longer welcome."

Jane's mouth opens as if she has something more to say, but when our eyes meet, she decides better of it, instead hoisting the behemoth of a vacuum from the back of the cleaning cart and setting to work on the pale blue carpet.

As I manoeuvre my cleaning cart toward my second guest room of the morning, Jane is called away to complete a task below stairs. I send her on her way with a friendly wave while refraining from muttering about how I am certain she is glad to be rid of me and my sour disposition.

My mind winds back to last night, when Papa and Cookie arrived home laden down with the remainder of her possessions. I've felt squeezed in our small space for weeks, since boxes started showing up. But yesterday, I braced myself, afraid of being shoved right out the apartment door, when Cookie's beloved rocking chair took the place of Mama's trunk.

I am aware my feelings on the matter are unsubstantiated. My inclination to hold onto something of Mama's that I seldom peeked inside is silly at best. If I had to guess, the trunk's presence was more about the space it held for her, as if she had a permanent spot within our home. I never imagined she could be erased by a rocking chair.

I pull the bedspread from the mattress with more force than I intend and stumble back several feet, bumping into the opposite wall with a thud. "Off balance. That's what I am," I whisper to myself as I attempt to regain my composure and focus.

Jane is right. I've got to move forward. I must shake off this childish foolishness and direct my attention back to the stage. I tried to speak with Papa about the brush-off I've been receiving from the director. It's eating at me that Agatha Taylor in *Mr. Brown's Secretary* is nothing more than a cardboard cut-out of a woman.

I was desperate to get Papa's thoughts on the matter. A good long chat about the situation was all I needed to encourage me. Instead, yesterday evening was taken up with Cookie's chatter of good ol' Ireland. I cringe at my blatantly misplaced annoyance and slide the pillowcases off the four pillows lining the headboard.

I've no wish to dismiss Cookie's family tales, but once her rocking chair was situated in the living room, I couldn't focus on anything but Mama's missing trunk. From the moment we arrived home, through dinner and until Clara and I finally escaped to our bedroom for quiet, Cookie's furniture and her plentiful remembrances had taken centre stage.

With the bed stripped bare, I retrieve a fresh set of linens from my cart and begin tucking and folding until everything is in order. Plumping the last pillow, I stand up straight and examine my work. "Crisp and clean and ready for a fresh start."

With a nod, I pivot toward my cart, unlock its wheels, and relocate it closer to the door. "A fresh start." My words are drowned out by the humming of the vacuum, but my assuredness rings through loud and clear.

I need to sink my teeth into the role of Agatha Taylor. My acting career is on the rise. Even Mrs. Oxley-Barnes, now Ms. Oxley, the daughter of a motion-picture executive, said so when she visited Vancouver briefly last New Year's Eve. Despite our meeting taking place amidst a scandal involving her good-for-nothing husband—now ex-husband —her offer to help me launch my Hollywood career seemed sincere.

Secure a bit more experience on the stage, she'd said. I've been chasing down those credits ever since, determined to make it to Hollywood and let her know she wasn't wrong to believe in me. The thrumming of the vacuum is welcome company as I plan my next moves. I can portray a meeker Agatha Taylor if that is what the script calls for. Surely the director and I can find mutual ground for Miss Taylor's portrayal.

Papa may have offered some wisdom on the matter, but after last night, it's quite clear my father no longer has time for every conversation about my career. If I'm going to make it as an actress, I've got to try to make it on my own. It's not like my family could accompany me to California anyway. I shake my head and chuckle at my foolishness.

Besides, even though our apartment is cramped and Papa's attentions must now be shared, I still have the opportunity to gain acting credits while living in the comfort of my family home. This chance may not always be afforded to me. I must strike now.

There is no time like the present. Women have made huge strides over the past few decades by being persistent and tenacious. If I am going to do something big with my life, then I'd better not let anything stand in my way.

CHAPTER 19

SATURDAY, MAY 26, 1928

lara

"Honestly, Clara, can I get in there for two minutes?" Louisa's voice is inching toward a full-fledged whine.

I open the bathroom door, a scowl as firmly in place as the hairbrush in my hand. "I don't see why you are attempting to get ready for your day at the same time as us. Rehearsals don't start for another two hours."

Louisa pushes past me in a huff, her mood souring further each day. "I have to be the first one there today."

"Fine." I give up my spot in front of the mirror, dropping my brush with a noisy clatter to the small shelf above the sink to ensure my sister is aware of my displeasure.

Shaking my head, I move toward the kitchen. It too is occupied and cramped. I smother a groan and instead force a "good morning" through tight lips.

"Good morning, Clara." Cookie's sing-song greeting

has an effect opposite to her apparent intention. "I'll be out of the way in a jiffy. Wanted to make sure your father has a decent lunch today, with both of us working the Saturday shift."

I reach across her for a teacup, bumping her arm as I stretch. "If you'll let me pour a cup of tea." Retracting my arm, teacup in hand, my elbow knocks into Cookie's, sending the hot stew she's ladling splashing onto the counter.

"Clara." Cookie's gasp echoes through the apartment. I hear Papa rising from the sofa in the living room as she mops up the mess.

"I'm sorry. I wasn't thinking." I reach for the bowl to push it out of the way and end up spilling more stew over its rim. "Oh my word."

Cookie exhales a slow breath. "Could you please wait for me to finish here? Then you can have the kitchen to yourself."

"Sorry," I say as I slink backward out of the kitchen, licking my wounds.

Papa's arm wraps protectively around my shoulders as I step across the threshold. I resist the urge to sink into his embrace and bury my head in his chest.

"Maybe now is a good time to talk about moving into a bigger home." Papa's words are lined with excitement, and I wonder how long the topic of moving homes has been in discussion without Louisa's or my knowledge.

Cookie's face lights up at the mention of a new home, and even though I'm aware it's irrational, this news feels like a slight instead of a happy announcement.

Papa squeezes my shoulders, clearly delighted, as Louisa appears from the bathroom. "What do you say, Lou? A new home for the Wilson clan? A bigger bathroom, maybe even two so you girls can stop fighting over whose turn it is."

Bustling around the kitchen, Cookie puts the stew in the refrigerator before pouring four cups of tea. Handing one to each of us, she gestures toward the dining table. "Perhaps we could talk about it some this morning before everyone heads out for the day?"

Louisa's expression mirrors the emotions running amok within me.

"I don't want to move houses, and I don't have time to talk about any of it today." She grabs her bag from the hook in the hall. "I have to go or I'll be late." Lou sneaks a glance in my direction, and I indicate with a subtle nod that, in this, we agree.

Louisa pulls the apartment door open with exaggerated force, but instead of stepping through, she takes a step back.

"What are you doing here?" She takes another step into the apartment and waves someone through. "I'm sorry, but I have to go or I'll be late. It's nice to see you though." Without another word, Louisa walks out, leaving William standing a few paces inside the doorway with a puzzled expression blooming on his face.

Cookie is the first to greet him with a whoop. "What a lovely surprise." She dashes toward him and pats his cheek before he leans down to wrap her in an embrace.

"Well, how is the new Mrs. Wilson these days?"

His teasing tone pulls me from my shock. Papa's arm falls from my shoulder as I move forward tentatively. "William?"

Realizing she is monopolizing the man, Cookie shuffles sideways down the hall toward Papa, leaving room for William to approach me.

William takes my hands in his. "Clara."

My name is all he says, and yet, it's all I need to hear. I feel moisture gather in my eyes, aware I haven't let myself miss him nearly as much as I wanted to.

Papa takes three long strides toward us with his hand outstretched. I move to the side to let Papa shake William's hand and clap him on the back. "It's good to see you. Are you in town long?"

William's genuine smile tells me he not only respects Papa as my father but enjoys his company as well. "I tried to come sooner, but I've got a case that is dragging its feet. With Eliza still convalescing, I figured I'd make the journey, even if I have to dash back on short notice."

Papa winks knowingly. "Two birds, one stone."

"Something like that." William chuckles, and I find myself puzzled by the exchange.

"We're about to sit down for tea." Cookie returns to her favoured spot in the kitchen. "I'll whip us up some pancakes."

William and I take the long way around to the dining table. While we are momentarily hidden from sight, he takes my hand and fleetingly kisses it. I feel my stomach flip.

We reappear in the living room side by side, and William continues the conversation. "I won't turn down Cookie's pancakes, but are you sure I'm not intruding?" Lowering his voice, he says to me, "I had hoped to walk you to work this morning."

I smile at his considerate nature. "I haven't eaten yet, and no, you're not intruding. We'll have a quick bite and be off. My duties are quite a bit larger now, and I try to arrive ahead of the rest of the staff."

"I'd like to thank you for that. For stepping in to help while Eliza recovers."

"I'm happy to help." I feel a wave of relief cascade around me. William is indeed supportive of the role I've taken on. Seeing his genuine expression, I've no idea how I could have worried he wouldn't be.

Thirty minutes later, we are out the door and walking toward The Hamilton. A crisp gust of ocean air whips my hair, freeing a few strands from my tight bun.

William's hand cups my cheek. "I love it when your hair comes loose."

"You do?" I scrunch up my nose at the constant, unwinnable battle I engage in with my hair.

"I do." His smile reaches his eyes in a way that makes me feel as though I'm melting from the inside out.

"When did you arrive? And why didn't you tell me you were coming?" I narrow my sideways gaze at him.

His laugh rumbles through me, and I find my whole being leaning into his orbit. The effect he has on me is unnerving. An inclination to forget my aspirations to be a hotel matron catches me by surprise. Embracing my dream of having both a career and William is much easier without his steady presence monopolizing my heart's desires.

"I arrived this morning." He steps behind me to make way for a stream of people. "My bags are still with the porter. I'll collect them once I've sorted out where I'm staying."

"Oh, I figured you'd be staying at the hotel." I'm brought up short by my wish to have him close while wondering how I could possibly concentrate on my job with him in such proximity.

"Eliza has a small apartment at the side of her house. Now that Cookie has moved in with you, it's once again vacant."

I realize I never once asked where Cookie lived before marrying Papa. "I hadn't realized they shared a home."

"They didn't. Not in the true sense of the word. They lived quite separately, though they did spend many an evening playing cards or listening to the radio. And of course they used to walk to and from work together." William leans in, and I feel his breath on my neck. "I think Eliza misses their walks the most."

"So, it's an apartment inside a house?" I didn't notice any such thing when I visited a few days ago.

"Yes, it's all very proper. Looks like a single house, but there is a side door that leads to a one-bedroom apartment. Has its own kitchen, a bathroom, and even a tiny sitting room. Though when Cookie lived there, that monstrosity of a rocking chair took up most of the room."

I press my lips together, not wanting to sour the mood with a discussion about Cookie's rocker. "I've never imagined such a thing." I bob my head in greeting to the doorman at the Hotel Georgia as we pass.

"Apparently, it's quite common in Europe." We pause to wait for traffic to clear. "I wanted to tell you that Robert, I mean Mr. Olson, is quite pleased by your handling of things as matron." William smiles as though the compliment were for him.

"That's kind of you to say. You speak to Mr. Olson regularly?" I think back to our telephone conversations, always short due to the cost.

"He telephoned to inform me about Eliza and then again when the doctor prescribed several weeks of rest."

The way William's gaze shifts away from mine to take in the view across the street tells me there is something he isn't saying.

I decide not to press the issue and instead take the victory that William is proud of my work, even if it means I'm not available to marry him at the moment. I chide myself as we step into the street to cross. The man hasn't asked for my hand in marriage. No sense putting the cart before the horse.

"That reminds me," William says, smoothly changing the subject. "How did you make out with the fundraiser for the former maid who lost her husband?"

"Very well indeed." I take his offered hand to step around a small mound of debris on the road. "I don't suspect her life will be easy, but we've gathered enough supplies and financial support to help see her through until her wee one arrives. I am hopeful though. Mr. Hamilton heard of Mrs. Whitmore's situation and offered to set her up with some work she can do from home as she raises her little one. I don't know the details, but I think it has something to do with ledgers and accounts for one of his other business interests."

"Well done you." William beams in my direction. "You have taken quite nicely to your new position. It is wonderful to see, Clara."

By the time we have crossed the street and are moving past The Hotel Vancouver, a new wave of panic grips me. He's being awfully generous with his compliments of my work. What if William doesn't intend to marry me after all? What if the something important he wanted to talk to me about is us not seeing one another anymore? Oh my word, I hadn't even considered the possibility. I suddenly feel too warm inside my light spring jacket.

I avoid his glances as we round the corner and walk down the alley toward the hotel's back entrance. Worry takes up residence like a long-lost friend, and I squeeze my eyes shut to stop the moisture from gathering as William opens the heavy door.

I hurry my steps down the corridor toward the basement, but William keeps up, matching my pace. We pass three second-floor maids on our way.

"Good morning, Miss Wilson," they all say in unison.

"Good morning, ladies," I reply with a tight smile.

I feel eyes on the back of my head and glance over my shoulder to find the most recent second-floor hire, a girl named Agnes, ogling William's retreating frame. She's a cute, petite thing with a pretty face and cascading blond locks, and her nerve concerns me. Even when our eyes meet and she knows she's been seen, she lingers a few seconds more before turning on her heel and catching up with the others.

CHAPTER 20

SATURDAY, MAY 26, 1928

*L*ouisa

Frustration whooshes from my lips as I step onto the sidewalk. This is the third day in a row I've had to fight for space in our little apartment. Since Cookie has been mixed in with us, everything has shifted—the bathroom schedule, space in the kitchen, and even where each of us sit at the end of an evening. The unease inside the apartment has been mounting for days, but now it feels as if it's about to boil over.

Walking toward the rehearsal hall, I contemplate the situation. I've tried to remain calm, even going so far as to conceal my annoyance behind tight-lipped smiles. Cookie's continuous joy over her new life does little to ease the strain of forced proximity. With the pressure Clara feels over her role as hotel matron along with the daily opposition I've been receiving at rehearsals, individual tensions are on the rise. My mind buzzes with agitation as I stride purposefully down the sidewalk.

In my already disagreeable state, Papa's mention of moving houses felt like the final nail in the coffin. As if I'm not already under enough pressure to fulfill my acting credits and unearth the courage to secure my passage to California.

A bitter taste fills my mouth at the thought of it. I don't enjoy change. Especially when it's being forced upon me. All I want is for us to stay where we are until my next steps on the road to Hollywood are clear. The memory of the strangers' words at the wedding reception presses in on me. My time with a home full of support is slipping away from me. *Be ready to fly, girlie.*

No. I shake my head at the offending notion. I need more time to gather myself, to find my footing within the safety of my family home. I want big things in my life. But I'm still not certain I'm brave enough to follow my dreams on my own.

I've never admitted it to them, but Papa and Clara's grounding presence enables me to be bold and fearless. Without their assuredness tucked into my arsenal, I'm left to flounder.

The pressure is real, and I'm running out of time. There is little choice. If I am to succeed, I must face the challenges as they come, and somehow, I must learn to do so without the support of my family. If I can just get my character in this play on track, then surely, I'll find the strength to stand on my own two feet and be ready to head to Hollywood. If I must relocate, I'd rather be the one determining the path forward.

The warm breeze catches my attention, reminding me today is a fresh start. I push aside my sour disposition and lift my chin, forcing myself to focus on the task before me. I have a full day of rehearsals ahead, and I have plans to speak with the director about improving my character's place in the production.

"Lou." A gust of wind whispers my name.

"Louisa." Louder this time. I turn toward the voice and see Thomas jogging toward me, with a wide grin and joy emanating from his whole being.

"What are you doing here?" I ask, smoothing out the question with a laugh. "I didn't think I was going to see you until tonight."

"Happy coincidence." He shrugs before wrapping an arm around me in a brief embrace.

I inhale his scent and feel my worries dissolve. Thomas, I'm reminded, never fails to steady me. Perhaps I've been fretting over nothing at all. He is my future, after all, and I am sure to have his unwavering support.

He gestures in the direction of the street at his back. "I'm heading over to see Mr. Johnson at the theatre."

I step back to gain a better vantage point of his face. "Mr. Johnson?"

Thomas' chuckle vibrates through me, and I swear I can feel his good-hearted nature all the way to my toes. "I would have waited for us to visit him together, but he sent word that the production currently in the works at the theatre is struggling. Says the director is a good man but he's lost his footing."

"So, you're going there to see if you can help?"

Thomas runs a hand through his hair, and right on cue, my stomach does a somersault. "Only if the director is open to receiving help. I have no intention of treading on someone else's production."

"I'm sure Mr. Johnson wouldn't have asked if assistance

wasn't being sought." Knowing the theatre's janitor is quite attuned, as a Black man, to the limitations of societal constraints, I am certain he wouldn't say a word unless he knew it would end well.

I remember the kindly man's understanding and care toward me when I found myself in the middle of a plot to ruin Thomas' production. "Mr. Johnson is one of the kindest people I've ever met, but he is also a force to be reckoned with. His morals are lofty." I place a hand on Thomas' forearm. "He knows his place in society, though it pleases me none. But more than that, he understands people and is aware enough to know whether someone is willing to receive assistance."

"You are probably right about that." Thomas beams affectionately at me.

"He's an example for all of us. I hope someday to have the gumption to become half as impactful as he is in the lives of others."

Thomas covers my hand with his. "You will be, Lou. I'm quite certain you've got enough moxie for all of us. We all need to find the thing that fuels us." He checks his wristwatch. "Anyway, I won't keep you, but I will see you tonight?" He places a light kiss on my hand before backing away with a silly grin.

"See you tonight." I send him off with a quick wave and watch him take long strides toward the intersection, where he crosses the street and disappears behind a block of buildings.

I spot the newspaper stand on the opposite side of the street and move toward it, my sour mood erased by Thomas' surprise appearance.

Returning my thoughts to the task before me, I go over this morning's plan. After mulling it over for several days,

I've decided to appeal to the director's achievement-orientated nature. Every director wants their play to be a success. I am certain a few tweaks to my character will help ensure *Mr. Brown's Secretary* is a hit worthy of newspaper headlines. If the director allows me to reach for more, then the rest of the cast will want to as well. I've seen it before, and I have no doubt that, together, we can create a production worth talking about.

It took me a few days and some long chats with Clara to come up with a plan. I originally wanted to have my father's ear on the topic, but I have to admit my sister asked some tough questions. I had to think long and hard about why I wanted to be onstage in the first place. In the end, it's less about money or fame, though those are both nice. For me, I love the way acting makes me feel alive and the joy that comes with working as a group for the same outcome. That is where I thrive.

Dashing across the street, I pause at the newspaper stand and purchase a copy of today's paper. I want to show up prepared, and today's theatre headlines are going to help me sell the idea to Mr. Max Barker. I find a park bench and scour the newspaper. The familiar inky scent hangs in the air as I fold and smooth the paper into a manageable rectangle, with the theatre reviews front and centre. With my pencil in hand, I circle descriptions that rave about the audience's enjoyment.

With a clear handle on my dreams, Clara's encouraging words, and a newspaper to prove my point, I feel my mood lift as I stride into the rehearsal hall. If I can align my goals with those of the director, our audience will leave the theatre happy every single evening and we'll have proudly done our jobs.

Rose Oxley's words run through my mind as I tug on

the interior door that leads to the makeshift stage. A few more credits and I could be on my way to Hollywood.

But first, I need to convince the director that making Agatha Taylor shine will make the production of *Mr. Brown's Secretary* sparkle like he never imagined it could.

CHAPTER 21

SATURDAY, MAY 26, 1928

lara

William's lips curve upward as he steps to the side and gestures for me to go ahead of him. As I step onto the landing that leads to the basement offices, the incident with Agnes, the new second-floor maid, slips into the recesses of my mind, and appreciation for William's chivalrous nature takes its place. Another warm smile and the gentle pressure of his hand on my back makes me confident, at least in this moment, that he only has eyes for me.

After a quick morning greeting to Mr. Olson, I leave the men to catch up and turn my attention to the eight floors of roll call awaiting me. As I navigate the back-of-house corridors, I allow William to monopolize my thoughts. At first, they are happy musings. Excitement courses through me when I admit how much I've missed him since he returned to Toronto.

By the time my feet are marching up the first flight of

159

stairs, my thoughts are muddled. William's presence, though inviting, forces me to face my doubts about our future together. How will I tell him the truth when doing so could tear us apart? The irony is not lost on me. I've got a good man in William Thompson, yet the very reason our paths crossed may also part them. There is a hotel between us.

I smother an exasperated sigh and greet the first-floor maids with a pleasant, albeit coerced, disposition before going over the events of the day. Within ten minutes, I need to politely remind them to quiet down in order to get through the roster. The giggles are endless as I head for the stairs. I don't bother turning back. Instead I roll my eyes and move on to the next guest floor.

By the time I complete roll call on the fourth floor, I fear I am facing an uphill battle. The warm spring weather seems to have brought forth the giddiness of the maid contingent. Something I might once have considered amusing is now hindering my day. I decide to check on each floor throughout the day and will suggest that the maids get out of doors during their midday meal. Hopefully that will allow them to burn off some energy.

When I agreed to fill in for Ms. Thompson, I didn't anticipate needing to roll with the moods, expectations, and shortcomings of many different personalities. Now, though, with a month as matron behind me, I'm no longer surprised by the continual antics. I am, however, still baffled by how to properly address such shenanigans.

I busy myself in Ms. Thompson's office by sorting out the upcoming week's schedule. Louisa's rehearsal schedule adds an extra layer of complication to the juggling of maids' days off. Thankfully, we are not dealing with the threat of a spring flu taking out the lot of them, at least not this week.

Closing the scheduling book, I remind myself to point out to Louisa how accommodating Ms. Thompson has been with her theatre schedule. Drafting up a calendar to meet the needs of both the hotel and the individual maids is not for the faint of heart. If anything, I've gained an even deeper level of respect for our matron, and I must make certain Ms. Thompson feels my appreciation when she returns.

A knock on the door startles me from my thoughts, and I pull the stack of papers containing next month's banquet room schedule toward the centre of the desk. "Yes." I raise my voice a touch to ensure it reaches the other side of the closed door.

William pokes his head through the half-open door. "I'm heading out to see Eliza. Didn't want you to think I'd forgotten to say goodbye."

"Please give her my best. I'm certain she will be beyond delighted to see you."

"I will." William hesitates, lingering in the threshold. "I will be tied up for the rest of the day, but are you free tomorrow? Perhaps a walk through Stanley Park?"

"That would be lovely." I don't bother hiding my smile at the thought of a slow stroll through the park with William at my side.

"Great. I'll come by after breakfast, then." William winks at me before ducking back toward the basement hallway.

"I look forward to it," I call after him, a vibration of exhilaration thrumming through me in anticipation of tomorrow.

Fifteen minutes later, after perusing the banquet room

schedule, I gather the papers and head toward Cookie's pastry kitchen. Several of the scheduled events are simple tea and pastry bookings, each of them requiring Cookie's input and baking expertise.

The hotel has become accustomed to renting out the smaller event rooms for business meetings and the like. We even host the Vancouver chapter of the National Council of Women of Canada from time to time, though I am relieved to see their organization missing from next month's calendar. With the Persons Case lighting a fire in women throughout our city, I am thankful to avoid any ruckus under this roof.

I hear William's voice as I near the end of the corridor. He must have been detained by someone he knows, I muse, thinking of how generous he is with his time.

Shuffling the papers to my left arm, I free my right in preparation to wave him good-naturedly on his way. I am stopped short by the scene in the hallway. William's back is to me. And Agnes is beside him, her hand resting on William's forearm.

Her coy shyness doesn't fool me for a second. When she bats her eyes, her giggle rips through me like a hot knife through butter. The blatant manner in which the girl is flirting with him, a man she met only this morning, sends warning sirens screaming through my head.

Last year, an eighth-floor maid was caught canoodling with a bellboy. The incident cost the boy his job, while the maid kept hers, thanks to her well-to-do father's connections. It takes less than a second for me to grasp the heartbreaking ramifications of dealing with a similar situation as matron, with William at the centre of it.

The door's hush draws my attention. I catch the back of William's head as he leaves the hotel, waving goodbye to the overly friendly maid. Unaware that she's being watched, Agnes' expression stretches taut with unmistakable triumph as the door closes with a thud.

When she turns in my direction, our eyes meet. I tilt my head to one side while raising my eyebrows high in question. Who behaves this way? I wonder. Though we've never flaunted it, I'm quite certain my relationship with William is far from a secret among the staff. I watch as her victorious expression transforms into a scowl, before she brushes past me and down the back-of-house corridor, in a hurry to remove herself from my line of sight.

CHAPTER 22

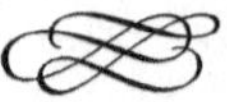

SATURDAY, MAY 26, 1928

ouisa

The rehearsal hall has a few early birds, and I'm grateful I'm not the only cast member eager to get to work on making this production a success. Taking a few steps into the hall, I notice two actresses huddled together, their heads bent toward one another while hushed words fly from their lips. Curious, I think but decide to stick to today's plan of action.

Glancing around the room, I note the director's absence. Intent on seeking him out, I turn back toward the door to the hall.

"Louisa." The actress named Judith calls me over with an enthusiastic gesture.

She plays my character's best friend and confidant, and I've come to know her fairly well over the last two weeks of rehearsals. It hardly seems polite to ignore her, so I veer right and greet them with a good morning.

"We're discussing the latest in the Persons Case." Judith leans in conspiratorially.

"The latest?" I ask. The decision continues to press in on me from every angle, though I skipped right past the front-page news today and went straight for the theatre reviews.

"The papers are saying the women are appealing the ruling to the Privy Council."

Marie, the understudy for Judith's role, adds, "It's the highest court."

"I thought the Supreme Court was the highest court." Feeling slightly out of the loop, I'm kicking myself for not reading the front-page news this morning.

"It is, but as a dominion of the United Kingdom, we can further appeal a Supreme Court's decision to the— what's it called again?" Marie looks to Judith.

"The Judicial Committee of the Privy Council," Judith affirms with a steady nod.

"Well that's something, then." I can only hope a favourable ruling will prevail. Maybe then the pressures pulling me under will ease, and I can return my attention to happier things.

Judith lolls her head to the side. "Even if the Privy Council upholds the Supreme Court decision, it's unlikely we'll lose our right to vote. At least we aren't in as desperate of a situation as those poor women in Quebec. They're still fighting the hard fight."

All three of our heads bob solemnly up and down, acknowledging Quebec women's lack of voting privileges.

Marie breaks our silence with a whisper. "Did you hear Archie, the male lead, is making two times as much as you, Louisa?"

I bristle, alarmed by any gossip regarding my wages. At

news of another injustice, I swear the fire in my belly is stoked enough that the flames lick my face. "I hadn't heard that." The desire to locate the director returns to the front of my mind, but I wonder which I should address first—my low wage or his lack of interest in directing a decent production?

I raise a single eyebrow, hoping to put this conversation to bed. I am about to excuse myself and continue on my mission to locate the director. Today, I decide, I've got bigger things to accomplish than worrying about what Archie is making. If this play flops, so might my career and any chance of earning the same wage as my male counterparts in the future.

Marie isn't ready to let this go. "It's true. Yesterday, I heard the men talking, and according to them"—she looks around to ensure she isn't being overheard—"the male stagehands make more than you too."

My calm demeanour evaporates in an instant. "What?" Pulling my expression into a tight smile, I say calmly, "If you'll excuse me." Then I turn and walk out of the rehearsal hall, fuming all the way to the director's office. Knocking with more force than I intend, I almost hope he isn't inside. I could use a moment to gather my wits and coax out the version of myself who smiles sweetly while edging toward getting what I want.

"Come in," Max Barker's voice booms from behind the closed door. As I step inside, he greets me. "Miss Wilson. Good morning." Though it's veiled behind a thin-lipped smile, I sense his displeasure at my presence within his office. The man clearly has no time for me.

I run the options through my head as quickly as I can. There are two choices. I can fight the consistently disappointing battle for pay equity, or I can set myself up for another successful career move, as I originally intended.

"Is there something I can help you with?" The director removes his spectacles from his nose and scrutinizes me.

"Actually, yes." I force my shoulders back and summon a brilliant smile. "I've found a way to elevate my Agatha character."

"Miss Wilson, as I've said before, the role doesn't need elevating. The secretary is fine as a stock character."

I push past his reservations, avoid rolling my eyes, and press on. I pull the newspaper, still open to the theatre reviews, from my bag. Thrusting the paper toward him, I continue. "If you'll read the reviews I've circled, you'll see the reviewers, and I imagine the audience too, are drawn to less prominent characters if they are portrayed with depth." I stab the paper with a finger. "See this one? We both know this Alice character is nothing to write home about, but the reviewer specifically praised her portrayal because the actress went above and beyond."

"Your point is?" He hands the newspaper back to me.

"Am I wrong to assume that you would prefer that this production receive rave reviews and sold-out performances?" I implement my single eyebrow lift and wait for him to acquiesce.

When he stares back at me, unmoving, I push my other concern into the conversation. "I suppose we could discuss how the cast is talking about the pay discrepancy between the male and female members of the production. Just a few minutes ago, I learned I was being paid less than the stagehands." I deliver the sweetest smile I can muster and wait for his response, knowing a director's reputation is not immune to gossip or newspaper headlines. Given all the fanfare over the Persons Case, I'm betting that Mr. Barker doesn't wish to have his production boycotted by women.

An exasperated exhale is the answer I'm looking for. "Fine, you can give it a try. But I'm not making any promises."

"Thank you, sir. I won't disappoint you. I'm confident I can bring Agatha to life and have the audience rooting for her."

"Well, I'm not so sure about that, but you're certainly a determined little filly, aren't you?" He waves me away before slumping back into his chair.

I bristle at his offensive comparison of me to a horse. Before I can summon a retort, I realize I've gotten what I came for. I hold my tongue and let the thrill of triumph run through me as I close the door. I may not have solved the inequality for women in the theatre, but I took a small step toward my career goals, and that is something to be proud of.

An hour later, my time to prove myself arrives. With the full cast assembled, I settle onto the makeshift stage, determined to convince the director I am right.

In the scene, Mr. Brown's board members are situated around a long rectangular table. Agatha sits in the corner of the room, notepad and pencil in hand, ready to take the meeting's notes.

Archie, playing Mr. Brown, inflates his chest as he struts the length of the boardroom table, spouting the words Agatha wrote for him. Giving me an opportunity, Archie pauses his monologue briefly and improvises. Archie, as Mr. Brown, knits his brows together as his character becomes aware the speech he is reading is not the speech he dictated to Agatha. Playing the role to its fullest, Archie dips his head in my direction and purses his lips as if he's about to question Agatha about the speech.

My cue, I think as I stiffen my posture in the slim office chair. I meet his gaze directly before ensuring my right eye is in the sightline of a would-be audience. With a wink to the audience, I showcase a put-upon smile for Archie.

Archie matches my smile with one of his own before continuing.

We banter back and forth, each of us playing off the other's cues. Together, we are on fire. I can feel the energy sizzling in the hall as the rest of the cast leans into their own characters' embellishments. Even Judith comes alive in a scene where Agatha and her best friend are having lunch, discussing Mr. Brown's lackluster attempts to be a successful businessman. Sometimes all it takes is a single nod of permission to encourage others to aim higher.

Near the end of rehearsal, the director steps onto the stage. His copy of the script is rolled into a tube, which he twists incessantly as he considers his words.

He looks directly at me. "Well, I said you could give it a shot, but frankly, all your theatrics only distract from Mr. Brown's character."

My mouth falls open. How can he not see the changes helped the entire cast improve? I have no words, and my mouth grows dry.

"Next week, we'll go back to doing it the way we were before." He scans the actors before him and then steps off the stage.

"But—" The word stumbles from my lips.

"No." The director booms from the stage steps. "Just stick to the script, Miss Wilson."

"Maybe if I give it another try, sir. Something a touch less flamboyant but still on point? Agatha wants to support Mr. Brown, clearly. But the audience needs to see her as a well-rounded character. More of a full, three-dimensional woman."

The director's eyes bore into me. "Miss Wilson, you don't seem to understand. Mr. Brown's secretary isn't a real person."

All I hear is a steady buzzing in my ears. Not a real person? The words play on repeat in my mind.

The director leaves the hall immediately after delivering his gut punch. I slump into one of the boardroom set's chairs while the cast and crew mill about for a few minutes, none of them sure of what to do or say.

Judith checks on me, but her words are garbled and indiscernible. In the end, she gives my arm a pat and says she'll see me next week.

Archie hangs around the longest, waiting for the others to clear out before trying to console me.

"You know," he starts, his voice breaking through the humming in my head, "I thought your version was better too. Not solely for you but for the entire cast. Everyone came alive following your lead. You made us all shine. You're a natural, Louisa."

With my defences kicked to the curb, a snort slips out. "Not so much, it seems."

"Well, I thought you should know. I think you were great today, and it's a pleasure to work with you." Archie stands and leaves me in the empty hall, disbelief wrapped around me like a heavy winter coat on a summer day.

Gathering what's left of my pride, I trek from the rehearsal hall to the diner where I'm meeting Thomas for dinner. My feet are as heavy as my heart, and I am thankful my legs know the route.

I almost crumple at the sight of Thomas waiting for me

at the diner's front door. Without my having to utter a word, he catches me in an embrace and holds on. I ignore the impropriety of the intimate gesture in public and instead breathe in his scent as my tears begin to fall.

We settle ourselves into a quiet booth, Thomas choosing to sit next to me. He waits patiently for me to detail the day's events, and he nods as I explain what happened.

When our meals arrive, I move my food around my plate with my fork until Thomas scoops up a mound of my mashed potatoes and encourages me to eat.

"You realize the director wasn't insulting you specifically?" He doesn't look at me as he speaks.

"The words are enough, Thomas." I let out a disappointed huff, a warning he doesn't seem to pick up on.

"He probably didn't connect what he said to what's going on in the courts. He's a well-respected man in the theatre. I'm sure he didn't mean—"

My fork drops to my plate with a clatter as I rotate against the booth's smooth bench seat. "He didn't mean what?"

"All I'm saying is he probably misspoke." Thomas' shrug does little to endear me to him. "Besides, right or wrong, you know it's your job to follow the direction of your director."

My eyes go wide in disbelief. "Even when he's wrong?"

Thomas lifts his burger while bobbing his head, clearly unaware of the angry heat emanating from my skin. "Yep. Even when he's wrong."

"How can you say such a thing? I didn't expect this from you of all people." My voice wobbles as my volume rises. I push my plate away and motion for him to get out of the booth. "Honestly, Thomas. I can't believe you are siding with that man."

Thomas, reluctant to let me pass, tries to reason with me, placing a hand dangerously on my forearm. "I think you might be overreacting, Lou."

"Overreacting. Me?" The scoff sails from my lips as my hands clench into fists. "Maybe you're not reacting enough. Did you ever think of that?"

Thomas' head tilts to one side as he considers what I've said. "This isn't personal. It's work, and sometimes a director has to make a tough call not everyone agrees with."

My gaze narrows on him, and I wonder if he's heard anything I've said. "That's the point. The entire cast thinks the director is wrong."

"Thing is, the cast isn't the director."

For a fleeting moment, I wonder if Thomas' position as a director is colouring his view of the situation. Maybe there's a code that says all directors must stand up for one another. But what about me? Who is going to have my back? Frustration and fear take over, and I wave my arms wildly, gesturing for him to move. "I have to leave. I have to get out of here."

"Lou, can't we finish our meal? Then I'll walk you home."

"I'm not hungry."

His defeated sigh tells me I'm getting my wish. Sincerity laces his words. "I'm sorry. I realize you've had a hard day." Thomas rises slowly but remains directly in my path to a clear escape.

He wants me to stay, to talk this through. But if I can't count on Thomas to support me when I need it most, who can I count on? I'm feeling too much despair to reconcile his actions with the man I know him to be, so I deliver a line to ensure my escape. "I don't accept your apology. Please move."

He slides to the left, creating a small opening. I slip past him without another word.

Not wasting a minute, Thomas calls out to the waitress that he's left money on the table and rushes after me.

I ignore him when he calls my name, too distraught to acknowledge his hurt-laced pleas for me to stop. I'm a mess, with tears streaming down my face, and despite wanting nothing more than for him to hold me in his arms, pride pushes me up the hill toward home. A few blocks later, Thomas walks silently three steps behind me. I assume he's following me home out of concern, whether he's worried about my emotional state or feels obligated to make certain I arrive home safely under the darkened sky.

I sneak a glance through the glass of the Newbury's lobby door as it closes behind me. My heart shatters at his despondent expression, telling me I may have just made the biggest mistake of my life. I wipe the tears from my cheeks before stomping up the stairs in manufactured defiance.

CHAPTER 23

SATURDAY, MAY 26, 1928

lara

I'm ruminating about flirtatious Agnes when Louisa tearfully bursts into our bedroom.

"What's happened?" I bolt upright in bed.

A fresh wave of emotion forces Lou to collapse onto my bed, sobbing. Sliding my legs from beneath the covers, I swivel my body so I can wrap an arm around her. "It's okay. It can't be that bad."

Lou's pained expression stares back at me. "It is that bad. Oh Clara, I think I've really done it. I've lost Thomas for good."

"What? How?" I rub comforting circles on her back. "You two are like peas in a pod. I'm sure you can work it out. Tell me what happened."

"The director, he won't listen to reason." Hiccups interrupt my sister's words. "He said my character isn't a real person." Renewed emotion trails down Louisa's cheeks. "And—and Thomas agreed with him."

I bite the inside of my cheek while I contemplate an appropriate response.

Lou looks at me, her mottled face puffy and red. "Don't you see, Thomas didn't stand up for me."

"With the director?" I do my best to keep my expression placid, not wishing to add fuel to Louisa's fire.

"No. Not with the director. Because of the director." A huff, strong enough to be deemed a light breeze, sails from her lips. "He should have agreed with me. Supported me. He should have comforted me instead of being all *it's your job to follow the lead of your director*."

I hold back a chuckle at Louisa's impersonation of Thomas and press on. "Ah, I see. You're upset because Thomas didn't side with you on something that happened with the director today. I'm guessing Thomas had on his director's hat?"

Lou nods while sucking in a sharp inhale. "He didn't even console me."

"I'm assuming you became upset and told him so?"

Another affirming nod.

"Well, it sounds to me like you and Thomas were having two different conversations."

Louisa wipes at her cheeks and sniffles. "What do you mean?"

"You told him about your day and wanted him to understand your disappointment with the director."

"Yes, but—"

"Thomas didn't understand you were seeking comfort from him, and instead he saw the issue from a director's point of view. I'm certain he wasn't trying to hurt you, Lou. He was actually trying to help you in a practical way. Thomas saw the director's obstinance as something you needed to get on board with. He's probably experienced cast members disagreeing with his own direction, and he knows that things go more smoothly when everyone agrees with a director's decisions."

"But—"

I shake my head slowly. "It sounds like a misunderstanding, not a breakup."

Her response is barely audible. "He hurt me, Clara. I'm not sure I can count on him to be there for me when I need it most."

My heart lurches for her. I refrain from offering further sensible advice. Instead, I wrap my arms around my sister and let her feel everything she needs to feel in this moment.

While Louisa cries quietly in my arms, my thoughts turn to William. He's never given me cause to feel unsupported. Even when I worried he might disapprove of me stepping in as hotel matron, he genuinely appreciated my decision to do so.

When my sister finally pulls away, washes her face, and slides into bed, I broach the subject of relocating from The Newbury. "What do you think?"

Never one to mince words, she says, "I don't like it one bit. They've surely been discussing a move for some time now, and I feel like they left us out of the conversation on purpose." Tugging her covers toward her, she shrugs. "Course, everyone I thought I could trust has been disappointing me every which way lately."

"Don't say that, Lou." I stretch my arm across the small space between our beds and wiggle my fingers. "You have me. You can always trust in me."

Grabbing my hand in hers, my sister smiles as a new

wave of moisture gathers in her lower lids. "And you'll always have me."

Louisa lets go and props herself up with an elbow. "What do you think about the two of us going out on our own? We could rent a little apartment, or maybe we could even stay right here." Her bottom lip finds its way between her teeth, a sure sign she is nervous about asking the question. "Could we afford it, just the two of us?"

I consider the options and recognize the opportunity for buying myself some breathing room. A little more time to continue my position at The Hamilton while courting William from afar. My solution of having both, at least for the time being, is right in front of me. "Yes." I sit up and face my sister, elation running through me. "I think with both our wages, we can afford an apartment on our own."

Louisa beams at me. "Then let's do it. You and me, girls of the city."

Laughter erupts from my chest, and I feel lighter than I have in weeks. "Let's do right by Papa and speak with him about our plans first. We've no reason to create extra tension."

"We'll talk to him tomorrow, then. Before they buy a house with all four of us in mind." Louisa falls back into bed, a silly grin plastered on her face.

~

SUNDAY, MAY 27, 1928

The late-into-the-evening talk with Louisa, in addition to a decent amount of tossing and turning all night, has not left me feeling refreshed this morning. My first thought at the break of dawn was an image of Agnes, that brazen maid.

Following close on its heels were the questions I've no answers for. Was William's smile merely a polite interaction, or was there more to it? Agnes certainly thought so, and since I can't be certain, my mind replays the incident on repeat.

I realize now there are more downsides of William living across the country than simply my missing him. We've not been afforded enough time together to give me the comfort of knowing his every mannerism. Maybe if we had been, I would be able to determine which of his smiles implies something more than politeness.

Then again, while I miss him when he's in Toronto, I've also found it rather convenient to organize my life into boxes. I have a work box, a home box, and a William box, which I can set aside without causing harm to anyone when another part of my life demands more from me. Given we correspond mostly through letters, I am afforded the luxury of a delayed response if I lack the time or words for an immediate reply. I'm aware my system will surely fall apart should I add anything else to the mix, including William as a constant presence in my life. I have no idea how things will unfold. I only know there are challenges ahead and difficult decisions I am not eager to make.

The bright of the day slips in through the thin break where the curtains part, reminding me that time marches on, regardless of whether I'd like to hide under the covers all day. I loll my head to the side and note Louisa's bedding is pulled taut and tucked like a Hamilton guest room's. Despite her tears, hiccups, and unyielding rants, she's managed to pull herself from despair this morning and get on with the day.

If my sister can, so must I. Sliding my legs from under the blankets, I let my feet absorb the cool of the wood floor before pulling my robe around my shoulders and heading into the living room.

Louisa is sitting on the sofa with a magazine draped over her legs and a cup of tea in hand. "I made a pot if you want some," she says without looking up.

I scan the room, my gaze landing on the oversized rocking chair. A pang of sadness squeezes my chest. Forcing my eyes to look elsewhere, I move toward the kitchen. Cookie's presence in our little apartment may come with its challenges, and even a few heartaches, but one advantage, aside from her fabulous cooking and genuinely delightful attitude, is my sister's new inclination to think about her role in the household. In the past few days, Louisa has made her own breakfast more than once and offered to wash the dishes. And this morning she is awake before me with a waiting pot of tea.

"Thank heaven for small mercies," I mumble to myself. The aroma of hot tea billows toward me as I tilt the pot toward my teacup.

Teacup in hand, I slide into the softness of the other side of the sofa and wait for the continuation of last night's conversation.

Louisa looks up from her magazine. "Papa and Cookie are out for a walk, but I spoke with them about the possibility of us staying in the apartment."

"You did? I thought we were going to have that conversation together."

"Time is of the essence, or so they say." Lou's sarcasm drips from every word, making me wonder whether her sullen disposition is due to last night's argument with Thomas or something else.

I deliver Lou a questioning stare, not wanting to beat about the bush with a groggy head.

"They've gone ahead and booked some houses to view with a real estate agent. So you see"—Louisa's expression is permeated with scorn—"time is of the essence."

"What happened to discussing these changes as a family?" I've been kept out of an important decision, despite making my concern known. A mixture of hurt and annoyance creeps in to keep me company.

Lou rolls her eyes, a clear indication I am annoying her by not keeping up with the conversation. "Time—"

"Yeah, yeah. I get it."

My sister flips a page of her magazine with a touch more force than is necessary.

"What did they say about the idea of you and me staying here?" I blow the steam from the rim of my teacup before taking a cautious sip.

"I think Papa was surprised, but Cookie seemed to understand. Then again, I don't imagine she'd complain about having him all to herself right now." Louisa's eyebrow lifts a fraction.

"Don't say that. Cookie loves us. She knew we were a package deal." My feelings are far too easily bruised this morning, but I blame it on lack of sleep.

Louisa's bottom lip makes its way between her teeth. "What do you think? Should we go forward with our plans since they've gone forward with theirs?"

I can tell Louisa is anxious for an immediate yes. Maybe it's due to her emotional uncertainty over Thomas, or perhaps she is simply desperate to stay put at The Newbury, something I never imagined would be the case when we first moved in. My mouth twists in contemplation. "In all honesty, I think I'd like to try."

She sits up straighter, her features brightening with enthusiasm, and reaches for my hand. "Me too."

The telephone rings, interrupting our bold announcement. I stand, placing my teacup on the dining table.

Before I reach the telephone, Louisa's wall goes up. "If it's Thomas, I'm not here."

I am about to argue back but decide better of it and simply answer the telephone. "Wilson residence."

"Well, you are exactly the Wilson I was hoping to catch." William's voice is tender and hushed, and I immediately picture him sequestered in a nook of Ms. Thompson's house in an effort to not be overheard.

A slow smile lifts my cheeks, and I instinctively turn my back on Louisa to afford myself a small measure of privacy. "Hello, you."

"It's a beautiful day. Are you still available for a walk through the park?"

"I am. What time were you thinking?" I look down at my robe and bare feet. "Actually, can we say noon? I slept late this morning and haven't had a chance to grab breakfast yet."

"Noon is perfect. I will see you then."

"See you then." I hang up the telephone with a contented sigh at the thought of an entire afternoon in William's company.

Returning to the sofa, I meet Louisa's gaze. "Are you okay? I'm sure last night was rough, but maybe if you talk to Thomas, you'll be able to work things out."

"I'm not ready to do that. He hurt me, Clara." Louisa's bottom lip quivers, and I sense a fresh onslaught of tears. "I thought I could count on him to have my back, but now I understand the only person I can truly count on is you."

"That's not entirely true. You have Papa and Cookie." I am taken aback by Louisa's adamant shake of her head.

"No, Papa and Cookie have one another now. They've made that perfectly clear by deciding to move without speaking with us first. You and me, we're on our own from here on out."

Louisa's firm in her stance, so I decide to leave things where they are for now, hoping as her heartbreak heals so will her perspective. I love my sister dearly, but even I am unprepared to be her sole source of lifelong support.

"I have to get ready. Did you want something to eat?"

Louisa shakes her head. Her focus is back on the magazine, but I sense she isn't reading any of it.

In the bedroom, I consider what it will be like to live on our own. I suspect it will be similar to life before Cookie moved in. Then again, I might be incorrectly assuming that I won't miss Papa's presence in the apartment.

I pull a dress from the cupboard, one William comments on every time I wear it. I wonder what he will say to my and Lou's plan to live at the apartment by ourselves. Will he be pleased with my inclination to strive for independence, or will he balk at the notion?

Sliding my feet into shoes, a realization hits me. I filter my every thought through the lens of what William will think. My bottom hits the bed with more force than I'm expecting, and I understand. I can no longer deny it. I am in love with William Thompson.

An image of that cheeky second-floor maid dashes across my memory, but I shake it off. I feel my resolve building. There are many obstacles ahead for us to navigate, and in time, I'm certain we will. But right now, I know precisely what I want, and that is William in my life and that flirtatious maid put back in her box.

My new awareness thrums through me. I feel as though my heart is beating in every corner of my body. I'm giddy at the thought of seeing William, though I do my best to hide my excitement from Louisa during breakfast.

Papa and Cookie come through the door, both of them chattering over one another. The toast pauses its trajectory toward my mouth as I try to make sense of what they're discussing.

"All I'm saying is it won't hurt to ask, love. Think of what's best for the girls." Cookie places a hand on Papa's arm, and like it's a magic touch, Papa acquiesces.

Louisa looks up from her magazine. "What's all this?"

Hanging his hat on the hook, Papa moves into the living room. He scratches his head before meeting Lou's expectant gaze.

"We ran into Mr. Watkins in the lobby." Papa hesitates.

"Oh, how is he? I've been meaning to bake him a pie since he appreciated the slice we shared with him at Christmas." I take a bite of toast while waiting for Papa's reply.

Papa's strained smile tells me he's about to deliver unpleasant news. "A pie would be nice. Mighty thoughtful of you, Clara."

Cookie and Papa exchange a look.

"We mentioned that we're looking for a new home to purchase, and Cookie brought up the idea of you girls remaining in the apartment after we relocate."

Louisa's magazine drops to her knees with a thwap. "And?"

"Well, according to Mr. Watkins, The Newbury property management hasn't ever permitted young women to reside in the building without a father or husband present."

Louisa is up from the sofa before I can process the information. "Are you saying we can't stay?"

"I'm sorry, darlin'. It's looking that way." Papa clasps his hands together, and I wonder if it's in preparation for the onslaught of ranting expected from Hurricane Louisa.

"Where are we supposed to go?" My voice is unsteady and subdued in contrast to Louisa's high-pitched one.

"You'll move with us." Papa glances between Louisa and me. "Together, as a family."

My heart sinks as our options are swallowed up with Papa's words. The plan we hatched last night seemed like the perfect solution, and now, this news is an uninvited guest taking up space in our little apartment, just like Cookie's rocker.

"Joseph." Cookie steps forward, her face set with determination. "I think we should ask The Newbury management. Mr. Watkins can only speak to what he is aware of. He doesn't make all the decisions."

Papa sighs, and I smother guilt over my previous thought about Cookie's rocker. Our friend is ardently standing up for our desire to remain in the apartment. My only hope is that Louisa can see Cookie's support for the caring and love-filled gesture it is.

CHAPTER 24

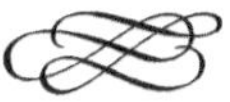

SUNDAY, MAY 27, 1928

ouisa

"I'm not moving." I cross my arms over my chest in defiance as the taste of bile rises in my throat.

The three of them gang up on me with their shared glances. Even Clara, my so-called ally, looks ready to cave at the first obstacle.

"You shouldn't have even started looking at new homes until we'd all discussed it. A decision like this affects each one of us." My angry stare lands on Cookie. She flinches, making me feel like the louse I am currently behaving like.

"Louisa." Clara beats Papa to the punch, condemning my harsh words with a sharp, disapproving tone. "Didn't you hear what Cookie said? She's trying to help. Surely you can rein in your quick tongue long enough to have a civil conversation."

I slump dramatically onto the sofa and mumble "sorry" with as much enthusiasm as I might muster for a root canal.

Clara places her breakfast dishes in the sink before joining me on the sofa. I will her presence beside me to be a show of solidarity, but given my rudeness, I can't be certain.

"Louisa is right about one thing." Clara reaches for my hand and squeezes it. "This is a big decision and should not be forced upon anyone."

Papa and Cookie exchange sheepish glances, apparently understanding their error. In their eagerness to fix the problem of our crowded quarters, they rushed to take action without fully considering us.

Clara has certainly grown in her ability to speak plainly, and I wonder if the matron position has helped her find her footing in both work and life.

"We understand." Clara raises our clasped hands a few inches off the sofa. "You desire to start your lives together. We don't wish to stand in your way. All we're saying is that we need time to determine our next steps. We want you to be happy. Both of you."

Papa's voice cracks with emotion. "I'm not choosing between you girls and Ruby." He reaches for Cookie's hand in an effort to include her in our conversation.

"We're not asking you to. The apartment is a tight fit for all of us. We are aware. But perhaps we could find another solution. I think we would all be well served by a chance to talk through our thoughts and fears." I sense Clara's pride at having taken up the charge of saying the difficult words as she releases my hand, clasping her own hands together in her lap.

Papa's head bobs in understanding. "When did you become so wise?"

Cookie beams proudly in Clara's direction. "They're growing up, Joseph. The both of them."

Spotting the opening, I raise myself from the sofa and

walk the few steps to Cookie. "I'm sorry. I didn't mean to hurt you. I've been known to lash out when I'm feeling uncertain, and right now, my whole life feels like it's on shaky ground."

Letting go of Papa's hand, Cookie grasps mine and squeezes tight. She regards me with a gentle expression. "When you're hurting, it's easy to turn that pain toward someone else. Only thing is, doing so seldom makes anyone feel better."

With her kindness shining on me, I'm plunged into the depths of emotion, crumbling into Cookie's arms as the first tears pave the way for my sobs of despair.

"There, there, dear. You know I love you like you're my own kin. Don't you worry one bit. Everything will work out how it's supposed to in the end. We'll take this one day at a time, all of us, together," Cookie coos into my hair, and this time, I choose to believe her.

CHAPTER 25

lara

The knock on the door pulls us from our emotional discussion.

"Oh, William. I said I'd be ready by noon." I rush toward the apartment door, trying to find the words to explain what's been happening within our walls. I'm passing the coat hooks when I make a split-second decision.

I turn back, poking my head into view of the living room. "I'll not invite him in. Save us all from an explanation." I look to Papa for his approval.

"Good idea." Papa winks to me as he stands to place a comforting arm around Louisa's shoulders. "We'll talk more later."

I nod in understanding, grab my pale blue spring jacket and pocketbook from the hook, and head for the door.

"Good morning." I open the door a sliver, just wide

enough for me to slip through, and shut it immediately behind me.

William's lips quirk into a questioning smile. "Good morning." He checks his wristwatch and chuckles. "Or rather, good afternoon."

"The day is getting on." I gesture toward the stairwell. "Shall we?"

"Your father isn't expecting me to chat with him before we go?"

"Not today." I feel my mouth twist, but before I can come up with the right words, William nods his understanding.

"Say no more. I'll trust that everyone is well, no matter the trouble." With a warm palm on my low back, William guides us toward the stairs.

"Thank you. For not prying, I mean." I attempt to hide my embarrassment by focusing on the steps. "We are adjusting to our new living arrangement. Still trying to iron out the kinks, you might say."

William opens The Newbury door to a brightly lit day. The sun is shining and the breeze is warm as we walk in the direction of Stanley Park.

I feel his gaze on me.

"Even the happiest of life changes come with challenges." William, the thoughtful observer that he is, intuits the discord I was trying to hide behind our apartment door. "I realize it's not what people expect, but I've found that more often than not, change of any kind brings about its own hurdles. It's best not to blame yourself, or anyone else for that matter, and simply try to understand that transitions take time and patience."

Lifting my eyes from the ground, I steal a quick glance in his direction. "Thank you for that." As the park appears in the distance, I mull over the idea of filling him in on the details.

An expansive lush green carpet is perfectly stunning, framed by views of the Pacific Ocean to the right. We take the path toward the pond and bridges, a favourite spot to view the turtles sunning themselves on logs.

"My father and Cookie are looking to purchase a home." I coerce a delighted tone into my announcement.

"I see." William's mind is as sharp as ever, and I consider, not for the first time, what a presence he must be in a courtroom. "How will a relocation affect you and your sister?"

Straight to the heart of it. I am pleased by his ability to grasp the crux of the issue without requiring tales about misbehaving family members.

"Louisa and I were considering remaining at The Newbury. Our current location is quite convenient for its proximity to the hotel and Louisa's theatre work."

"You said 'were considering.' Does this mean you are no longer considering the option?"

William tips his hat at a passing family as we step onto the arched bridge spanning the water.

At the crest of the arch, we rest our elbows on the bridge's railing and peer into the dark lagoon. The earthy scent of springtime water and damp embankment hangs in the air. Spotting a log wedged close to the bank, I point with an outstretched finger. "There they are."

The turtles lie tucked close to one another, some even resting on one another's shells.

"Funny little things, aren't they? All stacked up like building blocks." William chuckles.

"I'm afraid The Newbury, as far as we're aware, doesn't allow single women to rent an apartment on their own."

My shoulders lift in a *what are you going to do about it* manner. "She didn't say as much, but I imagine Louisa's feelings about the current barrier are heightened by the Supreme Court ruling about women not being persons."

"For good reason, I'm sure." William shakes his head. "I'm afraid justice doesn't move swiftly. I expect it will be months before the Privy Council has a chance to hear the argument."

"That long?"

William's woeful eyes find mine. "Afraid so."

"This probably sounds silly, but I never really knew women weren't considered persons before the radio broadcast announced the news."

"Not silly at all. Most Canadians were unaware of the narrow interpretation of the British North American Act. Women fought long and hard for the right to vote, and I imagine most Canadian women thought that was the end of it."

"That makes sense." We cross to the other side of the bridge, and I notice once more how comfortable I am in William's company. Daringly, I loop an arm through his bent elbow, briefly drawing him a touch closer.

His gratified smile and the press of his other hand on top of mine assuages all of my worry over William's interest in any other girl. I chide myself for thinking he would be anything but cordial to that flirtatious Agnes. Whatever was I worried about?

The echoes of children's voices raised high in play greet us as we near the playground. Mothers and fathers are scattered around, sitting on blankets and benches as they watch over the children.

"How nice to see so many people out and enjoying the day." William points toward an empty bench, and we walk toward it. "I'm not sad to be missing the last hurrah of winter in Toronto. Hopefully, anyway. We never know when the last snowfall will be. I must say, this is much more pleasant."

At his satisfied sigh, a wave of joy washes over me. Yes, I think, by my side is precisely where William belongs.

We are a few short steps from the bench when a small child, running too fast for his four-year-old legs, tumbles to the ground. Without pausing, William slips his arm from mine and takes two long strides to check on the lad.

The boy, shocked by his fall, begins to cry. I move toward them while craning my neck in every direction, searching the crowd for a concerned parent. The moment I am at William's side, the boy lunges from William's steadying arms to plant himself against my legs.

I bend at the waist and pick up the inconsolable child. Patting his back in a soothing motion, my body rocks back and forth, instinct kicking in.

"I'll see if I can locate the parents," William says. "Surely someone will be missing this one soon enough."

I give a quick nod while maintaining the comforting position. "Shhh," I coo. "You're all right. Just a little tumble. Not even a scratch. What a brave boy."

The boy's cries turn to soft hiccups, and I sense we are through the worst of it.

William, accompanied by a frantic-looking woman clutching a younger child to her chest, hurries toward me.

"Oh, thank heaven." Arms outstretched, she reaches for the boy. "Jack, you need to stay close to Mama." Though her words are reprimanding, her tone is pure relief.

The boy, hearing his mother's voice, squirms out of my arms and into her already full ones.

The mother bends toward the ground and plunks

down, liberated of worry and bearing the weight of two children.

I kneel beside her, rubbing little Jack's back as she repositions her younger child to one side.

"Can I offer you a lemon soda?" William asks the mother. "There's a cart right over there."

"Thank you. That would be much appreciated." Jack pops his head up from her lap at the mention of soda, and she ruffles his hair.

"Somebody likes lemon soda." I tease Jack with a playful tickle as William heads toward the vendor's cart.

"I can't thank you enough." The mother shakes her head. "It was foolish of me to think I could handle both of them on my own. The day was simply too inviting to keep them indoors, but clearly, that was a misjudgment on my part."

"Oh, no. Don't be hard on yourself. Children will dash from time to time. The park is the perfect place for them to do so."

"That is kind of you." The mother caresses both children's heads at once. "I don't mean to pry, but do you have children of your own? You're awfully good with them."

"Me? No." My thoughts flash back to the Murray children, eliciting a smile. "I had the pleasure of living close to some delightful children when I was younger."

"Well, you certainly picked something up. You're a natural."

"Here we are." William approaches with three lemon sodas, one for each of us.

When the cool, sweet drink hits my throat, I am grateful once more for William's thoughtfulness. We spend a few more minutes sipping our refreshments, allowing Jack's mother time to regain her composure.

"Thank you again," she gushes.

Jack waves goodbye with his free hand, his other one clasped tightly within his mother's.

"I don't suppose he will be free to roam about anytime soon. I thought the poor woman was going to faint." I pivot to meet William's gaze on me.

"She is right, you know." He lifts his chin toward the departing mother and children.

"Right about what?" I am lulled into the safety of his warm tone.

"You looked right at home with that child in your arms."

My heart plummets as the thought of having children reminds me of everything I would be expected to give up. "William, I'm not sure. I can't."

He takes a step closer. "What is it? Did I say something to upset you?"

"I—I'm not sure." I'm not making sense, but I have no idea how I will ever admit to him, the man I am certain I love, that he alone isn't enough for me.

His worried expression makes me reconsider my words, my thoughts, and even my desire to seek a career. Pangs of guilt over wanting more in my life than being a wife and mother make my knees go weak.

"Clara, are you all right?" William's hand is on my upper arm, steadying me.

Shame at my selfishness runs through my veins. I can't hurt this man with my grand notions. William is an upstanding attorney, a partner in his own firm. He is well respected in his community and among his colleagues. He is kind and generous, and I fear all of the things I love about him will coerce me into thinking I'd be happy enough being only his wife and the mother of his children.

I am quite certain William's career and affluent social standing will demand a wife who attends society events and volunteers for causes that, although surely important, interest me little. In my time as hotel matron, I've watched the high-society ladies, with their hats and fine dresses, attending society meetings in the hotel banquet rooms. Pomp and circumstance flows through the rooms full of women recognized solely for their husbands' achievements, never for their own.

I remember too how little respect Mr. Sampson paid Mrs. Tyler in the absence of her husband. If I hadn't come along, her and the children would have been turned away without another thought.

My head moves slowly back and forth. I've no desire to have my worth determined by my husband's status. I'd much rather put in an honest day's work and be valued for it. I may not have lofty dreams, but they are honest ones that will never require me to pretend to be something I'm not. No, I could never be both William's wife and a hotel employee. I search his grey-blue eyes and find only kindness and concern. My heart squeezes, and I clutch my chest in response. The mere thought of letting him go is enough to make me reconsider everything.

Pressure on my arm tugs my attention to the surface. "I'm feeling a touch light-headed. Must be the warm day."

"You had me worried." He moves his hand to cover my own. "Would you like to sit a minute?"

"Yes, that's probably wise." We stroll to the next vacant seat.

"Are you sure you're all right?"

I tuck my worry away, hoping to hide it behind a shy

smile so I don't ruin a perfectly lovely day with my overwrought mind. "I am. My apologies, I didn't mean to worry you."

"If you're certain?" William's lips twitch, and I sense there is more he'd like to say.

I nod, both affirming I'm fine and encouraging him to say what's on his mind.

"Do you remember our last telephone call?"

"Of course. I'm light-headed, not absent-minded," I tease in an attempt to humour him.

"I mentioned there was something important I wanted to speak with you about but I wished to do so in person."

"Yes…" I draw out my response, wondering how in the world we've managed to circle back to the one thing I'm terrified to discuss.

"Clara, I realize it's only been a few months and we haven't exactly spent a lot of time in one another's company. The thing is, I knew from the moment I first laid eyes on you. You are an extraordinary woman."

"William." I feel my cheeks burn at his admission, yet my heart, betraying my mind, silently begs him to go on.

"Please, let me finish or I might lose my nerve." He twists on the bench, our knees bumping as he gazes directly into my eyes. "Clara Wilson, I am in love with you."

My heart gallops in my chest as emotion rises in a rush of moisture to my lower lids. I have no willpower against his confession. I am my own worst enemy. I can't let this moment pass without acknowledging my feelings, but how can I do so without losing sight of who I am and what I want?

I take his hands in mine. "I am very pleased to hear it."

CHAPTER 26

SUNDAY, MAY 27, 1928

ouisa

By the time Clara arrives home from her afternoon stroll through Stanley Park, I have regained my composure along with a shred of hope. It didn't take long for Papa and Cookie to ask what was really troubling me.

My tears flowed freely as I told them about the challenges I've been facing. Though I began by sharing my heartache over Thomas, by the end of a second pot of tea, I realized that everything weighing me down—the director's refusal to see my character fully, the tension in our tight quarters and our impending relocation, and even the fight with Thomas—begins and ends with my displeasure over the Persons Case verdict.

"Why didn't you come to us sooner?" Papa asked, his brows furrowed with concern.

I felt like a small child as I confessed my juvenile worries about being forced to leave home before I was ready.

"We aren't pushing you out, love," Cookie exclaimed, gripping my hand in hers with a fierceness that conveyed her desperation for me to hear her words. "We're asking you to come with us."

"I see that now," I said. With no desire to hurt Cookie's feelings any more, I kept quiet about the fact that moving elsewhere in the city is not a viable option for me. Not if I want to continue both working as a maid at The Hamilton and earning the acting credits I need to eventually step out on my own.

Instead, I helped Cookie with dinner preparations, played a game of checkers with Papa, and begged off further conversation by turning in early.

Clara steps into our shared bedroom like she's walking on air, and a knowing smirk emerges on my lips. I see it clearly before she utters a single word. "You love him."

My sister does not deny it. She unabashedly plops down on her bed with a silly grin, which I expect will remain in place for several weeks.

"You're going to have sore cheeks if you keep smiling like that." Though my words are teasing, I am pleased to see Clara giddy and free. An hour later, we're tucked under our covers and chatting in the darkening room.

"They agreed to take it up with the property manager?" Clara asks after I inform her of Cookie's resolve to at least make an appointment with The Newbury property manager.

"Papa said he'd talk to them." I repeatedly fold and unfold the top corner of my bedsheet as I try to quiet my mind.

"Do you think we should offer to go with them? You know, show them we are responsible young women they can count on to pay the rent on time." Clara props herself on one elbow to look at me.

"We could ask, though I'm not certain Papa is keen to go in the first place."

Clara, not ready to let it be—and perhaps still on top of the world after her day with William—presses further. "We are the reason they were paid the overdue rent not that long ago. Surely that must count for something." She thinks a minute longer as she digests the information. "I'm not sure I'll be able to attend if it's during the workday. My days are already full to bursting. If Papa agrees, will you go for both of us?"

"I'll plan to go, but only if it doesn't conflict with a rehearsal."

"Then we're agreed." Clara rolls onto her back, the covers rustling as she settles into place. "Lou, if we can keep this apartment, I'm certain everything will work out for both of us."

"I hope you're right." I roll onto my side. Several minutes later, I'm still unable to break free of one awful thought. If William proposes, will my sister abandon me too?

I toss and turn, trying to find comfort in my bed and with my contemplations. Clara wouldn't do that, I finally tell myself. She promised to stay with me. To stand by me. If I know anything about my sister, it's that she is true to her word. Her promise coaxes me toward sleep. *You have me. You can always trust in me.* I snuggle deeper into the covers, pushing aside my unease and guilt. My need of Clara's support may be standing in the way of my sister's happiness.

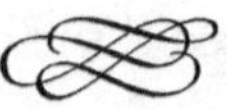

lara

The morning has barely gotten started when I'm summoned to the sixth floor. Having returned from roll call not five minutes ago, I stifle a groan and trudge back up the stairs to investigate the reported commotion in guest room 612.

Before my shoes even sink into the plush carpet of the sixth floor, I hear shouts emanating from somewhere beyond the back-of-house stairwell. I'm met on the other side of the door by a timid maid named Sally. I doubt the girl has ever caused anyone concern, so I find her worrying hands and stricken expression unsettling at best.

Sally's wide eyes shift to the guest room door across the hall. A loud crash erupts from behind the closed door and is quickly followed by a woman's emphatic shriek.

I place a calming hand on Sally's forearm before instructing her to find Cookie in the pastry kitchen, knowing my friend will take the girl under her wing and calm her nerves. "I'll be there soon. Ask Cookie for a strong cup of tea while you wait."

"Yes, miss." Sally dips into a brief curtsy before running for the door to the quiet back-of-house corridors.

Knowing my job is to re-establish order, I steel myself with a steadying palm to my midsection and march across the hall to guest room 612. My firm rap on the door may very well go unnoticed, given the concerning noises coming from inside.

The door flies open, and before me is a man with hair askew and shirttails hanging unceremoniously out of his trousers.

"Yes?" Mr. Riley—I checked who was occupying the room before arriving on the floor—is perturbed and in a hurry to wave me off.

"Mr. Riley, I am Miss Wilson, the hotel matron. There's been a disturbance reported. I'm here to ensure everything is as it should be."

A woman, whom I presume to be Mrs. Riley, pushes past both of us, a bag in one hand and her cloche hat clenched in the other. "I can assure you, Miss Wilson, everything is not as it should be. Not when the man you've loved for the better part of a year is nothing more than a lying, cheating, good-for-nothing scoundrel."

"Sylvia," Mr. Riley calls after her. His feeble attempt doesn't even garner him a look over her shoulder as she storms away toward the lift.

"Is Mrs. Riley all right? Should I accompany her downstairs, perhaps offer her a tea service in the lobby?"

Mr. Riley runs a hand through his dishevelled hair. "That won't be necessary." He has the decency to appear bashful as he utters his next words. "Mrs. Riley will be arriving within the hour. It's probably best to let Sylvia go."

I consider biting my tongue but change my mind when I catch sight of the state of the guest room behind him. "I imagine it would have been wiser to not have invited her in at all." I cast a pointed glance down the hall toward Sylvia's retreating frame.

I don't wait for a reply. "Now then, if you would be so kind as to vacate the room, I will have a team of maids set everything in order before the hour is up."

"Thank you, miss." A sheepish expression highlights his boyish good looks, and I see how Sylvia may have been drawn in by him. "I'm sorry, I've forgotten your name."

"Miss Wilson." I gesture for him to move aside so I can enter the room and assess the damage. "Well, Mr. Riley, it appears we will require the full hour."

Without another word, Mr. Riley tugs his jacket and hat from the coat rack. He gives me a nod of appreciation and slips out the door, likely hoping he never crosses my path again.

It's hard to believe, but an hour later, guest room 612 is restored to order. I've granted the four maids who tackled the mess, smashed flower vase and all, a short break outside to enjoy the warm day.

I make the trip down to Cookie's pastry kitchen to set Sally up with a task away from the sixth floor. Having recovered with a cup of tea and a friendly chat with Cookie, she goes to help the banquet staff set up for an event.

Cookie inclines her head, and I imagine her reading my thoughts. "How about a cup of tea?"

"Thank you, that would be nice." I settle myself in the

back corner of the pastry kitchen, where I hope I may remain undiscovered to enjoy a few minutes of peace.

Placing two cups of tea and a plate of sliced lemon loaf between us, Cookie settles into her chair. "The room's all sorted, then?"

I roll my eyes at thoughts of the kerfuffle. "All sorted. Mrs. Riley will be none the wiser, though I can't say that sits well with me."

"Not our business, I suppose." Cookie sips from her cup. "Happens more often than you'd think."

"Doesn't make it acceptable." I raise my eyebrows at the idea of behaviours being allowed simply because of the frequency with which they occur. "It makes me wonder how a woman is supposed to trust a man to be honourable."

"What do you mean?" Cookie bites into a slice of lemon loaf and chews before adding, "Not all men are inclined to such behaviour."

"I suppose not." I take a sip of tea but find myself unable to let the thought go. "Course, it wasn't that long ago that men could legally wrench children from the family home, sell the farm, and leave a wife penniless and destitute, all without her knowledge or consent."

Cookie pauses, her teacup hovering in front of her lips. "Well that's rather bleak, Clara. Is there something else bothering you? Something other than Mr. Riley's indiscretion?"

I lift a shoulder noncommittally and take another sip of tea. "This morning's encounter with Mr. Riley's wife in watercolour"—I use the euphemism for mistress, called such due to the impermanence of watercolor—"has gotten under my skin, and I wonder why women marry at all." I search my friend's face for an answer. "Why did you choose to marry?"

Cookie's expression tells me she's on to me. "I see. Worried about your William, are you?"

I feel the heat of a blush but offer nothing else in the way of words.

She waits me out for less than a minute. "I married your father because I fell in love with him. Frankly, I couldn't see a future without him. Or without you and Louisa." Cookie leans forward, placing a warm hand on top of mine. "I realize the transition of me moving into the apartment hasn't been easy for anyone. Having all of you in my life is worth a bit of discomfort as we find our footing. Nobody is perfect, love. We all do the best we can with what we've got. Speaking of…"

Cookie hesitates as she searches for the right words. "Your father told me about your mother's trunk, albeit a tad late." Moisture builds in her eyes. "Oh Clara, if I'd known what the trunk held within it, I wouldn't have suggested its removal. I never meant to hurt you, love. You can be sure the trunk will have a place in our new home. I don't mean to replace your lovely mother. On the contrary, I'm deeply grateful to her for raising such wonderful daughters and for teaching your father what it means to give his heart to another."

"Oh, Cookie." I swipe at the tears gathering steam on my cheeks. "Thank you for saying that. I didn't wish to hurt your feelings or ignore your family's history. You and your family have a place within our home now too."

"Thank you." Cookie squeezes my hand in hers before dabbing at the moisture gathering in her lower lids.

"Now, when it comes to your Mr. Thompson." Cookie

eyes me with a shrewd look. "If you're asking me, I'd say you've got a good one in William."

I'm certain the flush of heat colouring my cheeks gives me away. "I suspect you're right about that."

Twenty minutes later, I am back in Ms. Thompson's basement office. I slump into the hard-backed chair, with visions of Sylvia as she dashed toward the lift. She apparently loved Mr. Riley, but she obviously didn't know him. Love is more complicated than anyone ever tells you. The photoplays, theatre productions, and novels tout happily ever after, but I'm beginning to understand that when it comes to love, complications are simply part of the landscape.

Even among my family, love is complicated. Thomas and Louisa's disagreement has driven them apart, making Lou miserable these past few days. Cookie and Papa seem happy, but they too are navigating uncertain waters in creating their future. William's confession of love, which initially thrilled me, is now paralyzing me. The reality of the choice I may have to make is closer than I'd like.

Since our stroll around Stanley Park, questions have been steadily piling up. Will I be expected to move to Toronto? What would my moving mean for my sister, especially since I promised her I'd stay? Could I ever find fulfillment in a life without a career? These thoughts whirl through my mind, all because William told me he loves me.

Despite the disruption Mr. Riley's situation created, I felt immensely valuable while finding a solution to the problem. Acting as matron has helped me grow into a competent and forward-thinking woman. I've learned to spot a problem, address it, and get things back on track as quickly as possible. Somehow, my shyness has been overshadowed by the necessity of getting the job done, and

I suspect that has contributed to the strong sense of purpose in my life.

Worry is exhausting, but battling one's own mind is downright gruelling. Dropping the pencil to the desk, I let my head rest in my hands while I massage my temples.

A light knock at the door startles me from my thoughts. Ms. Thompson, appearing healthy and restored, walks into the room.

"Ms. Thompson, what a lovely surprise." I stand to greet the matron.

"At last, I've been let out of the house and am free to wander where I wish," she says with a slow, mischievous smile. "Naturally, the one place I wanted to go was here."

"It's good to see you looking so well." I note the colour in her cheeks and berate myself for immediately questioning what this means for my temporary position.

"How have things been going?" Ms. Thompson's strength is certainly restored. She takes the seat opposite the desk and gestures for me to return to the chair that has always been hers.

I begin by filling her in on the antics of the recently hired second-floor maid. "You'll want to keep an eye on her." I say, without sharing details. "She shares tendencies with Miss Lillian Roberts."

Knowing the reference is sufficient for the matron to understand the situation, I continue to this morning's events. "There was quite the ruckus on the sixth floor. It seems Mr. Riley's guest was unaware of his marital status, and when she learned Mrs. Riley would be arriving soon, well, let's just say she wasn't shy about showing her displeasure."

"Never a dull moment." Ms. Thompson's sigh is resigned. "Tale as old as time, I'm afraid."

I'm thinking that the sentiment seems contagious when our conversation is brought to an abrupt stop by William appearing in the open doorway. His flushed cheeks and laboured breathing imply he has run all the way here.

"William, is everything okay?" Ms. Thompson is the first to speak.

"I'm glad I caught you both. The case I've been working on was moved up on the docket. I got word a few minutes ago." His gaze lands on me. "I have to return to Toronto at once."

I notice the suitcase in his hand, and my heart drops to my feet.

"When are you leaving?" I ask, unable to smooth my knitted brows.

"I'll be on the noon train." An apology is written all over his face.

"I see." My words are barely audible.

Another apology reaches me through his gentle, grey-blue eyes. I feel my cheeks warm in response. "I'll write as soon as I can."

I tug a smile forward as he steps past his sister, an envelope outstretched toward me.

"Can you give this to Louisa?"

I'm taken aback, and he flinches, clearly sensing this is not what I was expecting. "It's something to encourage her, regarding the Persons Case."

"Of course." I reach forward and William slides his fingers down the envelope, closer to mine. His sheepish smile tells me he'd rather we had a moment alone. Either way, the touch of his hand makes my legs turn to jelly.

"I best be off." He gives his sister's shoulder a squeeze. "Don't overdo it."

Then he is out the door, and I am left calling to his retreating back, "Safe travels."

Ms. Thompson looks to me. "Well, that was quick."

"Certainly was." I immediately feel the unsettling weight of William's absence.

"Not to worry." Ms. Thompson leans forward in her chair, lowering her voice conspiratorially. "I don't imagine he'll be able to stay away too long."

Sadness mixes with embarrassment as I straighten the papers on the desk, doing my best to avoid the matron's knowing gaze.

"Anyway, I wanted to stop by and let you know I'll be returning to work next week." She clasps her hands, reinstating her matronly demeanour.

"So soon? I assumed you might require a few more weeks of convalescence, since you were just permitted to leave your house." The words stumble and stutter from my lips.

"My doctor says I can take this week to get out and about. As long as I get a full night's rest, I will be back in the swing of things by Monday."

"That is very good news. I'm sure you're pleased." The irony is not lost on me. In a matter of minutes, I have lost the best parts of my life. The ones I've come to cherish. William is gone, and now my role as hotel matron is about to end. Whatever will I do with myself? I wonder while forcing a delighted smile into place.

Ms. Thompson leans forward, placing both palms flat on the desk. "Miss Wilson, I am indebted to you. While I was recovering, you set my mind at ease. Mr. Olson told me how well the hotel was running. I knew you would perform excellently, and I am pleased to say you did not let me down. I can't thank you enough."

Feeling our roles shift back to maid and matron, I adjust accordingly. "I'm happy to help, ma'am."

"Well, I'm off to the market. I desire to surround myself with the aroma of the season's early berries." At the door, Ms. Thompson turns back toward me. "Thank you again, for everything. I will see you on Monday."

I listen for her retreating footsteps to disappear before allowing myself to sink into the sudden despair. How will I ever go back to being a maid after everything I've learned and gained these past weeks? Being hotel matron has been challenging and rewarding in equal measure, and I've no idea how I will manage to embrace my demotion come Monday.

CHAPTER 28

MONDAY, JUNE 4, 1928

ouisa

The Newbury property management offices are swanky, with gleaming wood surfaces set against polished chrome accents. Our home at The Newbury pales in comparison. The ornate, geometric-patterned ceiling catches my eye as the secretary's phone rings.

"Mr. Mitchell will see you now," the secretary, wearing enough perfume to paint the walls with, says in a nasal voice. She gestures a long, pink fingernail toward the closed office door, and Papa leads the way, knocking lightly before opening the door.

"Ah, Mr. Wilson. It is very nice to meet you." Though the man beams through his stiff handlebar mustache, his smile doesn't come close to reaching his eyes.

"Hello, Mr. Mitchell. This is my eldest daughter, Louisa."

"Nice to meet you. Please, won't you both sit." The

man settles into his own round-backed chair and sets it to swaying, forming a triangle with his two index fingers.

"We'd like to speak with you about my transferring the rental contract to my daughters. I've recently married, and my wife and I are looking to purchase a home. Louisa and Clara are both employed and can manage the rent quite well on their own."

Mr. Mitchell's façade of a smile drops. "Oh, I am sorry to say that won't be possible. Was there anything else?"

Papa leans forward, his elbows resting precariously on the chair's thin armrests. "As their father, I'd be willing to sign whatever papers you require, if you need a guarantee."

A tight expression flattens the man's features, and I wonder if this is the extent of his personality. "No need. As I already stated, your daughters will not be permitted to rent the apartment."

I shift in my seat, earning myself a cautioning glance from my father.

"Mr. Mitchell, is there a reason the girls are not permitted to remain in the apartment should I relocate?" Papa's impatience with the man's short and uninformative replies lines his voice.

"Yes." Mr. Mitchell's hands spread wide as if stating the obvious. "They are girls."

I clear my throat, ignoring my father's warning, and summon my most disarming demeanour. "Mr. Mitchell, I'm not certain that being girls is such a bad thing, since we are both employed and known to be hard workers. In fact, I currently hold down two jobs."

"The thing is, Miss Wilson, should your father decide to vacate apartment 3D at The Newbury, I have another renter lined up and waiting for your notice. In fact, he's willing to pay twice as much as your contract currently stipulates, sight unseen."

"Without formal notice, you cannot rent our apartment out from under us." Papa's agitation is no longer veiled. "I mean no disrespect, sir, but I will be taking this matter to the president of your company. Securing a future tenant prior to receiving our formal notice is a poor business practice, and I'm quite certain your boss will agree."

"Do you intend to vacate The Newbury, Mr. Wilson?" The man's smug expression is irritating at best.

Papa, knowing full well a relocation is imminent, acquiesces with a reluctant nod.

"Then I must inform you that our president is in the habit of making good financial business decisions. I fear your complaints will fall on deaf ears, though they may earn me a promotion."

"We're done here," Papa says. "Louisa." His voice pulls me to my feet. Mr. Mitchell hurls a final insult at our backs as we exit his overly decorated, posh office.

"I wish you luck, Miss Wilson. Finding a management group that will rent to two single women is likely to be a challenge, with all this news of women's rights not being what they used to be."

Halted in my tracks, I begin to pivot back toward the man, but Papa's large, calloused hand presses into the small of my back, forcing me out the door before I can utter a word.

"Good day." Papa's voice is as brusque as his steps, keeping us marching all the way out the building, onto the street, and two blocks away before we stop to regain our composure.

"I'm sorry, Lou." Papa washes a frustrated hand over

his face. "I wasn't hopeful for a change of heart, but I certainly wasn't expecting such a display of incivility."

Having been reminded of my childish temper only recently, I tuck my outrage out of sight, not wishing to spew it on those I hold dear. "It's not your fault. That man was truly dreadful."

"That he was." The June sun beating down on us brings droplets of sweat to Papa's brow. "I meant what I said. I'll be writing directly to the president of The Newbury."

An appreciative smile edges forward. "I appreciate your support, but I think it's time for Clara and me to start looking for a plan B."

"You are welcome to move with us. Nothing has changed there. Cookie and I have started looking at places closer to The Hamilton. They are smaller homes than what we initially intended, so you'd still have to share a bedroom with your sister, but your point concerning access to the city is being taken into consideration."

"You've already set your sights on the bungalow on the outskirts of town. Cookie told me it's a streetcar ride away and it will only take her thirty minutes longer to reach the hotel. I appreciate your willingness to keep looking, but perhaps it's time for Clara and me to figure this out ourselves." I note the time on the Birks clock across the street. "You'd better be off or you'll be late for the crew, and I've got a script to memorize."

Papa leans in and kisses my cheek. "I'm not through trying yet."

"I appreciate that." I wave goodbye before turning to head toward the building I'm certain will not be my home for much longer.

In the apartment a few hours later, I read through the script, intent to memorize my lines for the last quarter of the play. My impatience over this morning's meeting is mirrored in my opinion of the cardboard cut-out who is Mr. Brown's secretary. Rehearsals have been about as mundane as scrubbing bathtubs at the hotel, and I wonder for the hundredth time about the point of it all.

Nobody ever says so, but waiting for the next stage of your life to begin is excruciating business. Perhaps there is value in the space between knowing what you want and actually getting it, a built-in measure to protect us from human impulse. But in this moment, I simply want to leapfrog ahead to Hollywood, where I am certain my dreams will come true and my troubles will be small.

Although I'm eagerly chasing my dreams, I'd be kidding myself if I said I wasn't also looking to run away. I'd like to outrun the discourse between Thomas and me, the challenges surrounding our living arrangements, and even the distasteful nature of suppressing my instincts to appease a director without a vision.

I release a sigh weighted with the question that's been repeating in my mind for weeks. Where is my worth in this life? Where do I make a difference? As an actress, a sister, a daughter, or someone's sweetheart? The script lands on the coffee table with a light thud. The answer is that I have no idea, and this concerns me more than all my troubles combined.

Mrs. Kent's words, the ones she spoke to me after the verdict was announced, have tumbled through my consciousness since the radio broadcast. *Our worth is not theirs to take.* If only I knew my worth, perhaps then I could make certain I wasn't unknowingly giving it away.

Frustrated by my ruminating thoughts, I pick up the script again, determined to persevere. Opening night will be upon me in short order. "You must be strong," I tell myself in the quiet of our apartment. *Focus on the task at hand*, Cookie says. *The rest will fall into place when the time is right.*

I take her advice and spend the next two hours memorizing my lines. Despite having been cautioned by the director each time I've added a flourish to my leading role, I find myself unable to keep from embellishing Agatha's character. I wink and gesture and liven her up during my one-sided run-through of my lines.

As the play unfolds in my mind's eye, an idea begins to percolate. I push it aside at first, not wishing to be on the receiving end of a stern talking-to, or worse. But I wonder, tapping a finger to my bottom lip, what if…?

The telephone rings, interrupting my contemplations.

"Wilson residence." I answer with a smile in my voice.

"Please, Lou. Don't hang up."

My back goes stiff. "I told you I don't want to talk to you right now, Thomas."

"Louisa, I don't know how many times I have to apologize until you forgive me, but I will. I will keep calling and apologizing every day for as long as it takes."

"Apologizing isn't what it used to be." My retort is flat and a touch harsh, but it's out before I can reel it back in.

"Come on, Lou. You know I would never hurt you intentionally. I'm sorry. Really, I am."

A weighted sigh slips through my lips. "I know you didn't intend to hurt me. It's just that you sided so easily with the director, and though I realize you don't agree, I am right about this. The man is happy to let the male lead flourish while ensuring the female roles languish in the background."

It's Thomas' turn to sigh. "You're right. I can't see it

from your perspective, but I'd like to, if you'll give me the chance."

"Maybe," I concede.

"Maybe is better than a flat out no, Lou. I'll take it."

I try but can't smother my giggle. "Thomas Cromwell, you are insufferable."

"Yeah, but you love me anyway, don't you?"

My head bobs up and down, but I hold my reply close to my chest. "Can you give me some time? I really need to wrap my head around this script, and then we can talk."

"I won't stop calling." He's teasing, but I sense there is truth to his words.

"I'm not asking you to."

"Okay then. I'll talk to you soon. And Lou, whatever you decide to do with the script, just be sure you're doing it for the right reasons."

"Talk to you soon." I hang up the telephone, Thomas' words echoing around me.

Requiring reinforcements, I toss the script to the sofa and head to the bedroom to seek out William's note to me. I read it last week, when Clara brought it home. It was kind of him to encourage me with his thoughts, but now I see he may have been on to something.

CHAPTER 29

MONDAY, JUNE 4, 1928

lara

I arrived early this morning, disappointment cloaking me every step toward the hotel. Today ends my term as temporary hotel matron. As soon as I retrieve my maid's uniform from the laundry, I set to work tidying the office for Ms. Thompson's arrival.

Seeing my eighth-floor uniform only adds to my thrumming ruminations. I'm aware I must summon a pleasant disposition and press on, but in the quiet of Ms. Thompson's office, I allow myself time to brood.

My life choices have shrunk in less than a week. After worrying about how to speak my desire to have both William and a career, I now find myself without William at my side and climbing back down the ladder as a Hotel Hamilton employee. I shake my head, knowing my discontent at the descent is entirely my fault. I shouldn't have allowed the notion of a bigger, more important life to fool me into thinking I would have it.

I suppose women in general have been fooled into expecting a higher standing in life, given the legal case now waiting to be heard by the Privy Council.

A few years ago, I wouldn't have considered any future for myself other than becoming a wife and mother. Mama was happy being both, so I assumed I would be as well. Until desperately applying for the maid's position to avoid being evicted from our apartment, I didn't know a career working in a fine hotel was an option. This past year at The Hamilton has opened my eyes to the world around me.

I've learned to stand up for myself while navigating the joys and challenges that come with working alongside others. I've become good friends with the staff here, both the men and the women. As William's note to Louisa affirmed, *men and women are different, but that doesn't mean they can't be equal.* I've experienced this truth as matron, when all hands are needed for a positive outcome.

In the end, I am capable of far more than I ever imagined I might be. And I certainly can't forget that if I hadn't sought employment with the hotel, I never would have met William Thompson in the first place. That alone would have been a travesty, no matter what becomes of our relationship.

The office door flies open with a whoosh. My head snaps up as the papers I was sorting flutter to the ground. Ms. Thompson, out of breath and looking sick with worry, rushes toward me, forcing me to rise from my seated position.

"Have you heard from William?" The matron's tight voice emerges as a squeak.

I shake my head. "It's been less than a week though. A posted letter will surely take—"

She cuts me off with a sharp wave of her hand. "Clara." Another step closer and I notice the trembling of her lips. "There's been an accident." A sob erupts from deep in her chest. "William was on board. The train didn't make it to Toronto."

My knees buckle without warning, and I hit the hard floor. "No." The only word I can manage. "No."

Ms. Thompson kneels beside me. "There is no news of injuries sustained." She pauses, leaving enough space for dread to settle between us. "Or survivors."

I search her face for more, but she has none to offer. "But it's William. He'll be all right. He—he has to be."

We clutch one another's hands, and I wonder for a fleeting moment which of us is holding the other up.

A disturbance at the door demands our attention. Mr. Olson, looking far more unhinged than I've ever seen him, hurries toward us.

"Eliza, the train? I've just heard the news. Was it William's, my dear?"

My dear? I'm certain I've misheard, with the buzzing in my head.

A solemn nod is her only response, but it's enough to push propriety aside as Mr. Olson reaches for her and her for him.

I am struck by the oddity of the goings on before me. The shock of the news has yet to sink in fully, but from my spot on the floor, I become aware that Ms. Thompson and Mr. Olson are somehow devoted to one another.

Realizing they are not alone in the room, Mr. Olson delivers an apologetic glance my way before helping Ms. Thompson to standing. After bending to assist me as well, he helps us settle into chairs before excusing himself to order strong tea for all of us.

Several minutes later, Cookie arrives with a tray and an ashen expression. Placing the tray on the desk, she tugs free a bottle of whisky from her apron pocket. "I thought this might help with the shock."

"Roll call," I shriek, suddenly aware of the obligations currently being neglected.

'It's all right, Miss Wilson." Mr. Olson pours a finger of whisky into each teacup, the scent of alcohol filling the small room. "I've asked Miss Smythe to take care of roll call this morning."

"Oh." I deflate against the hard back of the office chair, unsure of what to do next.

Mr. Olson pours tea into a cup and hands it to me. "It will help with the nerves."

Trusting the man who has shown me a great deal of courtesy and guidance these past several weeks, I accept the cup and take a tentative sip.

Cookie, unable to remain across the desk from me any longer, squeezes between Ms. Thompson's chair and the wall to reach my side.

The moment her hand connects with my shoulder, my resolve vanishes and I crumble into a heap in her arms, spilling the contents of the teacup as I collapse.

Cookie walks me home, or rather, she supports me as I shuffle my feet forward, one step at a time. The morning disappeared between frequent bouts of tears, Mr. Olson's desperate attempts to learn more of the accident, and a mound of fears determined to monopolize my attention.

By the time he sent us home, Mr. Olson had left a telephone message for the president of the Canadian National Railway, a man he met once at a business event. Mr. Olson promised to telephone me with news, and then he informed Ms. Thompson he was taking her home.

Two blocks from our apartment, despair engulfs me. Cookie guides me toward a bench and rubs my back as the sobs rattle my body.

"I'll never forgive myself." The words stutter forth. "If he doesn't survive. I'll never forgive myself."

"What in the world would you need to forgive yourself for? You didn't cause the train accident. This isn't your fault, Clara." Cookie's voice is rounded with empathy, but she doesn't know what I've done.

"You don't understand. I put off choosing him." Tears cascade down my cheeks. "I was being selfish and trying to decide what was better for me. A career or William. I didn't once ask myself what was best for him."

I bury my face in both hands as Cookie squeezes closer to me, her arm wrapped around my shoulders.

"Ah, love. There isn't a selfish bone in your body. William would never expect you to choose." Cookie tilts my chin up with a finger. "Love isn't about choosing one thing over another. It's about finding a way to build a satisfying life for both people involved."

"Still." The defiance lacing my words steadies me. "If he doesn't come back to me, I'll never forgive myself."

"Shock has a way of making us say things we might not be able to live up to in the end." Cookie encourages me to stand. "Let's get you home and into bed."

CHAPTER 30

MONDAY, JUNE 4, 1928

*L*ouisa

Rereading William's note allows my mind to broaden with possibilities. I mull over his words. Men and women can be equal, he says, while reminding me to always be true to myself. He points out that, regardless of what others or even a court of law may say about a woman's rights, each individual has the obligation to understand and embrace what is best for themselves.

He cautions me that an awareness of one's guiding compass through life does not equal an easy or tranquil path.

I continue reading.

On the contrary, knowing oneself is sure to

lead to challenges and discord, but it remains the only true option for those who are compelled to seek truth and harmony for all.

This is who you are, Louisa. I've seen you confront injustice and live to tell the tale. You may feel social change is beyond your grasp, but know this. You will never be alone in your determination to do right by the world, not while I have breath in my body.

Your friend,
William Thompson

I am not expecting anyone home this early in the afternoon, so I'm startled when the apartment door swings wide open, thumping into the wall.

"Lou," Cookie calls out. "Can you lend a hand?"

Jumping up from the sofa, a shiver of unease runs through me. I understand in an instant that everything is not all right.

Clara, barely upright, is leaning against the wall closest to the kitchen, her head hanging low so I can't see her face.

"What's happened?" I rush forward, reaching out to support my sister's sagging frame. "Clara. You're scaring me. Tell me what's going on." I taste the unease rising in my throat. Something is very wrong.

The anguish in my voice jolts her, and I catch a glimpse of her tear-stained face before she leans forward and collapses into my arms.

"Let's get her to the sofa." Cookie bends at the waist

and hoists Clara's arm over her shoulders. "Get her other side." She spurs me into action with the tilt of her head.

"What is going on? You're scaring me." We struggle down the narrow hall, bumping and jostling until the hall opens in the living room.

We sit Clara on the sofa and guide her head and legs to rest against the length of the cushions.

I turn to Cookie with an expectant stare.

"There's been a train accident. William was on board."

I gasp, and my hand races to cover my mouth. My eyes flit to Clara, waiting for the worst. "Is he okay?"

"There's no word yet. Ms. Thompson received news of the accident this morning, but nothing more."

I have no reason to ask how my sister is taking the news. Her trance-like state speaks volumes.

William's words come back to me. *Know this. You will never be alone in your determination to do right by the world, not while I have breath in my body.*

My whole body shudders as I squeeze in beside my sister's limp frame. How is it possible that I may be losing another person who understands and supports me? My thoughts immediately turn to Thomas, and my heart lurches. Despite being angry with him, he is the person I want to weather this new storm with. I want Thomas by my side. I promise myself I will telephone him as soon as I know Clara is all right.

I shake the selfish thoughts from my periphery and focus my attention on Clara. "She loves him, you know." I intend the words to be about my sister, but as they emerge, I realize they are true for me as well. I love Thomas just as Clara loves William.

I look to Cookie, tears pooling in my eyes. "I'm not sure

how she'll survive another blow, not after losing Mama." Without meaning to, I'm aware I'm asking for myself too.

"We'll get through this, one day at a time." Cookie's hand rests gently on my shoulder, linking the three Wilson women together.

More than thirty minutes later, Clara is starting to emerge from her exhausted collapse. The cool cloth Cookie placed on her forehead plops onto the hardwood floor as she tries to sit.

"Easy does it," Cookie coos from her rocking chair before rising and moving toward the kitchen. "I'll make us some tea."

"Lou." Clara's voice cracks with emotion.

"I'm here." I run my hand over her hair, matted and wet from the cloth. "I'm right here."

"William." Clara's voice cracks.

"Oh, Clara." I lean forward and hug her tight. I remember Mama's hugs, her refusal to let go until the world was set right again, and I plead for her, wherever she is, to infuse that same strength into my hug right now.

A knock at the door feels intrusive, given our emotional state. Cookie's glance in my direction asks if I am expecting anyone.

I shake my head. She wipes her hands on a kitchen towel and disappears to answer the door.

The male voice is low and hard to make out. I cock my head in an effort to determine who is at the threshold. All I recognize is a mumbled apology. Dread grips my heart and squeezes as I fear the worst.

Cookie reappears in the living room, an envelope in hand.

My brow knits, bringing with it the beginnings of a

headache. "Who was that?" The envelope can't possibly be about William, I assure myself.

"Mr. Watkins. He said he was sorry to have to deliver the news." Cookie, unaware of the outcome of this morning's meeting, wears a puzzled expression.

The blood in my veins runs cold. That prickly little man from this morning's meeting flashes across my memory.

I stand abruptly, causing Clara's hand to slide from the sofa, and Cookie passes me the envelope.

"It's addressed to your father," Cookie informs me.

I can't tell if it's a warning or a statement, but either way, I disregard it and slice my finger through the envelope.

June 4, 1928

Dear Mr. Wilson,

At our meeting this morning, you confirmed your intent to vacate apartment 3D. The Newbury Property Management confirms receipt of your notice to vacate.

Please be advised that all belongings and persons associated with the Wilson household must vacate the premises no later than July 31, 1928.

Sincerely,

Robert J. Mitchell

Manager for The Newbury

"That low-life. Papa didn't give his notice. That slimy excuse for a human being has twisted his words."

I hand the letter to Cookie and wait less than a minute before the horror takes up residence on her face.

I glance over my shoulder at Clara and notice her nodding off to sleep again. "Papa is going to be furious," I whisper.

"Looks like we'll be putting in an offer on that bungalow after all." Cookie rests a steadying hand against the wall.

"Nothing like being forced into a decision," I mutter, distaste for today's events overwhelming me at every turn.

Clara mumbles something incoherent in her sleep, and my heart lurches for her. No matter what happens next, I think as I settle in beside my sister once more, we'll always have each other.

It's past midnight. The steady rhythm of the ticking clock should lull me, yet I am unable to succumb to sleep. The day's events have left me weary and emotionally drained. Despite knowing a good night's rest will rejuvenate me, my mind buzzes on a continuous loop, refusing to let me be.

Tears, lots of tears, have been shed by all four Wilsons today. Papa was met by three distraught women when he arrived home, tired and sun-kissed from a day working outside. We forwent a hearty meal and settled on a comforting round of toast and eggs instead. Our eyes roamed the room, occasionally connecting with one another's, while eating over our laps in the living room so as not to unsettle Clara's fragile state.

Worry for William mixes with frustration over the property manager's underhanded approach. So much is out of my control, and the desire to rein it all in is likely the cause for my current wakefulness.

After much contemplation, I decide the one thing I can stand up for is my reputation as an actress. The director may be willing to risk bad reviews reflecting poorly on the play, but a poorly orchestrated production affects the careers and livelihoods of the entire cast and crew. That is something I won't stand for.

I cringe at the thought of disappointing Thomas by not heeding his advice, but it's my career on the line—not the director's and certainly not Thomas'.

Mr. Brown's Secretary opens in three weeks. I will do as I'm directed and will gauge the audience's response. Assuming the reaction is what I expect, the director will have plenty of time to see the error of his ways and make a course correction. If he chooses not to, then my plan will be in place and ready to execute. This is my last resort, and though I hope things don't come down to it, I remain steady in my resolve and determined to prove to myself and everyone else that I can stand on my own two feet.

I tiptoe into the bedroom and crawl into bed. The one option that refuses to let me go is a bold one. If I send a letter to Rose Oxley in California to request her presence at the closing night of *Mr. Brown's Secretary* and the play is a disaster, I risk ruining my only chance at a Hollywood connection. With the Persons Case still undecided and looming over the heads of Canadian women, I can't count on having equal opportunities on the stage or in film. Without a guiding hand from someone who sees me as a talented actress, rather than just a pretty face, I may never have a future in Hollywood. Yes, women supporting women is the only path forward. I'm certain of it. But am I willing to risk everything to prove a point?

CHAPTER 31

WEDNESDAY, JUNE 6, 1928

lara

I've been staring at the same spot on the living room wall for the better part of the morning. The slight imperfection in the wall's painted surface, one I've never noticed before, blurs and clears with each blink of my eyes. My stomach rumbles audibly, but I pay it no mind. Food is the last thing I desire. Even the aroma of Cookie's fresh-baked cinnamon buns resting on the kitchen counter doesn't coerce my appetite. Their presence only reminds me of William's insatiable sweet tooth.

Cookie and Louisa returned to the hotel this morning. All hands are needed during this trying time. Until the apartment door closed behind them, I had welcomed the idea of time by myself. The boon of solitude disappeared shortly after their departure, making me realize I'd only thought I wanted to be alone. My defeated sigh, though quiet, punctuates the room with gusto enough to force my gaze upward.

Cookie fussed about returning to work, barely concealing her worry over both William and me. But after two days away from her pastry kitchen, it wasn't fair of me to ask her to stay and hold my hand. Ms. Thompson, she informed me yesterday, is back at home, waiting for news that is slow to arrive. I've tried, more than once, to turn my attention to the needs of The Hamilton. With no matron at the helm and everyone who knows William walking on eggshells, I shudder to think how things are limping along in our absence.

The telephone rings, startling me from my weary state. I almost trip over my bare feet as I dash toward the piercing sound.

"Wilson residence." My voice cracks with exhaustion, forcing me to swallow hard.

"Clara." William's voice is tinny, and the echo conjures images of deep, dark tunnels.

"William." I grip the telephone's handset, pressing it determinedly against my left ear. "Thank heavens."

"It's good to hear your voice." His chuckle lightens the weight of my heart tenfold.

"Are you all right? We've been worried out of our minds." The questions pile up, and I force myself to issue them one by one.

"I'm sorry to have worried you." His muted words zigzag between the line's crackles.

"Are you hurt?" My voice lifts into a shout, fearing we will be disconnected without warning.

"A bump or two, but nothing that won't heal in a few days." The line buzzes again.

"Where are you?" I try to make out the clicks and cracks coming through the earpiece.

"A small town in Saskatchewan. There was no telephone line near where the train derailed. No post office for telegrams." A loud hum swallows his words.

"William? William, are you there?" Panic rises in my chest. I am not ready to lose the connection with him. I understand completely, now, that I never was. Realizing my mistake, I vow to push aside my aspirations for a career. If the train accident has taught me anything, it is that William Thompson is more important than any career I could ever have.

"I'm here." The line crackles again. "The conductor was able to get word to the closest station, but it'll take time to get the train back on the track."

His soft chuckle puts me at ease in an instant. "I walked three hours to locate a telephone. Clara, I don't have much time. I've got a list of family members to contact for the others who were on the train with me."

"You're telephoning next of kin for all the passengers?" I lean my forehead against the wall, the cool surface steadying my whirring mind.

"Not everyone can make the journey, so I volunteered. Nobody was killed, thank heavens, but there are injuries. There's a telegraph office here, so I'll send the messages before heading back."

"I'm so sorry." My bottom lip wobbles as I hold back tears.

"I was desperate to telephone you." His admission brings a smile to my lips. "The six-hour return trip is worth it. So I could hear your voice."

The line pops and hisses again.

"William, have you spoken to your sister?"

"Yes, she was beside herself."

"She wasn't the only one," I whisper and wonder if he even hears me.

"Clara, I'm sorry but I've got to go. I have a long list of messages to send and a three-hour walk back."

"William." I can't let him go without telling him the truth.

"Clara, I can barely hear you," William shouts through the line.

"William, I love you," I holler into the telephone's mouthpiece. "Did you hear me? I love you."

Seconds feel like minutes as I wait for his response to come through.

"Those are the finest words I've ever heard."

I feel warm elation rise up and course through me.

"I love you, Clara Wilson, and I'll send word as soon as I'm back in Toronto."

The line clicks off before I can reply.

I stare at the telephone, unable to force myself to move as William's words play on repeat through my mind. I don't want to miss a thing as I embed the conversation into my memory.

Relief rains down on me as though I've been caught by an unexpected spring shower. Taking slow breaths, I urge my heartbeat to return to normal. William is okay, I tell myself over and over until my stomach interrupts, rumbling its displeasure more loudly this time.

I poke my head around the corner into the kitchen and snag one of Cookie's cinnamon buns. The soft, gooey centre delights my senses, and my state of mind gains traction with a rush of sugar and the happy news of William's safety.

In committing to William, I've also managed to ease my

worries over the future. The train accident, though horrid, was the push I needed to know what is truly important in my life. And that is William Thompson.

Glancing at my wristwatch, I note the time. There is plenty of day left for me to be of use. I head to the bedroom for a change of clothes before grabbing my bag and setting off.

I have good news to share, and I am eager to do so. With my bag in hand, I lock the apartment door and head straight for The Hamilton.

A bubble of resistance rises as my thoughts turn to Louisa. If William and I marry, what will become of her? She isn't likely to afford an apartment on her own, and I'm quite aware of her reluctance to move further out of the city. I push the worry aside as I step into the warm sun, deciding today is about happy news. Besides, though William loves me, he hasn't asked for my hand in marriage. So for now, I will keep my decision regarding my future to myself.

CHAPTER 32

WEDNESDAY, JUNE 6, 1928

*L*ouisa

"You've had news?" Clara's brilliant smile lights up the hallway as she strides toward me. I drop the feather duster onto my cleaning cart and meet her in front of the lift. Reaching for her, I draw her into a fierce embrace. "He's all right?"

"He's all right." Clara's words are muffled, with her head buried against my shoulder, but the joy in her voice is all I need to hear.

I tug her toward the linen cupboard, out of sight of fifth-floor guests coming and going. "What did he say?"

"He had to walk for three hours to locate a telephone, but he's fine."

"What a relief." A hand lifts to my forehead, and I'm aware my concern was not limited to the state of my sister's heart. It was also for the friend I've come to know in William.

"Have you told Cookie? Ms. Thompson?" William's presence has touched many within the hotel, and I feel the urge to spread the good news as quickly as possible.

Clara shakes her head. "Ms. Thompson knows. William telephoned her first. I'm on my way to tell Cookie now, but I needed you to hear the news directly from me. I realize I'm not the only one who cares for him."

"Does this mean you've decided to marry the man?" I lower my voice but raise a single eyebrow in question.

Clara bites her bottom lip. "I cannot tell the future. You should know that by now."

She is putting me off, and we both know it.

"Listen." I reach for her hand, wanting to ensure she hears me. "I don't expect you to make life decisions solely with me in mind. I realize I can be overbearing and single-minded at times, but that doesn't mean I want you to forgo your happiness for my contentment."

"We'll find our footing, Lou." Clara squeezes my hand. "I'm certain of it."

The door of the linen cupboard bursts open. Ms. Thompson and Cookie stand squeezed together at the threshold, wide smiles washing away the past two days of worry and dread.

"She's told you, then?" Cookie is the first to gush the news to Louisa.

"I was coming to find you next," Clara chimes in, her voice lifting with gaiety.

Ms. Thompson motions for us to move further into the cupboard so she and Cookie can join us.

"It's wonderful news." I let go of Clara's hand and reach for Cookie's instead. "And to think he walked so far to send word."

"Sitting idly by is not one of William's strengths," Ms.

Thompson teases. "Though I dare say, we could all use a touch of William's moxie in our lives. He seldom chooses inaction, and he is forever going after what he seeks." The matron directs her gaze at me before turning her attention to Clara. "What did he say? I got the scantest of details, given the quality of the telephone line."

Clara nods. "Yes, the line made it hard to hear. He said he had a few bumps and bruises but that he'd be good as new in no time."

"Yes, yes." Ms. Thompson's head bobs.

"He compiled a list of the passengers and their next of kin's contact information," Clara says. "I am sure he is still sending telegraphs as we speak."

"That's kind of him." Cookie fusses. "He's such a generous soul."

"I couldn't agree more," I add, delighting in the news that has joined the four of us together. "I've been on the receiving end of his generosity, and I can say for certain he isn't one to wait to be asked for assistance. He simply steps up to help."

"That's our William." I notice Ms. Thompson's inclusion of all of us, and I'm thankful to find myself within the folds of this dynamic group of women.

Her comments lead me to contemplate what it means to have the support of others. I'm aware of the immense value of a steady hand, but I see too, through William's actions, that individuals must be willing to step out on their own. Support is nice, but others can't take the chances or walk the roads for you. That, I understand now, is up to me alone.

As Ms. Thompson, Cookie, and Clara make their way back downstairs, my thoughts turn to Rose Oxley, my sole connection to Hollywood. As the daughter of a production company executive, she could have dismissed me entirely. Instead, she offered her assistance, telling me to get in touch once I had a few more theatre credits in my portfolio.

With Papa and Cookie on the verge of purchasing a new home and Clara falling deeper for William by the day, the expiration for my comfortable existence is approaching. I've delayed contacting Ms. Oxley for assistance, but now, with William safe and my future careening out of my control, there's no time to spare. I must push beyond my discomfort at asking a favour of someone I barely know. I must telephone Rose Oxley at once.

CHAPTER 33

SATURDAY, JULY 14, 1928

lara

"Ow." The corner of a box loaded with books jabs me as I make my way to the kitchen for a cup of tea. Weariness over our lack of space has become a steady companion, with the apartment bursting at the seams. Boxes take up every bit of floor space, turning daily activities into a gauntlet. We've even taken to eating wherever we can the past three evenings, given the sofa is pushed right up against the dining table to accommodate the teetering tower of boxes.

Between the suffocating sensation of the apartment walls closing in on us and Lou's sour mood over the poor reviews for *Mr. Brown's Secretary*, I'm out of ideas for easing the tension in apartment 3D.

"Argh. Look at this one," Louisa calls from the kitchen, the sole room left with a flat surface to spread a newspaper on.

I carefully shimmy between two stacks of boxes, purposely slowing my steps toward the kitchen, as I'm not at all interested in listening to yet another poor review.

She doesn't wait for my arrival. Instead she lifts her voice to the heavens, or at least beyond the kitchen wall. "Despite Miss Wilson's stellar performance in *All Souls Eve* and, before that, *Craig's Wife* directed by Thomas Cromwell, her character in *Mr. Brown's Secretary*, Agatha Taylor, offers this theatre critic little to talk about."

Lou's head snaps up as I appear at the threshold. "Do you see? It's exactly as I said would happen. A terribly directed production hurts the cast just as much as it does the play itself. It's enough to make my blood boil."

"I'm sorry." I reach a hand to rub my sister's arm, despite knowing my concern will do her little good.

"Yesterday, I was called *the actress who clearly missed rehearsals*." Crumpling up the newspaper, she tosses it out of the kitchen. "Might as well use that to pack the dishes." She grips the counter as if it is the only thing holding her in place. "If they only knew how hard I've worked."

"You know how hard you've worked. That's what matters at the end of the day."

"I'm not in the mood for a pep talk, Clara." She stalks away as well as one is able in an apartment that feels like a can of sardines.

I don't hide the sigh that whooshes from my body. Louisa isn't the only disgruntled Wilson in our midst. Recent days have been far from easy. The challenge of navigating Papa's and Cookie's delight over the purchase of their new house, while seeing the plentiful downsides of relocating for Louisa and myself, has stretched my agreeability to the limits. Keeping a pleasant disposition feels like carrying a bag of boulders uphill.

Worse yet, my work at the hotel has become mundane in a way I never expected. With Ms. Thompson back in full capacity as hotel matron, my role as an eighth-floor maid seems to have lost its shine. The first few weeks after news arrived of William's safe passage home, I was determined to remain grateful. We had been granted a reprieve from heartache, and I intended to take full advantage of it.

Now, though, more than a month since the train's derailment, I find myself struggling to accept the humdrum nature of my day-to-day life. I'm sorry to say I've even caught myself dreaming of a brighter future once more. One with both William and a rewarding career complete with engaging tasks. Reprimanding myself has done little to quell these fanciful notions, and I begin to feel I must confess them to William.

I've thought long and hard about confiding in him. There is risk in every relationship, Cookie told me over a late-night cup of tea, after my tearful confession about not choosing William. However, she elaborated that the greater risk is not sharing at all. If you can't give yourself fully and completely to another person, you need to ask yourself if they are indeed the right person for you. Her words compelled me to examine the issue more closely, and I am certain things between William and me will never succeed if I keep this part of myself from him.

With that bit of guidance tucked into my heart, I remind myself that William may not like what I have to say. This awareness unnerves me, and if I'm being honest, it's the reason I've held off voicing my thoughts on the matter. I feel guilty about wanting more when I've already been blessed with his love. Of course, if William takes offence to my desire to be more than his wife and mother to his children, that is telling too. Though I must admit that such a possibility troubles me deeply.

My conflicting thoughts remind me William has never shown a tendency to be closed-minded, nor unkind. Quite the contrary. He is a man of high morals and good deeds, and I owe it to both of us to be honest with him. I only hope confessing my true desires will not be the reason for William's departure from my life.

I shake my head to free my unruly musings. He has been my silver lining through these challenging days. The week he finally made it home to Toronto, he telephoned to say he was determined for us to spend more time together. He asked me to write as often as I could, and he promised to do the same. We sorted out our schedules and set aside an evening each week for him to telephone. His being three hours ahead of me means a sacrifice of sleep on his part, though he tells me hearing my voice is worth the cost.

Though our telephone conversations are lovely and the sound of his voice never fails to warm me through, our chats are far from private, given the Wilson telephone resides in the centre of our apartment. Instead, it's the letters we share that feel the most intimate, providing us a connection that grows deeper with each letter posted via Canada's Royal Mail.

Having wrestled with what I must confess, I've put off answering his letter for three days, and I can no longer do so. William has a right to know the truth of my heart, though saying such things to the man I am desperate to keep in my life scares me more than I care to admit. Out of time and with a nervous twitter in my stomach, I sit on my bed, using my hardcover journal as a makeshift table as I pen the most difficult letter I've ever had to write.

July 14, 1928

Dear William,

Your letter arrived a few days ago and with it more comforting words regarding the challenges we are facing as a family as we prepare to set sail across the city. Your kindness and understanding are like a balm to my weary mind, and I am grateful for them.

There is one matter I have been quibbling over, and I fear I cannot keep it to myself any longer. I do hope this doesn't come as a disappointment or a shock to you, as my intention is never to disappoint you.

The thing is, I've found great fulfillment while working at the hotel. To be plain, I relished the time I spent as temporary matron of the hotel. Though I do not in any way wish for your sister to be unwell, I find myself craving the bustle and problem-solving that is required for the role.

What I mean to say is I'd like to have a career as a hotel matron. Please forgive my bluntness on the topic, but I sense we are moving in the direction of a future together. I don't wish to keep such information from you, in the event you feel you are unable to embrace a lifelong relationship with a woman who wishes to remain employed.

I fear I may be putting you off by mentioning such things, but I do hope that is not the case. I've *also come to know that having you in my life is a gift and is of the utmost importance to me. Either way, I have made the dreadfully difficult decision that if I am to be truly happy in my life, I wish to have the freedom to have both a career and a husband. If that is something you simply cannot abide, I can't say I won't be disappointed, but I will do my best to understand. At the very least, I feel I owe it to you to be honest. Should you not wish to pursue a future with me under these circumstances, please know I am utterly grateful for the time we've had getting to know one another. In any case, I would like to hear your thoughts on the matter.*

I remain forever yours.

All my love,

Clara

Emotion pricks my eyes as I fold the paper in three and slide it into the addressed envelope waiting beside me on the bed. Holding the letter in my hands, I run my thumb over his name repeatedly. I consider tucking the letter into my bedside table, never to send it. But regardless of whether the Supreme Court of Canada deems me to be a person, I am quite certain William Thompson does, and for that, I owe him my truth, always.

Unable to keep the tears at bay, I let them fall freely, hoping with all my might that William's answer won't be no.

CHAPTER 34

SATURDAY, JULY 14, 1928

*L*ouisa

I place a steadying hand on my knot-riddled stomach. The plan I was so certain of a month ago now seems foolhardy, with the play's closing-night performance upon me. If Ms. Oxley hadn't confirmed her plans to travel to Vancouver and attend tonight's show last week via letter, I might be inclined to forget the whole thing, lick my wounds from a less-than-stellar showing of *Mr. Brown's Secretary*, and carry on as though the production never happened.

Pulling her letter from my pocket, I reread its contents. Rose Oxley is the one woman I trust to steer me well when it comes to the theatre.

Dear Louisa,

I have confirmed my travel plans to Vancouver. After we spoke on the telephone, I took your predicament to my father for his advice. My father has had numerous dealings with directors and the like, and I am happy to say he agreed wholeheartedly with your assessment. Though I imagine you may fear the ramifications of stepping out from under your director's thumb, we both support your decision to do so as a last resort. Clearly the man is unable to see past the tip of his nose.

The play's reviews have been dreadful, and sadly none of the critics have picked up on the fact the director's decisions are responsible for sinking the production. Be strong, Louisa, and know that my father and I are behind you all the way.

I will be arriving on the 4:00 p.m. train. Please leave a ticket for the play at the box office, just in case theatregoers who haven't read the reviews decide to sell out the show's final night.

I'll be cheering you on from the audience, my dear.

Yours truly,

Rose Oxley

A knock at the apartment door yanks my head up before I have a chance to reread her postscript. I place the letter back in my pocket and step around the maze of boxes. With Papa and Cookie visiting the new house, which became theirs yesterday, and Clara sequestered in our bedroom writing to William, I go to answer the door.

His presence is such a surprise it almost sends me stumbling backward. "William." I reach for his hand and squeeze. "I'm so happy to see you. What are you doing here? Does Clara know you're coming?"

A good-natured chuckle lifts his cheeks. "It's good to see you, Lou. I'm here to see Clara, and no, she's not expecting me."

"Well, you'd better come in and I'll fetch her." I step aside and let William pass.

I head down the hallway, hollering in a singsong cadence for my sister. "Oh, Clara. There's someone here to see you."

The bedroom door opens, and Clara steps out. The flash of a question crosses her features before her gaze finds William.

"Hello there." His tone is teasing and full of love. I take the cue and step away to give them a shred of privacy.

Returning to the living room, I hear Clara ask why he didn't tell her he was coming. William's reply is one that stills my beating heart. He didn't want to worry her, given the last train ride he took.

I smile as their talking ceases. I imagine a long embrace, and my thoughts venture to Thomas. We've continued to speak on the telephone every few days, rebuilding the trust we lost in the heat of the argument. I've even agreed to see him tonight after the play closes. Though he wasn't pleased by my insistence that we take some time and regain our footing, he respected my need for space.

In truth, I've been afraid I might slip and confide in him my plans for tonight's performance. Fearing his disappointment at my blatant disobedience of the director,

I needed to ensure I wouldn't be talked out of doing what I know I must. I've told no one, save for Rose Oxley, what's in store for the closing night of *Mr. Brown's Secretary*. If I am going to be able to trust anyone's judgement, that person needs to be me.

My lips twist as I contemplate my options. I've done a good job of convincing myself that somehow Clara and I will gain our independence. I've fooled myself into believing that, after a few months with Papa and Cookie at the new house, we will venture out to live on our own.

Seeing her with William, I am certain the time has come for me to step up and be the big sister. I must choose a path forward for myself so Clara will feel free to set a course all her own. What kind of sister would I be if I let my desires hold Clara back?

I reach for a stack of magazines, placing them in a new box. We women must do our utmost to ensure we all rise together. I'm certain it's the only way for all of us to comprehend our value in life. The question is how?

The answer pops into my head with a memory of Rose Oxley, and I see where my journey begins. Stilling my concerns, I force myself to face reality. My family was never going to follow me to Hollywood so I can chase my dreams. This is something I have to do for myself. Of course, I had hoped to have Thomas by my side, but things with Thomas aren't as certain as I imagined they would be. I rest my hands on top of the box, considering my options. He loves me. This I know is true. Maybe there's a way to take more than one risk tonight.

Regardless of how things unfold this evening, I'm aware it's time for me to fly from the nest. Not because I'm being pushed out but because I'm choosing to discover what I'm capable of on my own.

CHAPTER 35

SATURDAY, JULY 14, 1928

lara

I can hardly believe my eyes. William Thompson in the flesh. My cheeks burn as I consider the forthright words written in the letter still clutched in my hand. I throw my arms around him, and he lifts me from the floor, swaying lightly as I sink into his embrace.

My words are smothered, with my mouth pressed into his shoulder. "I've missed you." I inhale his scent and feel the surge of love as he squeezes me tighter.

"Would you care for a walk?" The stubble of his cheek brushes against the crook between my neck and shoulder.

"Yes, but not yet. Don't let me go just yet." I want to memorize this moment, put it in a time capsule in my mind in case the things that must be said alter our path forward.

William's breath near my ear sends my stomach into a flurry of somersaults. When he chuckles, I feel as though the whole world is turning upside down, and I lean in, not wanting the sensation to stop.

Several minutes later, my feet are back on solid ground. I hurriedly stuff the letter in my dress pocket and grab my pocketbook from the hook. With a feeble goodbye to Louisa, I promise to be in my seat at the theatre with plenty of time before the show begins.

Without William or me having to utter a word, we both turn at the end of the block and stroll toward the ocean's edge. A light breeze brings the salty air to my nose, and out of habit, I lick my lips, anticipating the taste of brine. I sneak glances at William as we walk, not believing he is here, beside me. Gratitude rushes through me at seeing him safe and recovered from the train accident.

My hand brushes the skirt of my dress, and I'm reminded of my letter to him pressed into by pocket. Tugging the letter free I lift the envelope up to eye level and stumble slightly on the sidewalk.

"Careful." William catches my elbow. "Do you need to post that?" He inclines his head toward my letter.

Heat flushes up my neck and licks its way past my collar. "It's for you, actually."

"Well, I am delighted to know you were thinking of me." His grey-blue eyes sparkle playfully in the sunlight.

"I was." My mind shifts to the contents of the letter. Wariness rises within me, and I hurriedly shove the letter into my dress pocket. The realization that I will now be forced to have the conversation in person slows my pace.

Changing the subject, I press him for details on his recovery. "Are you sure you're feeling better?"

William rolls up one sleeve and then the other, twisting his arms this way and that to show me he is free of bruises. "I was fortunate to be sitting near the front of the train. My only bruising was from the sudden jerk as the rear slid off the rails."

"We were all quite beside ourselves with worry." I catch myself using the collective "we" and steal a glance in his direction. "I was quite worried, that is."

William takes hold of my hand and tugs me off the sidewalk and into the shadows of an alleyway. His intense eyes lock on mine.

"I assure you I am more than fine. I'm here with you, and I couldn't be happier."

The left corner of his mouth twitches up as he dips his head to mine. A warm rush spreads through me and I link my arms behind his neck, drawing him toward me. My back presses against the cool brick wall as he leans closer. His tender kiss makes my knees go weak, and his hand in my hair sends me spiralling, unable to tell which way is up.

We come up for air several minutes later, William bracing his hand against the wall behind me. "I've missed you, Clara." His voice is deep and throaty as our breaths mingle. "I want you to know—the train derailing made things very clear in my mind. I'd like to talk with you about our future, if you'll allow me?"

I capture my bottom lip between my teeth and nod. I'll have no option but to be completely honest with him. Whether it's a blessing or a curse, I will tell William the truth today.

We pick a spot on a bench overlooking the ocean. The lapping rhythm of the waves soothes my soul, while I clasp my hands tightly in my lap to steady my nerves. I clear my throat, suddenly desperate to put off this conversation for even a few seconds.

"William." I pivot on the bench, determined to meet

him straight on. "There is something I need to tell you." I unclasp my hands and extract the letter from my pocket.

He tilts his head to one side, waiting for me to continue.

"I wrote it all here. In all honesty, I didn't expect to tell you in person." My voice wavers, already dreading what I must say.

William's face shifts, a thread of concern lacing his expression.

I chide myself for stalling and making things more difficult than they need to be. Thrusting my shoulders back, I meet his gaze. "William, I love you. I am quite certain you have taken up residence in the entirety of my heart."

His face relaxes as his warm eyes send adoration washing over me.

"The thing is, I have discovered that I enjoy working. The short time I was matron of the hotel, I thrived. I felt useful and valued. Others looked up to me, and I gained a sense of pride in myself that I've never felt before."

William leans toward me, a genuine smile lighting up his face. "Your abilities clearly shined. Eliza and Robert have said so themselves. You should be proud of your efforts."

I tuck my chin as sheepishness rises at William's flattery. "Thank you. It's nice to hear I haven't imagined my usefulness."

"Forgive me, but I don't see where your concern lies." William places a hand over top of mine. "What has got you worried?"

Releasing a long, weighted sigh, I push the words out. "I know that telling you I loved you meant choosing a future with you. The thing is, I can't seem to let go of my desire to keep working at the hotel. If I'm able, I would like to work toward a permanent position as a hotel matron, and I realize it isn't a woman's place, especially a woman married to an attorney, to have both a family and a career. I am sorry, William, but I fear if I marry you, I will lose another part of myself, and I simply can't see that being a good thing for our relationship in the end."

Moisture gathers in my eyes as I shift my gaze to my lap. "I'm sorry. I never meant to hurt you or imply you aren't enough for me. But I couldn't marry you without telling you the truth." I hold back the sob that is lodged in my throat.

"Clara." His voice isn't angry or hurt. Instead, he remains calm and steady. His tone is unbothered enough for me to steal a glance upward. "How long have you been worrying over this?"

A shrug of my shoulders is my only reply.

"You should have come to me. There is no need for you to fret over things where no worry lies. You can always speak plainly with me. Even if you don't know precisely what you want to say yet." William takes my hands in his. "I never want you to be afraid of having important conversations, and any discussion that involves you is important to me."

"I went about this all wrong." Tears roll down my cheeks, part heartache, part shame. "You were so pleased I had stepped in to help when your sister fell ill. I convinced myself it was the right decision to put our relationship on hold while I focused on work. I figured I could manage both in equal measure, with the geographical distance between us."

William's mouth quirks up into a humorous expression. "You put me off? I hadn't noticed." A laugh erupts from his lips. "I can only wonder how delightful things will be for me when you aren't trying to distance yourself at all."

At his teasing, a flush of colour replaces my tears. "I was worried about having to choose between you and work, and for a long time, I wasn't sure I could choose one over the other. But after the train accident, I understood what is important. It's you. William, I choose you."

William's chin drops to his chest, and when he lifts his head, his eyes dance above a wide smile. "I am very happy to hear that, but Clara, I haven't even asked you yet."

He's stifling a bemused chuckle—I can feel it—but I'm grateful for his transparency and ability to set me at ease.

"The thing is"—William holds my chin in his hand as his thumb dries the trails of tears on my cheek—"you don't have to choose. Not when it comes to me and a career. You can have both."

I inhale sharply, ready to remind him of how things are done in polite society. Given his status, surely he can't risk becoming the talk of the town. Oh, how those with little to do like to gossip. I can hear them now. *Did you hear she works? And in a hotel, at that.* Perhaps they would even be so cruel as to say, *I wonder what he sees in that plain, working-class girl.* My head shakes back and forth at the thought of such ridicule and scorn.

"Hear me out." William tilts my chin gently to stop my head shaking. "I told Louisa to pave her own road and live life on her terms, regardless of what the courts decide. I meant it when I said men and women are different but that they can be equal. I would never ask you to choose me over your career. I'm not the slightest bit concerned of what others think. I'm only interested in what you think. Besides, I already received your father's blessing."

William slips his hand out of mine and stands from the bench. I don't want him to walk away, but before I can say a word, he steps in front of me and kneels with one knee in the sand. He pulls a small velvet box from his pocket and lifts the lid.

A stunning platinum band with a glittering array of diamonds rests neatly in the centre of the box. My hand flies to my mouth, unsuccessfully hiding my gasp.

"Clara Wilson, will you do me the honour of becoming my wife?"

My heart swells within my chest, beating rapidly at William's imploring eyes. Every emotion under the sun vibrates through my body, mixing in a whirlwind of sensations. Fear, love, acceptance, passion, worry, joy. Tugged from my memory are Cookie's words, *William would never expect you to choose*, and the reminder from her wedding ceremony: *Love never fails*.

William waits a moment, watching me closely as I filter his words through my heart. Lifting an index finger, he positions it skyward to make a point. "Just know this, my dearest Clara, by saying yes, you are promising to be true to yourself as much as to me. I want all of you, Clara. Fully and completely."

My gaze darts between the ring sparkling in the late-afternoon sun and William. My mind whirs, barely able to comprehend how deeply fortunate I am to have this man in my life.

"Clara?"

My name on his lips tugs me from my thoughts, and I realize he is still waiting for an answer.

"Yes, William. A hundred times, yes." Fresh, happy tears build and spill freely.

William slides the ring onto my left hand before I grasp his collar and pull him into a fierce embrace. We remain in one another's arms, him kneeling in the sand and me seated on the bench, for longer than is appropriate in public. But in this moment, I care little about what others may think.

Several minutes later, he dusts the sand from his trousers and rejoins me on the bench, our hands woven tightly together. I feel like a brand-new woman. A woman worthy of having all she desires.

I'm marvelling at my brilliant engagement ring and my good fortune. I get to experience a life on my terms, with William at my side. "How did you become so open to the idea of having a working wife?" I ask, gazing lovingly at him.

"I've been familiar with the concept for quite some time. You could say it's in my blood." William's wink lets me know there is more to the story, but he's being cagey.

"Go on." I give him a cheeky sideways glance. "If I am to give all of myself to you, then I expect no less from you, sir."

His deep-throated chuckle brings a smile to my lips. "Touché. I imagine you're going to know soon enough, anyway." He eyes me dubiously. "In all honesty, I'm surprised you haven't figured it out yet."

My brows knit together. He is toying with me. My mind does circles around the possibilities. With so much consuming my life these past several months, I imagine I've been rather oblivious. I narrow in on topics that might concern William. Is this the secret he's been keeping from me all this time? I search his words for more clues. "It's in your blood." I puzzle out the riddle and feel my eyes grow wide. "In your family, you mean?"

William's laugh is a bellyful now. "Yes. I knew you were smart enough to guess."

"Mr. Olson and Ms. Thompson?" I clap a hand over my mouth. "They're married?"

William bobs his head up and down. "For going on five years now."

"But how? How have they managed to keep it a secret for so long?"

"They decided to keep their personal life separate from the hotel so tongues don't wag and all that. Eliza, Robert, and Mr. Hamilton agreed that it was in Eliza's best interest, to ensure her authority as matron was maintained."

I consider the degrees of separation. "She walks to work, and he drives."

"Eliza prefers to walk, though I suspect she misses Cookie's company. She's told me more than once that her walks help her transition from home life to work life."

I'm piecing it all together. "Cookie used to live in the apartment at the side of their house. She knew?"

William nods. "Yes."

"She never said a thing."

"It wasn't our secret to tell. Besides, she and Eliza go way back. Been the best of friends since Cookie arrived in Vancouver."

Ms. Thompson's words come back to me, clarity surrounding them with the insight of her marriage to Mr. Olson. I lift my voice to the breeze. "If you want a different choice, keep digging until you find an option that suits you."

"Those are wise words. Who said them?" William tucks my arm into his, turning my hand so we can both admire the diamond placed there.

I tilt my chin to meet his eyes. "Your sister. Wisdom apparently runs in your family."

Snuggling into his side, I note the sun is beginning its descent. "Oh, I hate for this moment to end." I battle my desire to remain nestled into William's embrace against the promise I made to my sister. "But speaking of family. I've got to get to Louisa's play. She didn't tell us why, only said to make sure we were there for closing night. She's had a rough go of it, with the harsh reviews."

"I'd better get you home so you can change for the theatre." William stands and offers me his hand.

"Will you join us? I'm sure tickets won't be an issue, given the play's less-than-stellar reception."

William's eyes squint in contemplation. "I have a feeling Louisa is up to something, and I wouldn't miss it for the world."

CHAPTER 36

SATURDAY, JULY 14, 1928

*L*ouisa

Nervous energy hurries my steps. Before going backstage to ready myself for tonight's performance, I have an errand to run. I purchase two tickets from the box office, leaving one with the attendant for Rose Oxley. The other I tuck into the note I wrote for Thomas and walk the several blocks to his apartment building.

Sliding the note and ticket under his apartment door, I hurry away, determined not to be caught in the act. Any explanation I can offer is unlikely to convince him of the validity of my plan. I must leave it to chance that he will bring this ticket and attend tonight's performance to see for himself.

I badly want to make things right with Thomas, but I'm aware I am asking a lot of him. He may not be able to accept my decision to go against the director's instruction, but I hope his trust in me, and the slew of bad reviews will have him reconsidering his thoughts on the matter. At any rate, Thomas deserves an explanation. I may not succeed in convincing him my actions are justifiable, but I must take the risk if I'm going to move forward in my life, with or without Thomas.

For the past several weeks, I have maintained the paltry role of Agatha Taylor without embellishment or fanfare. I've resisted the urge to veer from the letter of the script and instead took the punches that came in the form of negative theatre reviews. Being called out by name as "lackluster" and "boring to watch" stole my sense of self for days.

Tonight, though, that will all change. It's closing night for *Mr. Brown's Secretary*, and this time, Agatha Taylor has something to say. She is going to show the director, the audience, Rose Oxley, and, with any luck, Thomas Cromwell that resilience in a character and an actress is a very good thing indeed.

In the backstage dressing room, I examine my reflection in the mirror. I'm dressed in Agatha's simple and somewhat dreary ensemble. My hair is rolled to perfection in the demure fashion of a secretary whose sole role is to blend into the office furniture.

As I lean forward to apply the pastel pink lipstick, my gaze falls to the muted shade poking out from the silver cylinder. "Suitable for a wallflower," I murmur to myself. Then I pause and cap the lipstick. "You are not a wallflower, Agatha Taylor."

Tugging my handbag closer, I pull free the bright red lipstick that will undeniably make a statement. The audience might not know the importance of my resistance red lips, but I am quite certain their presence will not go unnoticed.

Standing at stage left, I calm my jitters with a few slow, purposeful breaths. The success of this evening may very well determine my future. I could certainly use a heaping spoonful of easy in my life right about now.

I remember the postscript of Rose Oxley's recent letter and feel emboldened.

P.S. The road to success is often paved with obstacles. Sometimes, it's prudent to raise one's head and examine the horizon, then forge your own path forward. The higher the mountain, Louisa, the steeper the climb. Dig in. It's time to start climbing.

Archie steps up behind me, nudging my shoulder as he speaks in a low voice. "I imagine this production hasn't gone anything like you thought it would. You're a talented actress, Louisa, and I'm sorry you've taken the brunt of a poorly directed play."

"Thank you. I appreciate that." I chew on my red-stained bottom lip, contemplating whether to let him in on my plan.

"If there's anything I can do…" His words trail off.

Pivoting to meet him square on, I beam. "There is one thing."

Archie's eyebrows quirk up, and I tug on his sleeve, pulling him away from the curtain to include him in my scheme.

With Archie on board, my confidence grows. Tonight

may not solve any of my troubles, but at least I'll have been true to myself.

The thick, red curtain is about to open. I take my seat behind the set's secretarial desk in the make-believe New York City office. The stage lights adjust until the spotlight lands on me. I catch the director watching from the opposite side of the stage, his arms folded across his chest, and I imagine him questioning what is different.

Whether it's the red lipstick or the assuredness rising within me, I give him a confident wink and smother a laugh at his puzzled expression. Then I swivel my head toward the audience, who is about to enjoy the run's best performance of *Mr. Brown's Secretary*.

"Miss Taylor." Archie strides in as the overly confident and quirky Mr. Brown, eliciting a round of chuckles from the audience. I pause my theatrical typing, tilt my head toward the audience, and lift my eyebrows in question. Then I stand to deliver my line, Mr. Brown's newspaper, and a steaming cup of coffee.

We sail through the first half of the production, with the audience roaring in their seats. I lock eyes with Archie and resist the urge to burst out laughing myself. Before the first scene is over, the rest of the cast is on board. From the boardroom men to Agatha's best friend, everyone's acting reaches for the theatre lights.

This, I think to myself while dashing backstage for a costume change, is my favourite part of acting. When everyone rows in the same direction, the boat moves with ease, grace, and an immense amount of strength. This is how we are better together, as the cast of a play and also as humans navigating a complicated and messy world.

I'm about to step onstage for the second half of the play when I spot the director heading my way, a scowl leading his charge. "Miss Wilson," he hisses. The redness of his face leaves no doubt: the man is hopping mad.

Desperate to avoid a confrontation, I dash toward the stage before the crew finishes setting up the next scene, a seedy speakeasy where Agatha and her best friend are about to have lunch.

"You aren't supposed to be here." One of the crew members shoots me a questioning glance.

"Just heading to the other side of the stage," I counter, knowing this move could throw off the cast. "Tell Judith to expect me from stage right," I whisper-shout over my shoulder before locating a hiding spot within the folds of the red velvet curtain.

The crew rushes off the stage, brushing past me in a hurry so the second half of the play can begin.

Judith enters the stage and settles into a high-backed stool in front of a tall, square table, where two cocktails of coloured water drip moisture from ice melting beneath the stage lights.

"Time to go." I let my worry of being discovered by the director fade into the background and turn my attention to the stage as I wait for the curtain to open.

The stage lights dim, adding another layer of dinginess to the pretend jazz club. A low hum of a soulful saxophone lulls me into character.

I ready myself to step onstage when a rough hand grabs my arm and spins me around. "Just what do you think you are doing?" Spittle flies with Mr. Barker's angry words. I instinctively jerk away, but his grip is firm on my arm.

"I'm doing what I should have done all along. You hired me to perform a role. The least you can do is let me." My words sound no less annoyed for their whispered delivery.

"I hired you because the script called for a woman."

The statement is so matter of fact it sends me reeling. "Believe me, if I didn't have to put up with all your whining and snivelling about equal pay and creative input, I wouldn't." The man's sneer oozes with arrogance, and I feel myself recoil. "You dames always think you know better."

The curtain opens, and a sideways glance toward the stage, where Judith sits alone, tells me we only have a moment before things fall apart for all of us. This is the mountain Rose Oxley spoke of in her letter. Dig in, Louisa, I tell myself with determination.

Wrenching my arm from his grip, I pivot and meet him toe to toe. "That just goes to show how little you know about women. This isn't about knowing better. It's about doing better."

I stride forward to Judith, playing Agatha's best friend, Winnie. From the corner of my eye, I see them—Clara and William, Papa and Cookie—sitting in the front row. As the stage lights follow my footsteps, the wide beam spills onto their seats. I almost pause mid-step at the sight of Clara's and Cookie's smiling, brightly painted red lips. The Resistance Red Brigade is on full display tonight, and my heart squeezes with appreciation.

Setting my mind to the task at hand, I turn my attention back to Judith and the waiting table. "I'm sorry I'm late." I place my empty clutch on the table's edge and plead forgiveness from my friend.

Winnie waves a hand dismissively. "What was it this time? Too busy writing his book?"

I take offence, putting a hand to my dress's neckline and the faux pearls that rest there. "I am not writing Mr. Brown's book."

"That's right." Winnie takes a long pull from her cocktail glass, meets the audience straight on, and says,

"You merely wrote the entire book and let him slap his name on it. I'm sure the signature was his."

My fingers twirl the cocktail glass in circles. "He dictated. I merely embellished." I give the audience a side eye, lifting one eyebrow innocently, garnering me another titter of laughter.

"With wit, grammar, and coherent thoughts?" This time it's Winnie's turn, and in my periphery, I sense the audience lean in and smile.

Brushing off her comment with a wave of my hand, I roll my eyes and retort, "Minor details."

The audience is invested, and I couldn't be happier as they laugh and enjoy themselves.

By the final curtain call, trickles of sweat are making tracks down my back. The audience is standing and applauding wildly as the cast gathers onstage to receive their praise.

With Archie on one side of me and Judith on the other, the entire cast clasps hands, raises our arms, and takes a final bow. The audience's cheers are so loud I can barely hear Archie beside me.

"You did it, Louisa," he says. "I'm so glad you didn't give up on the play."

A self-assured laugh spills from my lips. "I don't give up." I beam at him. "I simply keep pivoting until things fall into place."

Archie laughs, and I turn to take in the audience one more time.

On the far-right side of the theatre, standing apart from the crowd, like a director will do, is Thomas. He came. I sense understanding in his expression, and though I am certain there are conversations and apologies yet to come, I feel lighter knowing he showed up for me in the end.

Emotion wells behind my eyes, and I inch my chin slightly to let him know I see him. His wide smile tells me there is hope. For us. For Hollywood. For a future.

As the curtain closes for the final time, I spot the director at the edge of the stage, his dour expression letting me know he's not through with me yet.

I let the cast and crew vacate the stage before I do, not wishing for any of them to be caught in the crossfire. I don't dodge the director or avoid his gaze. Instead, I walk confidently in his direction, prepared to take whatever he wishes to throw at me. The show is over, and I've made certain his poor choices will not follow me in my career.

"Miss Wilson, you are far more brazen than I imagined you might be. If I'd known I would have to contend with such disgraceful behaviour, you wouldn't have made it past the first audition." His hands ball into fists. "An actress should know her place. Yours was to be demure and supportive, not attention seeking and commandeering of an entire production. Like I said before, you dames always think you know better." His voice growls, and I flinch, hoping the audience has already cleared out.

"An actress should know her place?" A familiar voice asks from the shadows. "Mr. Barker, I assume you mean *every* member of a cast should follow a director's lead. Not solely the female ones." Thomas steps forward, not taking his eyes off the director.

"Mr. Cromwell. I didn't realize you'd be attending the show this evening. Though I appreciate your productions, this situation doesn't concern you." The director splays his hands wide as if apologizing for me. "This one is as wild as they come, and I caution you to steer clear of putting her in anything in the future. You can be sure I'll be spreading word of her inability to take direction."

"Ah, you must have forgotten. Miss Wilson was the star of my production of *Craig's Wife*. A play that received rave reviews." Thomas inclines his head in my direction. "Due to Miss Wilson's role in it."

I bite my lip in an attempt to conceal my smirk.

"Oh." The director's face turns a fresh shade of red, though I'm unable to determine whether it's rage or embarrassment. "Well, at any rate, I'm glad to be saying good riddance to Miss Wilson."

"What you should be saying is thank you." Her husky voice arrives ahead of the clacking of her heels against the wooden stage. "I'm quite certain Miss Wilson has earned that tonight."

"And you are…?" The director looks baffled and a touch nervous at the growing number of people involved in this conversation.

"Ms. Rose Oxley." She adjusts the stole resting against her petite frame before addressing him again. "I'd also caution you against spreading rumours about Miss Wilson. For one, it's not nice. And two, little boys shouldn't play in big boys' sandboxes."

The director's head snaps backward. "Madam, I've no idea who you are, but you've no right to speak to me this way."

Rose Oxley meets my gaze. "Slow to catch on, isn't he?"

I nod in agreement but refrain from saying anything.

With a shake of her head, she tries again. "I'm Rose Oxley of Oxley Motion Pictures in Hollywood. I'm sure you've heard of us." Waving a hand dismissively, she returns her attention to me. "Anyway, I'm taking Miss Wilson with me, so you won't have to worry over her any further."

Our eyes meet and a rush of exhilaration floods me. "Thank you, Ms. Oxley. Thank you for believing in me."

"Honey, I've believed in you since the first time I laid eyes on you. Any fool could spot your talent a mile away." Rose's eyes narrow at the director. "Well, I suppose not any fool."

I catch Thomas' eye as he hides a laugh behind a clenched fist.

Placing a gentle hand on my arm, Rose provides a little direction of her own. "Louisa, I thoroughly enjoyed your performance tonight. Now, won't you be a dear and wash off all that makeup? We have dinner reservations and plenty to discuss." Rose gestures to Thomas. "Mr. Cromwell, I do hope you'll join us."

"Of course, Ms. Oxley. I'd be honoured." Thomas beams at me before Rose waves me off the stage to wash my face and grab my things.

In the dressing room, glycerin-soaked face cloth in hand, reality sinks in. I am going to California. The awareness thrills me through and through. I knew I would be leaving Vancouver, regardless of the play's success tonight. Before I stepped onstage, I fully accepted that my life is changing. Not because of Papa and Cookie moving into a new home or Clara and William falling head over heels for one another. Or even the pull I feel toward Thomas. I decided it's about time to know my own worth, and it's definitely time to start proclaiming it to the most important person in my world. Me.

lara

Almost two weeks have passed since William changed my world with his proposal and encouragement to pursue my goals of becoming a hotel matron. William thrilled me again later that week when he announced he would be leaving his firm and setting up shop in Vancouver.

"Why would we situate ourselves in Toronto when all of our family is here?" he countered when I asked him if he was certain a relocation west was in the best interest of his career.

Having little argument and quietly pleased with his decision, I quickly moved on to discuss the details of our nuptials.

I wave hello to the doorman at The Hotel Georgia and catch my diamond ring glittering in the sun. A ripple of bliss runs through me as I cross the street toward The Hamilton. Our engagement will be a long one, given the time it will take for William to close out his legal cases in Toronto, sell his business interests to his partners, and put his Toronto home on the market. Together, we settled on having the wedding in December of next year, at the Anglican church where Papa and Cookie were married. Though I am delighted to be having a traditional Anglican ceremony, given the church's connection to Mama, I am even more pleased by William's complete agreement to remove the words "to obey" from our wedding vows.

We'll have plenty of time to sort out the details. If I'm being honest, the planning to come excites me to no end, and I am comforted to know that William appreciates the thoughtful manner in which I approach these momentous decisions.

The warm morning is nothing compared to the heat billowing out of Cookie's pastry kitchen. The aroma of peach pie fills the air as I step inside, the scent urging my stomach into a grumble.

Cookie pops her head out of the kitchen, a towel in hand. "Ah, Clara. There you are."

"Something smells delicious." My mouth waters as another hit of sweetness wafts toward me. "You must have gotten here early if pies are already in the oven."

"I was keen to get an early start." Cookie quirks her head toward the lobby. "The ladies from the National Council of Women of Canada are expected this afternoon, and I wanted to present our best for them." Her glance up from downcast eyes tells me she is being sheepish. "You know, given all they're doing to keep the momentum going with the decision at the Privy Council."

"I think it's a splendid and very kind gesture." I pat her arm and move toward the back-of-house stairs. "Though I will admit the Wilsons would be delighted to enjoy such a treat at home too."

"Off with you, then," Cookie teases as she waves her towel at my back.

Before I am out of earshot, Cookie calls after me. "And Clara."

I turn and soak in her exuberant expression. "Only two more days to go."

She is over the moon. Though some boxes are already at the new house, this Saturday we will erase every trace of the Wilsons from The Newbury.

Forcing a smile, I nod my reply. My steps slow slightly as I meander down the hall, toward the locker room. Only two more days until our journey to work will begin from an entirely new direction, with at least thirty minutes added to each end of our day, depending on the streetcar schedule and delays. The days are already long, and the thought of making them longer is less than appealing. But with nowhere else to go, Louisa and I are bracing ourselves for the change.

I'm dressed and first in line for roll call when Ms. Thompson arrives on the eighth floor.

"I'm glad I caught you before the others arrive." The matron's colour has returned these past few weeks, the July sun giving her a warm glow. "There's something I'd like to discuss with you. Will you come to my office after roll call?"

"Yes, ma'am." Since William proposed, I find myself caught in between the professional and the familiar with Ms. Thompson. On the one hand, she is my superior, but on the other, she will soon be my sister-in-law. My brain has yet to reconcile the two, but in the meantime, I feel a bit foolish no matter how I address the matron.

Fifteen minutes later, I knock on the matron's open office door.

"Ah, Clara." She catches herself using my first name and offers an apologetic look, and I understand I'm not the only one struggling with the boundaries of our new relationship. "Miss Wilson, I mean. Please come in and have a seat."

Mr. Olson steps into the office behind me and closes the door. I take the offered seat, worried.

Mr. Olson settles himself on the arm of the chair positioned beside me.

"There is something we'd like you to consider." Ms. Thompson leans her forearms on the desk.

I swallow hard, uncertain of what could be so pressing that both the hotel manager and matron need to speak with me.

"The thing is, it's become quite clear to Mr. Olson and me that it is not sustainable for the responsibilities of the hotel matron to remain under one person's purview." Ms. Thompson's eyes dart toward Mr. Olson. "If we aren't proactive, I've been warned, I'll find myself saddled with another bout of exhaustion."

Ms. Thompson's lips twist at the idea of falling ill again, and I can't blame her for it one bit.

"You are, naturally, our first choice, and we'd like to offer you the permanent position of assistant matron."

This is not what I was expecting, and I stumble my reply. "Me? Assistant matron?"

Ms. Thompson's smile is genuine. "Yes, you are quite qualified for the role, I assure you. And I suspect we will get on famously."

"I would be honoured. Thank you, ma'am." My feet yearn to dance with the news, and I do my best to restrain them, forcing my black oxfords to the floor with sheer willpower. A new full-time position doing what I enjoy. My excitement knows no bounds.

"There is something we'll have to navigate though," Ms. Thompson continues.

The seriousness of her words halts my internal celebration.

Ms. Thompson tilts her head to one side as she considers me. "Shall I call you Clara when we're alone, or do you prefer Miss Wilson?"

Laughter erupts from my chest like a babbling brook. "Clara is fine."

Mr. Olson chortles from his side of the room. "I think you're forgetting that Miss Wilson is soon to be Mrs. Thompson."

Ms. Thompson laughs heartily. "That does confuse things, doesn't it?"

We all share in the humour of how our lives will be forever entwined.

"You could always start as Ms. Wilson, as Eliza chose to do, keeping her maiden name for the purpose of hotel matron."

Mr. Olson's suggestion settles within me. "I think I'd like that very much." There is no earthly force that could keep my smile from widening. "Ms. Wilson it is."

"Then it's decided." Mr. Olson rises from his perch. "I'll leave you to sort out the duties and schedule." He moves toward the door, but before opening it, he turns once more, his face lit with mischief. "Not that either of you asked, but Clara, you can call me Robert when we're out of earshot of the staff."

"I would be delighted to, Robert." I affirm the invitation with a resolute nod of my head.

As Robert opens the office door, I catch a glimpse of Louisa waiting in the corridor.

"Miss Wilson, did you need to see me?" Eliza asks.

"Yes, ma'am, but I can wait." Lou's face tells me she had hoped to see the matron without my knowing, and I'm instantly curious as to why.

"We'll only be a minute more," Eliza tells Lou before Robert closes the door.

"We can sort out the schedule and duties tomorrow." Eliza waves a hand, dismissing the importance of such things. "There is one more thing I'd like to discuss."

"Of course." I lean in, hardly believing there could be more.

"I hope this doesn't seem too forward. I appreciate how delighted Cookie is to be moving into the new house, and maybe you are as well. I thought perhaps—well, I don't want you to feel obligated, but I wondered if you might want to move into the small apartment Robert and I have at our house?"

My chin drops, leaving my mouth hanging open.

"The position of assistant matron is likely to come with a slew of early mornings and late nights, and I thought you might find it easier to be located closer to the hotel. At least until you and William are married."

"Eliza, this is a very generous offer."

"Well, I'm not being completely altruistic. I'm interested in spending more time with you. I'd like to get to know you better as a woman, and living in proximity to one another is sure to give us more opportunity to do so. We will be sharing a very big role as matrons of this hotel, but we will also be sharing the role of sisters, and that is more important to me than you might know."

"I am deeply touched." A nervous laugh slips through

my lips. "I will admit I was not looking forward to traipsing to and from the new house." As soon as the words are out of my mouth, my thoughts veer to Louisa. I wonder if there will ever be a fortuitous opportunity that isn't coated with disappointment.

Eliza beams from across the desk. "I should be up front. The apartment is really no bigger than a cupboard, but it's yours if you'd like it."

I consider how my accepting would disappoint Louisa. "Can I have a few days to think it over? I'd like to speak with Louisa first."

"Of course. Take as long as you need." Eliza stands and stretches both her hands toward me. Taking them in mine, she gushes, "I'm so pleased to welcome you into our family, Clara."

CHAPTER 38

THURSDAY, JULY 26, 1928

ouisa

Clara presses her hand into mine as she exits Ms. Thompson's office. "I have something I need to speak with you about. Come find me on the eighth floor when you're done here." My sister's hurried whisper forces my heart into my throat. Little does she know I have something to tell her as well, and I'm certain she isn't going to like it one bit.

I coerce a polite smile as the matron calls me into her office. My feet have barely touched the ground these past twelve days, with the memory of a successful closing night and plans made with Rose and Thomas playing on repeat in my mind. This morning, though, I woke knowing I could no longer delay the inevitable.

Stepping into the office, I search for the words I've come to say.

"Miss Wilson, it looks as though something is troubling

you." Ms. Thompson's head is tilted to one side, reminding me of her highly tuned abilities of perception.

"This is difficult to say, ma'am." I square my shoulders and meet the matron's gaze. "I am ever so grateful that you took a chance on me and believed in my abilities. You have been exceptionally patient and willing to schedule around my pursuits in the theatre."

Ms. Thompson sits up straight, clasping her hands together atop the desk. "I sense there is a 'but' coming."

"Yes, ma'am. I am here to hand in my notice."

"Ah, I see." The matron's expression holds no disappointment. Instead, she seems bolstered by my news. "Off to California, are you?"

"Yes. How did you know?"

"Miss Wilson, it may be hard to believe, but I've known yours would be a temporary position at The Hamilton from the day you were hired. It took very little time to comprehend that you were destined for greater things. When I first saw you on that stage in *Craig's Wife*, I knew neither The Hamilton nor Vancouver itself could hold you back."

I feel my cheeks flush with colour.

"You come alive onstage, Louisa. Hollywood will be lucky to have you."

I notice the use of my first name and feel as though we've crossed the barrier between matron and maid. "Thank you, ma'am."

"I wouldn't worry too much about your sister either. She'll be fine here."

My mouth falls open, but no words come.

Ms. Thompson dips her chin conspiratorially. "Sisters always worry about one another. You two are no different. When do you leave?"

"Well, if you can manage without me, I'll be on my way by the month's end."

"We have a few new maids starting next week. I'm sure we can manage. I'll ensure your wages are ready for you by the end of your shift on Saturday."

"Thank you, ma'am."

"I'll be sure to keep this news to myself, until you've had a chance to tell your family, that is."

I nod my appreciation.

"It's been a pleasure working with you, Louisa, and I'm confident the skills you acquired here will serve you well going forward."

"Quite well, indeed." I allow my good news to lift the corners of my mouth. "Ms. Oxley has arranged employment for me as a maid at The Roosevelt Hotel while we pursue my acting options. It's a stone's throw away from the boarding house she has secured for me." My smile stretches wide. "It all fell into place quite quickly, really."

"The Roosevelt. My, that is impressive." Ms. Thompson hesitates. "I am surprised you are choosing to work as a maid though."

"So was Ms. Oxley." I laugh. "It was the one thing I insisted on. I have no desire to find myself unable to pay my way. Besides, there's no shame in a solid day's work."

"Well said, Louisa. Well said."

I make my way toward the pastry kitchen to find the next family member to receive my news. In my bubbling excitement, I almost let it slip during last night's dinner, but I held back, knowing my decision is best doled out one Wilson at a time.

Cookie is sure to make a fuss, but I will hear her support in every word. At least that is my hope. The trick will be convincing her to remain quiet until I've had the chance to speak with Clara and Papa.

She is coming through the swinging door of Chef's kitchen, a towel draped over one shoulder. "Well, if it isn't Miss Louisa Wilson, the star of the theatre, in the flesh."

Her teasing is a welcome reprieve. I bend at the waist in a mock bow. "Always a pleasure to greet my fans."

"Shouldn't you be on the fifth floor, or does that no longer suit your famous status?" I doubt Cookie realizes how close to the truth her ribbing comes.

"Ms. Thompson knows I'm here. I have something I'd like to speak with you about."

"Oh, sounds serious." Cookie gestures me toward the pastry kitchen. "You'd better step in here, then."

Before I can utter a word, she is pulling out a chair from the small table in the corner and setting a piece of sweet-smelling coffee cake before me.

I sink my teeth into the cake and moan. "I'm going to miss this."

The delight drops from her face in record time. "I see. It's about that time, is it?" Tears glisten in my friend's eyes. "I'm not sure I am prepared for this, Lou."

My emotions quickly catch up, matching hers step for step. "I don't suspect there is ever a good time to say goodbye."

"When will you be off, then?" Cookie steadies herself, with both hands pressing into the hard wooden table.

"Our plan is to catch the train on Tuesday afternoon." I don't look away, not wanting to miss a moment.

" 'Our'?" Her eyes twinkle with mischief. "So, Mr. Cromwell will be accompanying you to Los Angeles, will he?"

"Yes." My reply is subdued, understanding a lecture on

the impropriety of an unmarried woman travelling with a man may be coming my way. "I have a room arranged at an all-female boarding house once I arrive in the city. Travelling with Thomas is surely safer than travelling by myself."

"Is that the argument you're planning to use when you tell your father?" Cookie cocks her head back and examines me with a scrutinizing stare. "Was I your trial run? See if you can get the plan past me before you lay it at your father's feet?"

I wear the accusation, knowing it is spot on. "I also wanted to tell you first because you are the one who will have to hold the family together after I leave. Both Papa and Clara will follow your lead, and I knew that if you understood, then they would too."

Cookie's chortle catches me off guard. "I suggest you lead with that bit about the boarding house before easing into the topic of your travelling companion. We're going to miss you, Lou, but we'll be rooting for you."

I push my chair back and stand, pivoting to be engulfed in her crushing embrace. "I'm going to miss you too."

A shuffle at the threshold captures our attention.

"Why are you crying, Miss Louisa?" Masao's innocent face scrunches with concern.

"Oh, hello there." I wipe the tears from my face with the back of my hand.

Cookie places an arm around the boy's shoulders. "Our Miss Louisa is going on a grand adventure."

His big brown eyes light up.

"She's heading to California," Cookie continues.

Masao's head swivels in Cookie's direction. "Isn't California a long way away?"

Cookie bobs her head a few times, likely buying herself

a moment to gather her emotions. "It is, but California is where Miss Louisa can follow her dreams and become an actress." She bends toward the boy. "Sometimes, even though it's hard to say goodbye, we must be brave. Fear has no business bossing our dreams around."

Masao's sombre nod squeezes my heart.

"You know what though?" I kneel to the floor and tug on his shirt sleeve. "I can write to you from California." His face lights up at the news. "And you can write back." Masao looks from me to Cookie and back again.

"I will, Miss Louisa. I will write to you."

I ruffle the boy's jet-black hair. "I'd like that very much."

My gaze lands on Cookie's with a sad sigh. "Now, I've got to figure out how to break the news to Clara and Papa." I say goodbye to my new pen pal. "I'll write soon, Masao." Then I climb the back-of-house stairs to the eighth floor. I'm not prepared for this conversation, but there is no backing out now.

Miss Smythe is walking toward me as I step from the landing onto the pillowy red carpet of the illustrious eighth floor. A sharp inhale is still my automatic response to the richness. The walls boast a gold-and-burgundy flocked wallpaper, demanding to be admired like fine art, while the glimmering chandeliers cast shadows the length of the hall.

"Are you looking for Clara?" Miss Smythe asks as a knowing smile plays at her lips.

"I am."

"This way." Miss Smythe inclines her head, and I fall into step with one of Clara's closest friends, marvelling at the ease with which she avoids getting caught up in the plush carpeting.

Rounding a corner, I spot my sister tucked behind a half-closed linen-cupboard door.

"I'll leave you to it," Miss Smythe says, though I suspect she is keeping something close to her chest. Before I can reply, she is off, gliding down the hallway.

Clara pulls me into a cupboard the size of our apartment's kitchen and closes the door behind us.

"Thank you for coming. Can they spare you?" Clara has yet to take off her matron hat, still concerned with everyone's work. I simply nod my head in reply.

"I have exciting news," Clara says eagerly. "Ms. Thompson has asked me to take on the permanent position of assistant matron. Can you believe it?"

"Yes, I can, actually. I had no idea there was such a position, but it sounds perfect for you. You've worked hard, Clara. I'm proud of you." My hands make their way into Clara's. As my joy at her happiness rises, I remember Ms. Thompson's comment about not worrying over Clara.

Clara's delight quickly clouds over as her smile morphs into worry. "There is more, but I'm not quite sure how to tell you." Tucking her chin, she avoids my gaze and examines the plush red carpet instead.

I jostle our clasped hands back and forth to reassure her. "If you're happy, I see no reason I won't be."

She says nothing.

"Come on, Clara. It can't be that bad." I tilt my head to catch her attention and tug her gaze upward.

Her lids are rimmed with moisture as she lifts her eyes to mine. "I don't mean to disappoint you, Lou, but Ms. Thompson has offered her apartment for me to live in. It's at the side of her house, and since Cookie vacated, it has been empty."

A small smile graces my lips at Clara's concern for my feelings. "I see. And you're worried about me?"

"I know we talked about moving out on our own and—"

"Clara, I understand."

"You do?"

"I do. It's wonderful news, and it makes far more sense than traipsing from the other side of town." I roll my eyes at the nonsense of the new house's location. "I honestly don't know how Cookie is going to do it every day."

Clara's voice is timid. "You're not upset? I know how keen you were to remain at The Newbury. I was concerned. Well, I thought you might be angry with me."

"Oh, Clara. I was afraid to face an uncertain future, not knowing if I am strong enough to stand on my own two feet. In all honesty, it was foolish of me to cling to a home we'd all outgrown." My bottom lip makes its way between my teeth. "The thing is, I will be moving on too."

"How? Where?"

"To California." It's my turn to become timid as my sister digests the news. "I leave on Tuesday."

"Oh, Lou." Clara pulls me into a hug, and I can't tell if she is crying or laughing. "I'm going to miss you dreadfully, of course, but this is it. This is your chance."

"You aren't upset with me, then?" I extract myself from her embrace so I can read her expression.

"Mad? How could I ever be mad at you for chasing your dreams? I told you months ago that I'd support you when you decided to take the leap."

Wrapping Clara in another embrace, I whisper into her hair. "You always were my biggest fan."

"And I'll keep being your biggest fan, no matter where you call home. I love you, Lou, and I'm so proud of you."

The tears between us are plentiful but happy.

We hold tight to one another, neither of us wishing to break our connection. Time is short. California is far away. But a sisterly bond knows no bounds.

TELEGRAM FROM CLARA WILSON
TO LOUISA WILSON

TELEGRAM   IO /20/ I929

SENDER: *Clara Wilson*

RECIPIENT: *Louisa Wilson*

PURPOSE: ◯ THANK YOU NOTE ◯ SECRET ◯ WARNING
◯ HOLIDAY HELLO ☑ SPECIAL DELIVERY

DEAR LOUISA,

PRIVY COUNCIL ANNOUNCED DECISION. WOMEN ARE PERSONS!

STATING. "THE EXCLUSION OF WOMEN FROM PUBLIC OFFICES IS A RELIC OF DAYS MORE BARBAROUS THAN OURS."

ALL MY LOVE,

Clara

AUTHOR NOTES

"The exclusion of women from all public offices is a relic of days more barbarous than ours. And to those who would ask why the word 'person' should include females, the obvious answer is, why should it not?"

The above quote is attributed to Lord Sankey, Lord Chancellor of Great Britain, when he announced the decision of the Privy Council on October 18, 1929.

To begin with, The Famous Five, as they became known in the media, were made up of five women from Alberta. Emily Murphy who was an author and Canada's first female magistrate led the charge by inviting four prominent activists to her home in August of 1927. Together Emily, Nellie McClung, Irene Parlby, Louise McKinney, and Henrietta Muir Edwards petitioned the government by way of the Supreme Court of Canada, to reinterpret the word "persons" within the British North American Act. The Supreme Court was tasked with answering the following question. "Does the word 'Person' in section 24 of the *British North America Act*, 1867, include female persons?" Their answer, a resounding "no" is where the story that unfolds in *Whispers of Her Worth* begins.

When I first heard the words "Persons Case" I thought my husband was pulling my leg since I had no previous knowledge of this piece of Canadian history. When I learned the Privy Council ruling is acknowledged every year on October 18 as Persons Day, I doubled down on my research since as a Canadian, I had never heard of nor celebrated Persons Day. The more I researched, the more I uncovered possible reasons as to why the historic legal case isn't as well-known as I would have expected it to be.

For starters, the Privy Council ruling was announced just days before the stock market crashed resulting in widespread fear and panic. Women becoming known as "persons" was suddenly less important in those weeks and months that followed as the reality of The Great Depression began to take hold.

There is also the issue with the five women being in favour of Alberta's Sexual Sterilization Act. In today's light, with what we know of eugenics, it may appear appalling to think that five women who stood up for the rights of women would also believe in forced sterilization. I am reminded of the phrase, *when we know better, we do better* and I would like to think I'd give the famous five the benefit of doubt that if they knew what we know today, their position on the topic would be reconsidered.

Times were different a hundred years ago. Knowledge was often restricted to limited regions and distributed by men in powerful positions whose goal was to control the narrative in order to support their own biases. The Famous Five can be remembered for not only their role in changing the history for women in Canada when it comes to female representation in the Senate. They contributed independently as well. Some were supporters of all women's right to vote and be elected into office regardless of social standing. One worked for decades supporting the rights of Japanese and South-East Asian Canadians. Another was instrumental in supporting indigenous women earning herself a sacred indigenous name. Regardless of their many efforts in support of Canadian women, I suspect their take on eugenics may be what holds us back from heralding them as heroines.

In the end, none of the women from the Famous Five were appointed into the Senate. Instead, Mrs. Cairine Wilson was sworn in as the first female Senator on February 15, 1930.

Women of non-white backgrounds often encountered racial barriers to voting and holding office in 1928. This didn't change for far too many years. Therefore, I'd like to acknowledge that, although The Hotel Hamilton is a fictional hotel, if it truly existed it would be located on the traditional, ancestral, and unceded territories of the xwməθkwəyə̓ m' (Musqueam), Sḵwx̱wú7mesh (Squamish), and Səlilwətaʔɬ (Tsleil-Waututh) nations in Vancouver, British Columbia, Canada.

It may seem unlikely that Canadian women were handing over their wages to their husbands in 1928 but in reality, this was entirely possible. Despite the Married Woman's Property Act being in effect since 1873 in British Columbia, women were actually unable to open their own bank account. The Act indicates women had the right to own property, earn their own money, etc. but a working woman still needed her husband's consent and signature in order to deposit her earnings at a bank. I reasoned that because of this stipulation, it wasn't easy for women in 1928 to have control over their own income. It wasn't until 1964 that a woman had the right to open her own bank account. Add to that, women were not permitted to apply for a credit card until 1974.

I love it when history and fiction bump up against one another. This was the case when it came to the phrase, "to obey" in Cookie's wedding vows. The Anglican Church of England actually changed the official vows, excluding "to obey" from the wife's vows in 1928, making it possible that "to obey" would be included or excluded depending on the views of an individual church, Reverend, and happy couple.

Though Louisa issues a veiled threat to the director, I did not come across any evidence to suggest that British Columbian women picketed or boycotted businesses after the Supreme Court's dismissal of women as persons or during the review of the case set before the Privy Council.

The phrase Wife in Watercolours comes from the Regency era where a mistress was referred to as the Wife in Watercolours due to the impermanence of the relationship. Unlike an actual marriage, the relationship with a mistress could be dissolved with ease.

To learn more about the research that goes into my novels, subscribe to my author newsletter, at tanyaewilliams.com.

ACKNOWLEDGMENTS

Whispers of Her Worth would not exist if my husband hadn't taken my passing grumble of not knowing what I was going to write about, seriously. Twenty minutes later, I had moved on and was immersed in a TV show when his head popped up with a "huh". Over the years, I've learned to take those non-words as significant and he immediately had my attention. Thank you, Dave for digging deep on my behalf, for making dinner when I'm lost in a story, and for loving me despite my many shortcomings. Maybe you'll actually read the acknowledgements this time since it's up at the top of the page:)

A huge debt of gratitude goes to my editor, Victoria Griffin. Despite finalizing the story's progression, you saw something more and pushed me to find it. Thank you for always having the story's back and for being gentle when you break the news that I'll have to move chapters and timelines around.

The Hotel Hamilton covers are a true group effort. Resulting from a photoshoot where my husband, best friend, and the most delightful model, descended upon Vancouver with a goal to capture as many cover options as possible. A huge thank you goes out to Ana Grigoriu-Voicu for taking a simple photograph and turning it into another stunning cover.

Thank you to Brianne Matheny. You are an author's

dream VA. I would be lost without the book bible you created for me.

I am extremely fortunate to be surrounded by strong, intelligent, successful, and inspiring women. They are my Resistance Red Brigade and I'm honoured to stand among them.

My beta readers are all accomplished authors in their own right. I am forever grateful to Kelsey Gietl, Kate Thompson, and Diana Lesire Brandmeyer for spotting the missing words, the duplicate words, the incongruencies, and more. Not only are you exceptional beta readers, you are true friends and I am lucky to have each one of you in my life.

To the ladies of The Eleventh Chapter, Jenn Bouchard, Kerry Chaput, Jen Craven, Sayword B. Eller, Maggie Giles, Caitlin Moss, Sharon M. Peterson, and Colleen Temple, your passion, talent, and sense of humour are a guiding light even on the darkest days. Hugs to each one of you. HOWARD!

A huge shoutout to my HNS After Party friends. From how to cut an onion to unending insight and support, you warm my heart, make me laugh, keep me thinking, and teach me something new every time we meet. Thank you!

Thank you to my advance reader team for the time and attention you give my novels. I couldn't do this without your help and I am eternally grateful for your continual support and interest in the stories I write. Thank you to each and every one of you!

To my newsletter family, thank you for opening my emails, answering my questions, and being just as excited as I am for each new cover, story, and milestone reached. You are the reason I keep writing books.

For the past several months, I have been MIA for many

people in my life. Despite being buried in more projects than I actually have time for, each of you is never far from my mind. Thank you for your support and patience as I wade through my "to do" list. To Michelle Cox, Carla Young, Kari, Tammy, Donna, Irene, Judy, Mom, Dad, Tamalin, and all of my family, I promise to come up for air soon.

To Dave (he won't see this one :)) and Justin, thank you for answering random questions I've provided little context for, not ridiculing me when I take on way more than I can accomplish, for being my safe place to land, and of course for pouring the wine on Friday night. I love you with all my heart.

Thank you to all the readers who allow my stories to share a spot on your bookshelf and a place in your heart. Thank you for taking time out of your day to read *Whispers of Her Worth*.

Hugs,
Tanya

ABOUT THE AUTHOR

A writer from a young age, Tanya E Williams loves to help a reader get lost in another time, another place through the magic of books. History continues to inspire her stories and her insightful view into the human condition deepens her character's experiences and propels them on their journey. Ms. Williams' favorite tales, speak to the reader's heart, making them smile, laugh, cry, and think.